"You've done well for yourself."

Yes, Laura had. She could detect a note of admiration in Nick's words and was proud of the hard-won fruits of her labor. She relaxed into her chair and put her feet up on the desk. Her skirt slid down her thighs. His gaze followed the movement, lingered, moved along her body slowly.

Good. Let him look. He certainly wouldn't get to touch. Never again.

"Showing off?"

"Maybe a little." She smiled, but there was no warmth in it. "Is it working?"

"Do you mean am I turned on?"

She nodded.

"Yes. How's that for honesty?"

"That's a lot more honest than you used to be."

He smiled and touched one pink toenail, then feathered his fingers along the arch of her foot. His fingers hadn't changed. They still knew their way around a woman's body.

"Does that turn you on?" he asked.

"No."

"Liar." He grinned and left the room.

Nick was still ruthless. And she still wanted him.

Dear Reader,

I love cooking and baking! And my heroine, Laura Cameron, has the vision and sensuality of a great cook. There's something so heady, soothing, invigorating, pleasing, inviting, sexy…about playing with food, especially in creating new recipes.

Both home cooks and professional chefs have used cooking and baking to make magic in their kitchens. There's nothing more satisfying than sitting down with a cup of tea or coffee and a freshly baked, hot-out-of-the-oven pastry.

All of this got me thinking. Could I create a little magic of my own? I gave it a shot and made up a recipe that Laura might use in her bakery. I've included Laura's recipe for chocolate chunk cookies at the end of the manuscript. I think of them as chocolate chip cookies for adults!

And maybe that time creating my own cookie recipe helped me with this story. To be honest, writing Nick Jordan gave me fits. In the first story about the Jordan brothers—the February 2013 book *In from the Cold*—he was self-centered and arrogant and, certainly, the least likable of the three brothers. Humanizing him was a challenge, but Laura helped him to see the light.

I hope you enjoy the fireworks Nick and Laura create in and out of the kitchen!

Mary Sullivan

P.S. I love to hear from readers! Please contact me through my website at www.marysullivanbooks.com.

Home to Laura

MARY SULLIVAN

HARLEQUIN® SUPER ROMANCE®

Recycling programs
for this product may
not exist in your area.

ISBN-13: 978-0-373-71837-5

HOME TO LAURA

Printed in U.S.A.

ABOUT THE AUTHOR

One of Mary's lifelong passions has been cooking, including baking. She has spent her life compiling folders and binders of favorite recipes she has collected. She has also created many of her own. One of her original recipes won her an ice cream maker in a contest put on by a national cooking magazine and, boy, has she enjoyed that many times over! You can reach her at www.marysullivanbooks.com.

Books by Mary Sullivan

HARLEQUIN SUPERROMANCE

Other titles by this author available in ebook format.

Thank you to Cathy for your valued friendship,
for your support when I needed it most and for the
medical background on preterm labor!
"Any errors are mine."

CHAPTER ONE

"WHAT DID YOU do to my granddaughter?" Mort Sanderson stormed into Nick Jordan's office, indignation pouring from him like lava.

Nick took his time placing his pen beside the documents he'd been perusing and struggled to remain calm. Mort's behavior was becoming more erratic with age. Sure, Nick could handle it, but Mort's eccentricities didn't belong in the office.

He also wished Mort would keep Nick's private life out of here, too. He worked hard to separate the two.

Mort was Nick's boss. He was also his father-in-law. *Ex*-father-in-law.

Too late, Nick had learned the danger of mixing his personal life with business.

He pointed toward the office door. "Would you mind closing that so this conversation can remain private?"

Mort stepped into the room and slammed the door.

That should impress the two clients in the waiting room, Nick thought. Thank you, Mort.

"What's wrong with Emily?" Nick asked.

"She called me last night in tears."

"What?" Nick shot out of his chair. "Why? What's wrong?"

"She's not happy with you."

Not happy with him? Why not? Old, familiar acid churned in his gut. His stomach troubles had started with his ex-wife's defection to another man. Was he about to lose his daughter, too?

Emily hadn't said a word to him about being unhappy. He

reached for the phone and dialed his home number before realizing Emily would still be at school.

His daughter had called Mort in tears.

You should have been there for her. She shouldn't have to go to her grandfather.

"What did she say?" he asked.

"That you ignore her and never have time for her."

"I work hard." Nick owned a beautiful home in a good neighborhood. Emily attended a private school. Every Christmas, he sent her to visit her mother. "That's what a man does to support his family."

"My granddaughter deserves to be happy," Mort shouted, leaning his fists onto Nick's desk. If he were a tall man, he would loom over Nick, but at five-five, Mort had learned to use the force of his personality to intimidate. At the moment, he leaned close enough for Nick to count the red spider veins on his cheeks—and to smell alcohol on his breath. Damn. It wasn't yet noon, too early for Mort to be drinking.

After Mort left the office, Nick would get his assistant to find out where he would have to do damage control.

What was happening to Mort? When had he started this slide into…what? Self-indulgence? Self-pity? Where was the astute businessman Nick used to admire, used to emulate? Nick was the one making all of the big decisions in the company these days.

If that involved putting out too many fires that Mort started and not enough time on creativity and problem-solving—the things Nick loved—so be it. That was the cost of running a large corporation—and a small price to pay for the money he raked in.

His stomach roiling, he stared at Mort, eerily afraid that he might be peering into the crystal ball of his future. No way did he want his life reduced to a string of wives and endless days of drinking, of depending on others to fix his mistakes.

How could Nick stop that future for himself? He didn't know when Mort's slide had started, or how.

"You couldn't make Marsha happy." Mort interrupted his thoughts. "Now you can't keep Emily happy."

"Enough," Nick shouted, anger spurred on by fear that this might be a problem even he didn't know how to fix. What then? What would happen to Emily? "How is this any different from you? You're on your fifth wife. Marsha complained about how little attention you gave her as a child. Keep your damn hypocrisy to yourself and stay the hell out of my relationship with my daughter."

"It's different because Marsha is my daughter and Emily my granddaughter."

"Each of your wives was someone's daughter and grand-daughter."

"That's beside the point. I want Emily to be happy. That's your job."

Nick mimicked Mort, leaning his fists on his desk and pushing forward into Mort's face. "That hasn't been my only job, has it? You've never once complained when I worked nights and weekends on end to bring in new clients or to complete your projects, have you?" The unfairness of the man's criticism burned.

"You've been my mentor," Nick continued. "You taught me how to deal in business. I'm following your example. *You're* the reason I am the way I am." He silenced a voice that nagged, *that's not completely true. You wanted so much. You were an ambitious SOB. Mort fit into your plan.* "I ignored Marsha and Emily because I was here making money for you and this company. How else do you think I did it? By twiddling my thumbs? By taking vacations with my wife and child? I made you a fortune." Nick struggled for control. Where was his precious cool head?

"As far as Marsha goes, we divorced as friends," Nick said, forcing a reasonable tone. "She knew who I was when we married, but wanted someone who could give her more attention. She wanted the money and the big house *and* me home evenings and weekends."

That was why she'd had an affair with Harry Fuller and why she'd divorced Nick and married him. Harry came from money—had never had to work and scrape for every penny as Nick had—and gave her the attention she craved. Yes, he'd understood, but it had hurt, which was strange considering it hadn't been a love match for either of them. Was he more of a dreamer, a romantic, than he'd thought? Had he been fonder of Marsha than he'd realized?

"Marsha wanted too much, just like her mother." Mort's voice came out as a growl. "I shouldn't have spoiled her."

"You didn't," Nick conceded. "She's a good person and she was right. I never paid her enough attention. I probably never gave Emily enough, either." He knew in his heart he hadn't. Now he was making her cry. He'd never figured out why Emily had opted to stay with him in the home she'd grown up in rather than follow her mother to Europe with her new husband four years ago. Maybe to keep her friends?

Had any of her decision been based on wanting to be near her father? He hoped so. Again, he reached for the phone. He needed to talk to her. Again, he remembered she wasn't home.

"Fix it," Mort said. "Whatever is wrong with her, take care of it now."

He planned to. Tonight. There wasn't a person on earth who mattered more to him than his daughter.

Nick winced. "I honestly never meant to hurt her. I'll talk to her tonight."

"That girl means the world to me."

Nick's anger softened. Mort had always treated Emily like gold. She was a shining light in his life.

"I'm not sure what can change," Nick said, but the fight had left him. Emily was his shining light, too. She kept the darkness at bay. "I have to work as hard now on this project as I ever have."

"Stop it now. Cancel it."

The Accord Ski and Golf Resort? He couldn't, and there was no way to explain to Mort why. Mort had been born with money. He would never in a million years understand how Nick had grown up, how poverty had shaped him, how important it was to build the new resort in his old town.

"Make Emily happy," Mort said, his eyes narrowing. "That's an order. Do it, or I'll pull the plug on the resort."

Nick stilled. Accord Resort was his dream, his baby, part homage to Mom and part revenge against his older brother Gabe—and partly to prove to the town that had barely noticed him when he was growing up that Nick Jordan had become a success and was a force to be reckoned with. His reasons were so confusing and convoluted even he didn't understand fully what drove him. He only knew that he had to annihilate that old house and build something bigger and grander than the Jordan family had ever owned in the past.

Why he worried about his name, and the family, was anybody's guess. He wasn't part of the family anymore, was he? In thirteen years, he'd gone back only twice, four years ago for Mom's funeral and in January to a town meeting concerning the resort. He spoke to Tyler occasionally on the phone. To Gabe? Never.

Mort couldn't possibly pull out now. They were about to break ground. Before Nick had even sent his former assistant, Callie, to Accord to work on getting his brothers to sell, he'd been working behind the scenes to have permits pushed through, greasing more palms than he cared to admit to Mort. Once Gabe and Ty had sold their shares to him, he'd increased his efforts. This resort had already cost him a bundle.

"You can't be serious about pulling the plug," Nick said.

"Look at me." Something in Mort changed, as though a

crack opened in that gruff exterior he painted on like shellac. "Take a good look at me. Do you like what you see?"

Nick stared for a long moment at things Mort had never laid bare before—unhappiness, regret and enough loneliness to bury a man. *No wonder he drinks.* The powerful man Mort had been shrank before Nick's eyes.

With one quick jerk of his head, Nick admitted that he didn't like this version of Mort, that it scared the daylights out of him. That it confirmed Nick's fears that he himself was on a slippery slope barreling toward his own version of Mort's life. And he wanted to stop.

"If you don't make a real effort to change for that little girl—" Mort pointed a finger at himself "—then you're looking at your future. You're going to lose Emily. She told me she's going to France to live with her mother. I want her to stay here. Make it happen."

He walked from the room, closing the door without slamming it this time, leaving Nick stunned.

Emily wanted to live with her mother? She was leaving him? He imagined that big beautiful house empty save for him and a housekeeper who came in to cook and clean.

He heard the silence he would live with every day, every evening, without his daughter near to fill it with joyful sound.

Nick. Alone. Truly, truly alone. The thought raised old—positively ancient—feelings in him that he couldn't name or place, and which made no sense. He'd never been alone. Had never been abandoned.

So why did Emily's desire to move to Europe leave him feeling so panicked?

How could he imagine coming home from work and Emily not being there to greet him, to share her gossip from school, to relieve the unending emptiness he felt here in his office?

He couldn't pinpoint when the emptiness had started, but the thought of what he felt at work spreading to his home terrified him.

For long minutes, Nick stood still, the man of action paralyzed, the man who took control in every situation momentarily lost. His heart rate kicked up and a shaky hollowness filled his stomach, as though he'd drunk too much coffee.

You're looking at your future.

It was true. Old before his time, Nick was plagued with headaches and stomach problems. At only thirty-two, he was already too far along on Mort's road. He'd skipped his youth, had lost it too early.

He paced to the window. He'd worked his butt off to become CEO of Sanderson Developments. He'd earned his beautifully appointed corner office with the floor-to-ceiling windows in the heart of the business district. He pressed one hand against the window as though he could touch Seattle where it lay far below him. At this height, he had a stunning view of Elliott Bay.

He'd given Marsha and Emily a gorgeous home and all of the best that money could buy. It hadn't been enough for Marsha. Good Lord, it seemed it wasn't enough for Emily.

He stared around his office, bewildered. He was known as a brilliant strategist, a problem-solver without peer, but how did he fix what was broken in his personal life?

He stepped away from the window, noting as he did so that he had left his palm and fingerprints.

I am here. This is real.

Then why did so much of his life seem *un*real, hollow, ephemeral?

Why did the business no longer fill him with fire? Why did he feel there should be *more?* That this life of shuffling papers and moving money couldn't possibly be the end-all and be-all, the sum total of life? When had he become two-dimensional, like those drawings on ancient Greek vases before mankind had figured out how to draw the third dimension? Why did Nick lack depth? Because he'd only ever focused on his job.

Thirteen years ago, when he'd started with Mort, it had meant everything to him, and had been enough.

It no longer was.

Now, he didn't have a clue what was wrong with him except that he wasn't happy.

And now he knew that Emily wasn't, either. His happiness didn't matter. Hers, though? Oh, yes, it mattered immensely.

He would do anything for Emily, but he couldn't run around half-cocked. What did she need?

He scrubbed his hands over his face. Damned if he knew. He opened the liquor cabinet built into the bookshelf unit that covered one wall and poured himself a Scotch. He emptied it in two gulps then stared at the empty glass, horrified at what he'd just done.

Was this how it started? He'd already spent thirteen years of his life emulating Mort. Was he about to spend the next thirty continuing to emulate him? To become the man in all of his self-destructive manifestations?

It started as easily as this? His daughter threatened to leave him and he started drinking in the office alone? Not socially with clients or to celebrate a deal, but to obliterate the hollowness, the loneliness?

He was turning into Mort. His wife had left him for another man and now his daughter wanted to leave him, too. It hadn't been so bad when Marsha had left. After all, how much had they loved each other, really? Not enough to sustain a lifelong commitment.

But Emily? He loved her to distraction. Mort had said she'd complained that Nick didn't spend enough time with her; therefore, the solution was simple. He would spend more time with her.

She wasn't happy.

She deserved to be happy.

Starting tonight, she would be. He dropped the bottle of Laphroaig into the trash then called Emily to tell her he loved

her and planned to spend more time with her, starting tonight, leaving a message on the machine for when she got
home from school. He would let her go to France to visit,
but to live? No.

He'd leave the office as soon as he finished with the clients in the waiting room.

He straightened his tie, made sure his hair was in place
and asked Rachel to send them in.

HE COULDN'T GET away until after six and didn't reach home
until six-thirty.

TGIF.

He rubbed the back of his neck, took his overcoat and
briefcase from the backseat, closed the door and locked the
car. He turned to walk up his driveway…

…and got a snowball full in his face.

"What the—?"

He swiped his hand across his eyes to clear them of wet
snow. Emily stood in front of the house with a dare in her
eye, and what might be construed as hope.

She's not happy with you.

So. She'd received his phone message and wondered how
sincere he was.

Did he intend to follow through on his promise to spend
time with her? You bet!

He tossed his briefcase and coat onto the hood of the car
and grinned.

When had he last had a snowball fight? He caught a
glimpse of a memory. Ah, yes. Snowball fights with his two
older brothers. He'd forgotten about that—a rare good memory.

His cell phone rang, its blare a harsh discord in this quiet
neighborhood covered with softly falling wet snow.

"Dad, don't answer it," Emily shouted, still with that dare

in her eye. She stood ten feet away from him with another snowball in her hand.

Dad? When had his daughter stopped calling him *Daddy?*

She'd turned twelve this week. He'd missed so much. Where had the years gone? Into building a business. Into making more money than he could ever need.

The phone rang again and it took all of his self-control to stay focused on Emily and ignore it.

If he answered it now, he'd lose her. He sensed it as surely as the snow soaking his shoes. He needed to change. That change started now. This minute.

The wrinkle of his vibrating cell phone required superhuman control on his part to ignore.

She lobbed the second snowball at his head. Bull's-eye.

"You want a fight, kid?" He laughed and picked up a handful of the wet snow left by a rare late-April snowfall and formed it into a ball with his bare hands, the bite of cold bracing on his palms. "You got it."

He threw it at her, making sure he didn't hit her above the shoulders. She hid behind the only tree on the front lawn. A moment later, a snowball hit his chest. He ducked behind the car and lobbed one over the hood. It landed beside the tree.

He watched a pair of hands in fuzzy red mittens build a small stockpile of snowballs beside the tree.

Nick sneaked around the back of the car and made a run for it, swooping around the tree to catch her by surprise from behind.

He lunged at her, picked her up and tossed her into a pile of snow left by the man who had cleared his driveway. She squealed. Emily was getting heavy, too big for this, but fool that he'd been, he'd missed innocent, spontaneous play in her childhood.

He breathed a sigh, feeling young rather than the thirty-two-going-on-fifty that he felt in his office.

Emily giggled and picked up a handful of snow and threw it at him, but he dodged.

"Look what you did to my shoes," he said, his words harsh, but his tone not. "You could have ruined my suit." He dumped handfuls of snow onto her, scraping it from the two inches covering the dormant grass until her torso was covered, all the while still dodging snow she threw at him.

"Do you give up yet?" Nick stood arms akimbo laughing down at his daughter.

She lay on her back and panted. "Yeah."

"Yeah, what?"

"Yeah," she said, making a snow angel while she talked, "I shouldn't have thrown snow at you until you changed out of your business clothes." She sat up. "But, Dad, if I waited for that, we'd never have gotten to play in the snow."

"That's not true," he said, reaching a hand to help her up.

His growing-up-too-fast daughter rolled her eyes. "Seriously, Dad? You're kidding, right?"

He didn't have to think about it hard. All he had left of Emily's childhood was a slim handful of memories.

He loved her more than anyone or anything and yet still he worked too much.

"You're always working," she said, her tone accusatory.

Well, not for the next few hours.

"Not tonight," he said.

He picked up his overcoat and briefcase before wrapping an arm around Emily and opening the front door of his opulent house and tossing his things onto a chair. He stepped out of his ruined Gucci loafers.

"I'm not working tonight. For this evening, I'm all yours," he said and, still high from their snowball fight, expanded. "In fact, I'm not going to work all weekend. You want a movie and pizza for dinner?"

She threw her arms around his neck. "You mean it about the whole weekend?"

"I mean it." He hugged her hard, getting a little choked up that it was so insanely easy to make Emily happy. "Go order the pizza and choose a movie."

She ran to the phone in the kitchen on legs that were growing longer and faster than her coordination could keep up with. Someday soon, though, she was going to be a knockout, model beautiful with her long legs and body, a drop-dead face, blue eyes with an odd ring of hazel around them and a killer smile. And skin that had never known a blemish. Her rich auburn hair flew in every direction courtesy of static electricity and the hat she'd just pulled off.

How did he, Nick Jordan born to poor parents in podunk Accord, Colorado, deserve such a beautiful girl?

He picked up the mail his housekeeper had left on the kitchen counter and leafed through it. His cell rang and he checked the number. His assistant. He sighed.

"Yes, Rachel?"

"There's a problem at the work site."

"Which one?" Callie MacKintosh would have rattled off all of the details, the most important ones. In fact, Callie would have just taken care of the problem herself. But she no longer worked for him, thanks to his damned older brother Gabe, and it was taking too long for Rachel to learn the ropes.

Back off, you impatient bastard. A month is hardly long enough to become another Callie. If he weren't careful, he'd lose this one just as he'd lost the other two he'd hired in the three months since Callie had decamped to marry his brother.

He tried to ignore that Callie had ever existed.

Rachel shuffled papers on the other end of the line. "The problem is at the work site in Accord."

Great. Just great. The one development he wanted to run more smoothly than the others. He might want the new resort built on the old family land, but that didn't mean he wanted to *be* there, overseeing everything and problem-solving.

"Did Rene mention what the problem is?"

"No. He just said that you need to get down there ASAP."

Rene was a brilliant foreman. If he thought Nick should be there, the problem was serious. He called Rene.

"What's going on?"

"We got a bunch of Native Americans here blocking access to your land. They said they aren't moving until they talk to you."

"Why?"

"There are ancient burial grounds here, sacred to the Utes."

"This is the first I've heard of it."

"They accept that your family already owns the land, but you try to build, to expand that house into a lodge or hotel, and you'll alienate them."

"They don't own the land. I do. Build anyway."

"It was one thing with your brother not wanting to leave, but this is spiritual. I'm Catholic. I wouldn't want anyone tearing up my cemeteries. You gotta have respect for the dead."

"If it's true."

"Is there any way you can find out?"

Nick thought about it. He could check with the university in Colorado and try to find historians who might know something. No one would be available until Monday. He couldn't wait that long. Otherwise, he'd be paying Rene's crew to stand around and do nothing. He needed to go to Accord to reason with the Native Americans.

"I'll fly down and take care of this. I'll leave in the morning." He hung up.

And turned to find Emily watching him.

Even though her expression was closed up tighter than a clamshell, he knew disappointment lurked beneath her careful neutrality. He'd taught her that poker face. Here he was, yet again, disappointing his daughter. Story of his life.

He'd fallen back on his normal pattern and had answered the phone without thinking, because it was part of his life, because the damn thing was part of his hand. He'd answered without thought and was now involved in a problem he could neither ignore nor delegate. He had committed to flying to Colorado without a thought for Emily and his promise to her. He couldn't turn back now. He had said he would go. He would go. He didn't break promises. In business at any rate.

He'd made that commitment to Emily, too. But surely she would understand.

"Where do you have to go tomorrow?" All of the teasing had fled her tone, erased by his never-ending need to excel, to have more, especially with this project. If he could just finish this one project, he could spend more time with her.

"To Accord."

She perked up. "Great! I can go with you. I can meet my uncles and I can see Callie."

"No!" He hadn't meant to shout and brought himself back under control. "I told you I don't want to hear her name mentioned in this house."

She lost her excitement and closed up again. What did he expect?

"Why not?" she asked. "I don't get why you're so mad at her just because she stopped working for you, Dad. She was getting married to your brother and moving to Colorado, for Pete's sake. It was time for her to get a life. Was she supposed to waste her whole life working for you?"

Nick winced. *Waste.* That's probably exactly how Callie had thought of Nick once she'd met Gabe. A waste of her time.

He prided himself on his rational mind, but he was unreasonable where Callie was concerned. Ditto for Gabe.

"Dad? Are you listening to me?"

He dropped the mail he'd been staring at but not really seeing. "I heard you."

"She was your assistant, not your girlfriend. So what's your problem?"

No, she wasn't his girlfriend, and *that* was the problem, which wasn't something he could discuss with his daughter.

"I miss Callie," she said. "She used to be my friend. I want to go with you."

"No."

"Why not?"

"I'll be busy."

"So what? I can spend time with—" she crossed her arms and intoned "—the Woman Who Can't Be Named."

Her sarcasm hurt, had barbs that surprised him. She used to be sweet. "You want to know the honest-to-God truth, Emily? I don't want you in Accord." He saw that he'd hurt her feelings and rushed on. "I don't have good memories of that town. I don't want you to see where I grew up."

Heaven forbid that she should see the poverty he'd grown up with, the boy he used to be compared to the man he'd made of himself. *This, here,* was him—the Gucci shoes and expensive house and successful business. Not his childhood. Not Accord.

"But—" she started.

"Case closed." For the third or fourth time that day, he pulled his unruly emotions under control. What was wrong with him? He didn't *do* emotion.

Nick approached Emily and put his hands on her shoulders. "Go choose a movie while I change. Let's not spoil the little time we have together tonight. Okay?"

"'Kay." She wasn't happy about it, but he knew Emily. She would bounce back.

Except that she didn't. Nick didn't know whether it was teenage hormones kicking in or Callie's move to Accord, but Emily remained subdued for the rest of the night and through Saturday morning's breakfast. He knew he was doing the right thing in keeping her away from the town he'd grown up in, from that house he wished he never had to set foot in again, that would be obliterated as soon as he solved this problem.

Before he left for his morning flight, he tried to cajole her.

"Maybe I can catch a flight back tonight. We can spend to-morrow together."

"Sure." She didn't sound as if she believed him.

Damn. He didn't have time for this. "I have to go, honey. I'll see you tomorrow."

As he got into his car to drive to the airport, he watched her in his rearview mirror standing beside his housekeeper.

Emily looked small and sad and lost, and it was all his fault.

He turned the key in the ignition.

You're looking at your future, Mort had said.

What if he turned his vivacious daughter into a miniature version of himself, a one-trick pony, a person for whom work was the only thing? A man whose life was passing him by as though someone else was in the driver's seat? And how weird was that for a man as driven as he, as crazy for control?

With a flick of his wrist, he shut off the engine and stepped out of the car.

"Pack a bag."

"What?" She stared openmouthed, afraid to hope.

"You're coming with me to Accord."

Her face lit up. "Seriously?"

He grinned. "Seriously." He checked his watch. "You've got ten minutes."

Emily squealed and ran into the house.

While she packed, he called Mort.

"There's a problem at the work site in Accord. I'm tak-ing Emily with me. We should be back by Sunday evening."

"Good." Mort didn't sound right, his voice low, subdued.

"What's up?" Nick asked.

"Lesley just left. Another damn woman without the gump-tion to stick it out, to see things through."

Mort's fifth wife was walking out? Man, how rotten would that feel?

"Mort." Nick hesitated. It was hard to tell the man the truth, but if his drinking affected things at the office, how did it feel to live with? "Maybe you should look at your drinking."

"I don't have a problem."

No? Then why had Nick just heard the clink of ice cubes in a glass? Chances were good that it wasn't lemonade that Mort was chugging. It was most likely Scotch—and it was only nine in the morning.

"I'll call when I get back on Sunday. Do you want to come over for dinner one night?"

"Yeah. Sounds good."

Nick hung up, but uneasiness clung to him. Despite the drinking, the screwups that Mort caused at work, he was still the world's best mentor. Over the years, he'd been a good friend to Nick. Nick's problem, though, was that while he could fix problems at work, he didn't know how to fix people. Hell, he didn't even know how to fix himself, so how could he help Mort?

Emily ran out of the house with a knapsack and a big grin.

Maybe he wasn't completely useless with people. He'd made his beautiful daughter happy.

An awful feeling of doubt screwed up his gut, though. He was about to show her his hometown and his childhood. He'd never exposed his past to anyone outside of Callie, and look what had happened then? He'd lost her.

CHAPTER TWO

"HOLD ON A SEC."

Laura Cameron held the phone against her chest and leaned her forehead on her hand, needing a minute, just one blessed second, to figure out how to prevent the tornado that was barreling down on her.

She and Vin had been circling around the same old argument for twenty minutes and they still weren't any closer to solving it than when they'd started. After Laura had lost their baby, Vin had left Accord to "clear" his head in Las Vegas. She'd been devastated by her miscarriage. He'd been relieved. He'd said he needed time away.

She put the receiver to her ear again. "Vin, I know you don't want children yet, but—"

"I'm not coming back, Laura."

He'd said it so quietly she wasn't sure what she'd heard. "Pardon?"

"I'm not coming back."

Her breath hitched in her throat, her shock too great, too large, to have a voice. Nothing coherent, nothing but denial, the one word *no,* formed inside of her.

"We want different things," he said. "You want babies right away. I want to wait."

"Of course I want babies right away. We've been engaged for five years. I'm thirty-five and running out of time." Vin could afford to wait. She couldn't.

"We're not getting married, Laura. Sorry."

"But…" She didn't know what to say, how to change his mind.

Pain burned in her chest. It was over? That was it? After five years she was losing her fiancé and the beginning of a family and all it merited was a simple *sorry?* Her world was falling apart and all she got was one lousy, measly *sorry?*

"There are no buts, Laura. You shoulda seen it coming."

Yes, part of her had seen it coming, but the larger part had resisted.

"I gotta go. You okay?"

She couldn't respond, had nothing inside of her at the moment for the man who was walking away from her.

For a long time after disconnecting, she sat with her head in her hands, rocking, until she realized she was grieving more for the baby she'd lost in her miscarriage than for Vin. What really saddened her most about losing him was that she would miss him more for the chance at a family she'd have with him rather than for *him*. How sad was that? How screwed up?

She doubled forward holding her stomach. She wanted her unborn baby back. At least then she would still have a chance at children. But no. She wanted a *family*.

Sick with herself, with botched opportunities and lost chances, with hope shattered, she ran downstairs to the one thing that worked in her life—her bakery café.

In the kitchen, she swiped a hand across her stomach, across her empty womb. *I miss you.* There had been butterfly kisses of movement, things that Vin had never felt, tiny filaments that had never bound him to the baby as they had for Laura.

She breathed deeply, calling on reserves that were depleting too quickly, and pulled herself together. At least she still had her baking and her business, her driving passion.

The café was full so she put on her game face, but smiling hurt. Her empty body hurt. The memory of the flutters of an "almost" little being ached.

She stepped up to the counter so she wouldn't wrap her arms across her belly and cry. She was stronger than that.

A lineup eight- or nine-deep awaited service. Good. *This* she could do, even if she couldn't hold on to a fiancé or an unborn babe. This she could do, and do *well*.

HUNGER GNAWED A hole in Nick's belly. Or maybe it was in his psyche. Standing in the town he'd grown up in, he couldn't tell the difference.

He and Emily stood on Main Street in Accord in front of a bakery, with his stomach grumbling as it had done too often in his growing-up years in Accord.

As a boy, he used to stare at baked goods in this very window while his mouth watered and his belly grumbled. He'd been too poor to walk into the place all those years ago, let alone be able to purchase anything.

He wasn't poor now. He could buy this place ten times over without feeling a strain.

So was his hunger a Pavlovian response to returning to Accord? Hell, all he knew was that, despite his wealth, here he stood feeling small again.

When he used to leave fingerprints on the glass, Mr. Foster would come running out to shoo him along. From a block away, he'd watch the old guy spray the window with glass cleaner. A second later, no trace of Nick would remain.

Wasn't that a disturbingly apt metaphor for how Nick had felt growing up in this town? Invisible?

"Dad, can we go in?" Emily looked up at him, clearly puzzled by his hesitation.

He wanted to walk into the place as if he owned it, but he knew who really did own it these days, and he knew she wouldn't be glad to see him. Laura Cameron was the first woman to come between him and his brother Gabe, long before Callie had.

"I'm hungry," Emily said.

He opened the door and let her step inside then followed into warm cinnamon-and-vanilla-scented air that wrapped seductive arms around him, luring him in with the promise of home, but it was something he'd never smelled in his house growing up.

Mom had worked two jobs while Gabe had learned to cook the basics to keep his brothers fed.

Nick was perfectly happy with his life in Seattle. True, he didn't see enough of Emily. Her childhood had slipped away like windblown clouds, but he was changing that, starting here, starting now. So he didn't need the homey-ness of the scent of baked goods to make him feel homesick. Because he wasn't.

"Wow," Emily breathed. "This place is great, Dad."

"Wow is right."

Inside, the shop looked like no ordinary bakery, splashed as the walls were with red and yellow. Dominating the far wall, dots of orange popped from spring greens in an unframed oversize print of Klimt's *Field of Poppies*.

Laura had transformed the plain old bakery into a harvest of the bold and the sensual, a feast for all of the senses.

He nudged Emily gently. "Go figure out what you want."

She ran to the display cases.

Amid the hum of conversation, music danced from speakers somewhere in the ceiling, Imelda May performing a Les Paul classic with her sexy *kitty, kitty, kitty* chorus accompanied by Jeff Beck's insanely difficult guitar riffs.

The bakery cum coffee shop was an original. He knew there was nothing like it in Seattle. He looked through the closing door at Main Street, to make sure he was still in small-town Accord. He turned back to the inside of the bakery. *Alice through the Looking Glass*.

Laura had turned the original bakery into a small café, had squeezed tables and chairs into every available spot and had covered them with brightly colored tablecloths. All seats were taken. There was a sizable lineup at the counter. Popular place. A going concern. As a businessman he could appreciate her success.

Just to the left of the door, she had hung a bulletin board with notices and business cards stuck all over it. One of the pamphlets read Keep Our Youth Here. Ha! Good luck with that one. You had to offer them something worth staying for. He'd never found anything to keep him here. Why would today's youth stay?

He'd offered to pay tuition for any kid completing high school and willing to study Hospitality or Culinary Arts then guarantee two years working in his resort.

So far, he'd had a lot of interest.

It wasn't charity, but a keen move calculated to get the town on his side in convincing his older brother Gabe to sell his portion of the land. Once Gabe had capitulated, middle brother Tyler had soon followed.

Another notice asked for volunteers to coach a basketball league. God, he used to love basketball. He'd played in high school. It had gotten him through his adolescent years sane, in one piece. He touched the phone number at the bottom of the page. He hadn't played since then.

He should have taught Emily how. She had those long coltish legs. He stifled a sigh. He'd missed so much.

Impatient with himself, he took his place in line. Regrets were a waste of time and energy.

A table cleared against the wall. "Emily, do you know what you want?"

"Yeah, Dad, one of our sandwiches and a brownie."

"Go grab that table and I'll bring everything over."

The music changed to Texas country rock. Steve Earle. "Copperhead Road." Where were the vapid pop songs that flooded radio stations these days, or the rap, or the country music he'd expected in rural Colorado?

He glanced up toward the chalkboard that listed drinks and baked goods, but a flash of rich chestnut hair caught his eye and quickened his pulse.

Laura.

In the past thirteen years, he'd seen her only once in the high school auditorium, when he'd come in January to give his sales talk to the people of Accord. The second he'd gone up onstage, she'd run from the room so he'd seen her only from a distance. He hadn't been close enough to get the full impact of her beauty and her personality. He was now. There was no other woman on earth like her.

Even Callie paled by comparison.

Crap. It all came crashing back. He was fifteen years old again, his heart was pounding like a snare drum, his hands were sweaty, and he'd just figured out he was in love with an older girl and wanted to rip his brother's arms off because he was holding her and kissing her on the veranda as if he had a right to. Well...he did. She'd been Gabe's girlfriend and later his fiancée.

Nothing was simple here in Accord.

Half earth mother and half seductress, Laura stood in the doorway from the back of the shop, even more tempting than she'd been in high school. She'd grown up beautifully. Maturity added fullness to her figure and depth to that intriguing face. Her body had developed curves only hinted at all those years ago.

Lush didn't begin to describe her.

Small pale freckles dotted the perfect white skin of her cheeks. Her crocheted top slipped from one shoulder, revealing a lavender bra strap.

The woman breathed sensuality as effortlessly as she'd slipped on those clothes.

He'd slept with her only one night, when he was nineteen, and it hadn't been nearly enough.

The young girl working at the counter deferred to Laura with a question about cinnamon buns. Laura laughed—God, still so husky—and said to the crowd in the lineup, "You people are insatiable. I'll make a larger batch next time."

The decor and music made perfect sense. She'd always been original, unpredictable and deep.

The music changed again. Keith Jarrett's jazz piano floated through the bakery along with his signature grunts and moans. Describing Laura's taste as eclectic would be an understatement.

She hadn't seen him yet so he looked his fill, that hunger inside of him morphing into something that lunch wouldn't satisfy, into something as strong as a kick to his solar plexus. Where before he'd stepped into the bakery he'd been hungry, now he was ravenous.

"CHARLIE, WHAT CAN I get for you today?" Laura asked, shocked that her voice sounded normal.

"Coffee and two chocolate éclairs."

She'd never noticed before how deep Charlie's voice was. She knew he was reliable, supported himself and his mother with construction work. Came in here like clockwork every day.

In her vulnerable state, she found herself looking at him differently, as a potential father, as though she could just ask, "Hey, you want to have a baby with me?" and *poof!* she would be pregnant. No strings attached.

Stupid, foolish thought. She didn't want single motherhood. She *wanted* strings attached, heavenly binding forever strings. She wanted her life tied up with a man's, not because she felt incomplete without one—lord, no, she was independent—but because she loved families. Babies did well in families.

Even so, she couldn't stop herself from seeing the men she knew in a new way.

When Geoff stepped forward and ordered his usual, two bran muffins and a caramel latte, she watched him from the corner of her eye.

She hadn't noticed before today that he wasn't half bad-looking. She packaged his coffee and muffins and took his money.

Geoff had to be in his mid-fifties. He was a nice guy, but she couldn't imagine sleeping with him, the age difference too broad for her. That she'd considered it even for a split second spoke of her desperation.

Sheila McCabe and her daughter were next in line.

After Sheila placed her order, Laura asked Tilly to fill it then took a serving paper and picked up a tiny cookie perfectly shaped like a duck. She stepped around the counter and crouched to address little Shawna.

"Do you remember how much you liked these cookies last year?"

When she saw the yellow icing and orange beak and two dark dots for eyes, Shawna's own eyes grew big and round. "They were good."

"This is a spring present from me to you."

Impulsively, Shawna threw her four-year-old arms around Laura's neck. Oh heaven. Laura squeezed her right back. Oh, the urge to just have a baby somehow, anyhow, overwhelmed her, warred with her beliefs, had her considering calling adoption agencies.

When she stood up, she said, "You enjoy that, sweetie pie," and waved off Sheila's thanks. She kept that batch of cookies on the side to hand out to children.

Last in the lineup, a man checked out the goodies left in the glass cabinets while she wrapped the duck cookies so they wouldn't go stale.

Her stomach grumbled. She hadn't gotten around to eating lunch.

With a quick glance at the stranger's clothes, she noticed he was overdressed for Accord. They didn't get a lot of suits here. Ranchers, yes. Plenty of cowboy hats, sure. But business suits? On a Saturday? Not so much.

"Can I help you?" she asked while she wiped the counter.

"I'll have a coffee and two turkeys on rye with avocado. I also want a hot chocolate and two brownies."

He pulled a couple of twenties out of his wallet and handed them to her. He held himself unnaturally still and it gave her pause. She glanced up…and her heart stopped.

Pain took her breath away.

Nick Jordan stood on the other side of the counter. Clean-cut. Rich. Gorgeous in his refined way. Not in the way of the men she usually went for, like his rugged brother Gabe. But then, Nick had ruined her chances with Gabe, hadn't he? Before that, her life had been right on track.

This man had upset her plan, had stolen her dream. She'd had it all worked out—marriage to Gabe, then a pair of children, then starting a bakery when they were old enough to go to school.

After the heartbreak of losing Gabe, throughout her twenties, she hadn't worried, but no man had tempted her until Vin and he wasn't ready to settle down. So…here she was, with minutes turning into days and weeks into years. And years into frustration and loss. And still no family.

Nick watched her steadily. He'd changed from the young man who had seduced her. Gone was the cockiness, replaced by a quiet confidence. He watched her with those dark coffee-colored, almost-black eyes that were the Jordan trademark.

Nick's, though, were set in a more streamlined face than either Gabe's or Tyler's, his high cheekbones strong, his jaw fine-boned. In Laura's opinion, he was the best-looking of those three handsome boys.

To her disgrace, her heart rate stuttered. She still found him attractive and that was *awful*. The man was a snake. Lower than a snake.

The breath he'd just robbed her of returned.

"You have a lot of nerve." Her hard tone could cut glass. "What are you doing in my shop?"

A ruddy blush rose into his cheeks and, for a moment, his gaze shot away from hers. As it should have. He deserved to be ashamed of himself after what he'd done.

She couldn't serve him, couldn't stand there and make small talk with the man who had robbed her of her chance at marriage and children with Gabe.

"Go to hell."

She turned and ran from the room, not caring that she rushed, not giving a rat's ass that, heaven forbid, he should think she was running from him. She was. She hurt. And she was afraid. Not of him, but of herself and her reaction to him. It had been a long, long time since a man had her sweating, had her wanting to lose control, had her wanting reason to take a backseat to passion.

No, she ordered herself. None of this again.

In the kitchen, she leaned her hands on the counter, straight-armed and rigid so she wouldn't fall apart, and closed her eyes. She hurt.

NICK HEARD WHISPERS spin around the café.

Who's that? What's happening? What's up? Isn't that Nick Jordan? Curiosity flashed through the room like sheet lightning.

Did Laura know she'd yelled in her anger?

He felt all eyes on him.

Not so invisible now, are you, Jordan? his psyche mocked. *You should have checked whether she was in here before entering.*

He was a thirty-two-year-old multimillionaire, a successful businessman who didn't let others run roughshod over him. He controlled people. He controlled his emotions. Laura Cameron shouldn't be able to turn him back into that callow teenager he'd been around her, but he felt like that boy, sick in love with his older brother's fiancée. He'd kept his secret deeply hidden, until that one night.

She'd been three years older than him. To a nineteen-year-old boy/man, that was a lifetime. In his fevered nighttime sweats, his dreams had been deeply erotic. Then, that one night, she'd been even better in reality.

They needed to talk.

He flew around the end of the counter and into the back.

"Hey," he heard the girl named Tilly call.

Stalking into an industrial kitchen, he pulled up short.

What he saw on Laura's face stunned him. Grief. Misery. He had expected anger, but not pain, or whatever it was that made her look as if she wanted to crawl into a dark place and curl into a ball.

Why would seeing him affect her so much? That one night had been thirteen years ago. She was a successful business-woman. So what was her problem?

He had to have it out with her, whatever *it* was. He couldn't leave it alone, had to give it the perspective of time passed so it wouldn't eat into his stomach any more than it just had.

"Laura," he said, quietly.

Her eyes flew open.

Emotions flitted across her features like fireflies—anger, loss, regret and grief. For the briefest moment, the woman he'd always thought of as invulnerable looked lost.

"What's wrong?"

Her face turned red.

"What's wrong?" After her yelling out front, her voice was now too quiet. "You have to ask? After what you did?"

They had never talked about it.

"I know what I did, Laura, but that was only one night

thirteen years ago." *Then why do you still feel it as though it happened last night? As though your marriage and daughter and career never took place?*

"I know it was only one night."

"I didn't exactly seduce you."

Her cheeks flamed. "You—"

Nick felt someone approach behind him.

"I'm sorry, Laura," she said. "He ran in here before I could stop him."

"It's okay, Tilly. Go finish with the customers."

Tilly's footsteps whispered away.

He stepped closer to Laura. She'd opened an old wound and he wanted to heal it, to finish with it here and now, and euthanize like a rabid dog the insanity he hadn't realized until this moment still foamed inside of him. "You were as hot for me as I was for you."

Her expression took on some of the guilt with which he lashed himself. "Yes," she conceded. "I was. I turned out to be a willing partner. I hadn't planned that night, though. You had."

"True." While she might have given in to temptation in the spur of the moment, she hadn't had the ulterior motive he'd had when he'd returned to town with the aim of sleeping with her.

He'd wanted to destroy his brother, to shame and embarrass Gabe the way he'd shamed Nick in front of the man he'd wanted to work for. Nick had left college with Marsha. They had gone to Seattle to meet her father. Nick wanted to marry Marsha and work for Mort.

"You arranged for Gabe to find us," Laura said.

"Yes. What difference did it make?"

"I was engaged to him. I was going to marry him."

"Did you honestly think you could still do that after we'd slept together?"

"No. I was guilty of infidelity. I wouldn't have made Gabe

try to live with that." She huffed out a breath loaded with anger. "I would have softened the blow, though, and found a better way to tell him than to have him walk in on us."

She pressed a hand against her mouth. "It must have been awful for him."

"I wanted him to find us."

"I eventually figured that out. Why?"

"I'd left college and run off with a girl. I wanted to marry her. Gabe caught up to us and dragged me back to college. He shamed me in front of her and her father." He still remembered how deeply his embarrassment had run, how humiliated he'd felt, and how afraid he'd been that Gabe had ruined his chances with both Marsha and Mort permanently.

"So? He'd worked for five years to save enough money for you to go. You should have been grateful. You should have been down on your knees kissing his feet." She leaned forward, speaking with a feverish intensity. "You and Tyler would have been the first in the family to attend college. All thanks to Gabe."

"So? It wasn't what *I* wanted. It wasn't the way *I* wanted to start my career. The girl's father was a big deal in development. He had a lot of money. I wanted him for a father-in-law. I knew I could learn more from him firsthand than I would ever learn in school."

"So, why didn't you just run away again? Why come back to Accord to seduce me?" He would have objected, but she rushed on. "Yes, you did seduce me, even if you didn't find it hard to do. I would have let my attraction to you slide. I would have had a good life with Gabe."

"I saved you from a mediocre future."

"Not true. Gabe is a good man."

"You couldn't have loved him too much if you were tempted by me so easily. Marriage to Gabe would have been too tame for you. I rescued you."

"Don't," she bit out. "It wasn't a charitable act. What you

did had nothing to do with me and everything to do with hurting Gabe as much as you could."

"Yes." He'd wanted to hurt Gabe, the meddling bastard, but seducing Laura had been magnificent. Yeah, it had everything to do with hurting his brother, but so much to do with Laura, too. Lovely, breathtaking Laura.

"You were a selfish bastard concerned only with your own revenge."

"I was only nineteen. I regret it now."

At his even tone, her eyes narrowed. "What are you? A robot? Don't you have feelings?"

Too many at the moment. "I don't see the value in indulging them."

They stared at each other, apparently at an impasse.

"I have to go," he said. "My daughter is waiting for her lunch."

Something changed in Laura, as though a whirlwind fanned a flame higher. A blush flared on her cheeks.

"You have a daughter?" she asked, her voice quiet again, but pulsing with anger.

He cocked his head. "Why does that make you angry?"

"You have no idea what you took from me, do you?" Laura asked. "How unfair it is that you have a child while I don't? You stole my chance at a family."

Ah. He understood. "You didn't want Gabe as much as you wanted children. Gabe was a means to an end."

"I loved him. He was a good man. He would have made a brilliant father."

For the briefest moment, he thought she might cry. Over ancient history?

"You owe me so much."

"Were there no other men in this town who would marry you and give you babies?" Were they blind?

She shook her head, once, quickly. There were things going

on here that he didn't understand, that she didn't want to share with him. He didn't blame her. They were strangers.

The longer she stared at him, the more he got the impression of something forming inside of her, something calculating and sly, of that wind fanning a twister.

"You owe me," she said again, with conviction this time.

Her smile worried him.

"What do you mean?" he asked.

"You owe me a baby."

CHAPTER THREE

"WHAT?"

"I'm planning to collect on an old debt."

"You're—" Had he heard her right? She couldn't possibly mean—? "You're asking me to *impregnate* you?"

"If you want to be technical about it. I'd rather call it love-making."

"You're not even talking in vitro fertilization. You're talking *sex*."

"Yes."

"You want to use my body."

"You used mine to get your petty revenge on Gabe."

Yes, he had. Gladly. Passionately.

"Today is the perfect day."

Meaning she was ovulating.

The idea was ludicrous.

She was insane.

She was glorious.

Glorious, but out of her mind.

He would make love to her in a heartbeat, but give her a baby? No.

"I barely have time for my own daughter, let alone having another child."

"I don't want you involved. The baby would be mine."

"No."

"Why not? All I need is a little sperm."

It angered him that she wanted to use him as though his

penis were nothing more than a syringe. Talk about being made a sexual object.

Thirteen years ago, you used her for your own ends, didn't you?

Yes, but I also wanted her.

And yet, you walked away.

I had bigger fish to fry.

You were heartless.

It was business.

So is this for her. A means to an end she obviously wants desperately.

He sympathized, he really did, but her demand left him cold. He leaned back against the counter and rammed his hands into his pockets, because they were having ideas of their own, of giving in to Laura. "Besides, I'm only here for one day."

"My apartment's upstairs."

"Now?" he sputtered then choked on his own spit.

"Now."

The look on her face—of hope and…hope—made him wish that he could give in, but no. He didn't want another child. He refused to have a baby if he couldn't be part of its life. He wouldn't do that to a child again. Never again.

He barely had time for his daughter. Look what that was doing to Emily. He'd just made a commitment to her, wanted to get to know her better. A baby would take all of his attention away from her. No way was he having another kid.

"I can't," he said, sidestepping the issue. "My daughter is with me and I have to deal with a problem on the business site."

"It only has to take fifteen minutes."

To pay homage to a masterpiece? No. If he were going to love her, he would do it right. If he was going to sin, he was going to *sin,* and he sure as hell wouldn't rush.

He shook his head.

She drew a shaky breath. "It was worth a shot."

"I have to go."

Something inside of her had turned off and she merely nodded. She seemed diminished and he hated that.

He felt responsibility, but didn't know what else to say to her, or what to do, so he returned to the bakery at the front of the building, unsettled and shaken. That was saying a lot. Nothing much shook him.

Hadn't he more than once been called a cold bastard?

The bakery was humming again with conversation, so Nick placed his order with Tilly, paid for it and waited at the table with Emily. Laura wasn't going to kick him out of the café, not with Emily here. Laura wouldn't hurt a young girl if her life depended on it.

"Dad?" Emily sounded uncertain. "What was that about? Why did you go in the back room?"

"Laura and I had a misunderstanding a long time ago. I tried to settle it."

"Did you?"

"What?"

"Settle it?"

He shook his head. Not by a long shot.

Music still rang from the speakers overhead. He recognized Dr. John and Rickie Lee Jones. "Makin' Whoopee." It suited Laura, made her earthy laugh sound as if it held a world of secrets whispered on hot nights. Nick wanted to make whoopee with her. He just didn't want to give her a baby.

I CAN'T BELIEVE I said something so idiotic.

Laura took a pitcher of iced tea out of the walk-in cooler, poured herself a glass and added ice. Needing to cool down, she trudged up the back stairs to her apartment, the ice in the glass clinking because her hands were shaking so badly.

Telling Nick Jordan he owed her a baby was so far removed from what she wanted in her life and how she wanted it. Upstairs, she lay on her bed and stared at the colored gauze draping the ceiling.

She'd hung it there to create a sexy harbor, a haven for sex play. She loved sex. Adored it. Loved both the noisy sloppiness and the exquisite pleasure. She used every sense to heighten her enjoyment—sight, scent, sound.

She found no haven here at the moment.

Her cheeks, her chest, still burned. She replayed every speck of her conversation with Nick.

You owe me a baby.

Temporary insanity.

What else would explain it?

Desperation?

Yeah, that, too.

She'd propositioned the worst man on the planet, the worst man for her. When he'd mentioned his daughter, something inside of her had snapped. Where was the fairness in life? He had ruined her chances with Gabe then had gone off and fathered a child of his own.

He might not have been responsible for all of the guilt in their one-night affair—she understood her own culpability, her own weakness in giving in to him all those years ago, and accepted it—but she hadn't planned that night. *He had.*

She could have resisted Nick for the rest of her life, but that one night, he'd put real effort into getting her into his bed. And it had worked.

Damn her passionate nature and her unruly attraction to Nick. What was it about the man?

She would never in a million years have had Gabe find them together. She couldn't let go of her anger at Nick for that.

Her throat ached with the urge to scream. *He* shouldn't be a parent. *She* should.

She lay on her bed with the weight of shame and chagrin and envy hurting her chest and with tears leaking from the corners of her eyes. She'd never been a weak person. She'd always depended on herself.

At this moment, she needed someone. She couldn't be alone right now.

She couldn't stay here harming herself with jealousy and bitterness and anger. She had to get out, to find support.

She'd always been independent, but it was time to ask for help. She needed someone to hold her.

Against habit, natural inclination and history, she needed her mom.

OLIVIA CAMERON STEPPED out of the office in the gallery she owned called Palette. The door chime had sounded. She hoped it was a customer. It had been a slow day.

When she saw who had entered, she halted.

Aiden McQuorrie.

He didn't realize she was there, so she just watched him. Dear God, he was beautiful.

He prowled the gallery studying the current artwork on display. She'd always thought *prowled* an odd verb to use for a man, fanciful and too romantic, but if ever it fit a man, that man was Aiden.

Sculpting stone had broadened Aiden's shoulders, had built powerful biceps and had kept his midriff so trim and hard it was concave.

His hard handsome profile was softened by too-long hair. When he worked, he often forgot about things mortals did as a matter of course, like eating and getting haircuts. Aiden was an artist. When he was sculpting, time meant nothing to him.

Olivia wished she were an artist so she could paint him, but she wasn't. Her deepest regret was that she couldn't paint, or sketch or sculpt, or fashion art of any kind. Instead, she funneled her passion into enjoying the art others produced, like Aiden's stunning stone sculptures and divine crazed metal abstractions, and into promoting artists.

She loved his artist's eye and his lack of inhibition.

He prowled closer and the hard planes of his face reminded her of a laird in ancient times in Scotland surveying his holdings and his clan. She could picture him in a kilt. His legs would be strong to match the rest of his body.

Aiden McQuorrie was gorgeous and passionate, and she loved every particle of his temperamental genius. She loved him.

And there wasn't a damn thing Olivia Cameron could do about it. In two days, she would turn fifty-eight. According to Aiden's press release, he was forty-three.

"Aiden, what can I do for you?" Her voice sounded extra sultry today. She didn't know why. People had remarked on it often, on how at odds it was with her cultured manner. It wasn't something she put on. It was just the way her voice came out of her throat.

"Come to my place," he said without preamble.

What? Her imagination stirred. Why did he want her there?

"I have work to show you."

Oh. Work. *Of course, you foolish old woman. Why else would he want you there?* She called herself an old woman, but didn't feel like one. She didn't even feel middle-aged, had yet to figure out when middle age ended and old age began. One thing was certain—she was foolish to think of Aiden as anything but a client.

"Of course," she said. "I'd be happy to come over. Monica is covering for me tomorrow. Would that work for you?" Since she had hired Monica Accord, Olivia had been able to take Sundays off for the first time in years.

"Aye."

The slightest trace of a Scottish burr softened his speech every so often, a reminder that he hadn't been born in Colorado. It made her want to swoon, foolish, middle-aged, not-quite-old woman that she was.

"What time should I come over?"

"Noon."

He wasn't much for words.

He left the gallery and Olivia ran to the window to watch as that body, a piece of artwork in itself, strode down Main Street.

For Pete's sake, he was fifteen years younger than her. She had no right to drool over a forty-three-year-old man, even if he was as gorgeous as Michelangelo's *David,* albeit more rough-hewn.

So what if he was handsome? She'd known good-looking men, including her late husband. She wasn't that shallow. Oh, but there was that talent, that artistic genius that had her drooling over his work. And that intensity. When he gazed at a woman, he really *looked,* deeply, as though searching her soul for all of her secrets.

She'd only ever known one man—her husband. He'd died ten years ago. She didn't have the experience to deal with a man like Aiden McQuorrie.

The bell above her door chimed.

"Mom?"

She stepped away from the window, but not until after Aiden had entered the food market down the street and she could no longer see him.

"Mom? Are you okay? What are you looking at?"

"Nothing." She forced images of Aiden from her mind and turned to her daughter. When she saw misery and pain on Laura's face, her gaze sharpened. "Something's happened. What?"

Laura shrugged and studied one of the paintings. Olivia took her arm and spun her around.

"Laura, tell me what's wrong."

"Nick Jordan's back in town."

"Oh, honey, come here." She embraced her daughter, fully understanding what this meant to Laura. Coming on the heels of losing her baby, it must be devastating.

Why on earth was Olivia so worried about a simple business meeting with a man when her daughter was suffering so?

"Come." She led her into the back office and plugged in the electric kettle. "We knew he would come to town once they started building the resort."

"I know, but the timing couldn't have been worse." Laura fell into a chair, her lack of grace a sign of how upset she was. "Vin called while I was on lunch. It's over. He's not coming back."

Olivia turned from dropping a tea bag into a pot. "Didn't you suspect he might not?"

Laura worried a chip in one of her nails, concentrating so hard Olivia wondered whether she were trying not to cry. "I tried to stay positive."

Olivia sat across from her and took her hand. "It's hard to accept the truth."

"I feel like he was my last chance."

"You don't need a man to have a baby. Not these days."

"I do, Mom. I want a family."

Olivia didn't have to ask why. She and Laura had been down this road before. She wanted what they'd had before her sister died.

"Mom, do you ever think about Amber?"

As though Olivia had spoken the thought aloud, Laura mentioned her. Anger flashed through Olivia. "Why?" They never talked about her. Never spoke her name out loud.

"I do," Laura said quietly. "All the time."

"Why?" *Why open this wound I've spent twenty-one years cauterizing?* Twenty-one long years.

"Because I miss her so much. Don't you?"

All the time. "I live for the present."

"Do you?"

Those two words spoken so quietly, as though her daughter could look inside her heart and know her better than she knew herself, shattered her.

She exploded. "Yes! Why would you do this?"

Laura's jaw dropped. She stared at Olivia as though her mother had two heads. "Do what?"

"Bring up the worst period of my life?"

"I need to talk about Amber."

"Stop it." Olivia slammed her hand onto the table. "I have a good life. I run a solid business. I've come to terms with the past. Why are you people coming around stirring things up?"

"You people? Mom, it's only me. What's going on?" Laura stretched a hand toward her but Olivia stood up from the table, dodging it.

You're dredging up all of that sorrow, that crippling guilt, reminding me of what Amber's death cost me and your father, of how he took his solace in another woman's arms—a woman twelve years younger than me. Of how I lost twice. Never in the ten years after that were we close again. Then he died. Now you're trying desperately to turn me into a grandmother while there's a man fifteen years younger than me, fifteen years, *with whom I've fallen in love and can't possibly have.*

How could she say any of this to Laura?

"Mom?"

"I can't talk about it. I—I have a headache today."

"I didn't know. Can I get anything for you?"

Olivia sat down at the table again and rubbed her temples. "I need some time alone."

"Maybe you should close the shop early today."

Olivia smiled weakly. "Maybe I will."

Laura touched her shoulder as she passed to leave. Olivia grasped her fingers. "I love you."

"I know, Mom. I love you, too."

Laura left and Olivia knew in her bone marrow that she'd disappointed her daughter.

NICK FOUND THE entire demolition team standing around. He and Emily had driven straight out to the old homestead after lunch.

The workers were supposed to be taking down trees this weekend, specific trees worked out with the architect, disturbing nature as little as possible and incorporating it into the design of the building.

"Rene," he called, and his foreman turned from the man he was talking to and walked over.

"Nick, good to see you here." They shook hands. "Nothing's changed since last night. The Native Americans are still here."

Nick eyed the row of men and women blocking his big machinery from entering the work site. He tapped his fist on the hood of the car. Emily waited quietly beside him.

"They don't quarrel that your family already owns the land," Rene said. "Like I said on the phone, this is spiritual. You gotta respect the dead."

Nick approached the group.

"Can we talk?" he asked.

"Sure," the tallest man answered, maybe eighteen years old with high cheekbones and straight dark hair that hung past his shoulders.

"My family never mentioned burial grounds here," Nick said.

"They weren't formal burials. This was part of a migratory route. Our ancestors were buried where they fell, either from injury or old age."

"So you don't know *exactly* where they are?"

"Nope. Just on the land somewhere."

Nick pinched his lower lip, thinking. Contrary to what most people thought, he wasn't completely insensitive. This was a serious issue. He would be smart to take it seriously.

"There should be a solution to this, a win-win that would benefit everyone." He stepped away for a minute and then came back as a solution started to form. "Who wants to act as the representative of this group? You?"

The boy nodded, took Nick's outstretched hand and shook it. "I'm Salem Pearce."

"Nick Jordan. Do you have access to elders who might know stories of this land?"

"I can locate them."

"Good. I'll find out whether there's a professor or some kind of expert in Native American history at the university in Colorado Springs or somewhere in the state. See whether there are records anywhere."

"Good luck with that," Salem said. "Ours is an oral history."

Nick slipped a business card out of his jacket pocket and wrote his cell number on the back. "Let's aim to meet ASAP, ideally on Monday, to sort this out. I'll get an authority here by then. Think you can pull your elders together by then?"

"Yep." The young man took a convenience-store receipt from his pocket and wrote his number on the back. "Call me if you have trouble locating an expert. I'll see what I can do."

"Good. You and your friends can go home. I'll send the crews home, too. Nothing will happen here before we talk."

As he turned away, Nick heard someone ask Salem if they could trust him.

Over his shoulder, Nick said, "You have my word. We won't touch the land until we settle this issue."

A thought occurred to Nick. "Won't you be in school on Monday?"

Salem shook his head. "I graduated from high school last year."

"How old are you?"

"Eighteen."

"You graduated *last* year?"

"Finished a year early," he said with quiet pride.

"Why aren't you in college?"

A faint blush tarnished the flawless dark skin. "No money."

"What about my offer of a college education to anyone who wants to work in my resort?"

"I don't want to cook or book rooms in hotels."

"What do you want to do?"

"I want to document my people's history before it's lost forever. To educate everyone about my culture."

"Good luck finding a job in that area." Nick wasn't being cruel, just honest. Unless he could afford years of university to become a prof, the kid wasn't going to find the kind of work he wanted. "See you on Monday."

Nick paced away toward the car. After all he'd gone through to make this resort a reality, now he had to deal with this?

Rene followed him. "I'm beginning to think this deal is doomed."

Nick turned on his foreman. "I don't want to hear that kind of talk. This ski resort is getting built. Period."

"How? We can't tear up their ancestors."

"I'll figure out something." He returned to the car and Emily while the Native Americans and construction workers dispersed to different vehicles and left the site.

Emily watched him expectantly. She would want to go inside that house.

Time to face it, and all of its issues, down.

Laura stepped out of the Palette and stopped short, lost. She'd gone to her mother for support, but there hadn't been any. It brought up an old sensation, a familiar one, of times when she'd gone to her in the past only to come away dissatisfied, and feeling so alone, the worst time, of course, after Amber's death.

She needed her now, though, desperately, but something was going on with Mom these days that Laura just couldn't sort out.

Never in her life had Laura felt so…without an anchor. Without a purpose, especially not on a Saturday night when she was usually up for a good time.

She and Vin used to go out for dinner, sometimes just with

each other, sometimes with friends, and would have a blast. Then they would return to Laura's apartment, to her sexy haven, and make love for hours.

Saturday night was usually Laura's night.

The bakery was closed on Sundays, so she didn't have to bake tonight for tomorrow's customers.

She didn't know what to do with herself when she had so much on her mind, including that asinine demand she'd made of Nick.

You owe me.

That wasn't how she wanted a baby, but his presence had rattled her. As did her unreasonable attraction to him. What was it about Nick Jordan that brought out the worst, and the best, in her?

She started down Main, drawn by the small white chapel on a small hill past the end of Accord proper. She needed to visit Amber, as she had done so often since she'd lost her baby.

As soon as she opened the gate in the white picket fence and stepped into the cemetery on the outskirts of town, a measure of peace settled over her. Row upon row of white headstones stood out on green spring grass.

White oxeye daisies and yellow-green northern paintbrush dotted the grass. When the grass became long enough to need cutting, the flowers would be mowed down, too. She was glad she was here this early in the season to catch them in bloom.

The small white wooden chapel had been built sometime in the 1800s and was framed by the mountain in the distance on Jordan land. This early in spring, there was still snow on top of Luther.

In the children's section, she sat on the well-manicured grass in front of Amber's small grave and plucked weeds curled up against the headstone.

Amber Cameron. 1985–1991. Taken Too Soon. Rest In Peace, Sweet Angel.

Laura ran her hand across the grass covering the short grave.

"Mom called." Laura turned at the sound of her brother's voice. "Said you were probably here."

Noah was two years older than her and a throwback to the sixties. On this unseasonably warm April day, he wore thick gray socks with Birkenstock sandals, jeans and an ivory Aran knit pullover with a hole in one sleeve. He owned the Army Surplus, he was a survivalist and an organic farmer and never, ever apologized for who he was.

"I thought I should come make sure you're okay."

"I'm okay. Just a little blue."

"From losing the baby?"

She nodded. Noah, bless his heart, was the only one who wasn't urging her to forget about it, to go for drinks with well-meaning friends who sympathized and said things like, *Don't worry. You'll get pregnant again.*

But with whom?

Five months had passed and Noah thought she had the right to still grieve, bless him.

"Vin broke up with me today. For good."

"Aw, Laura, I'm sorry."

"Me, too."

Noah crouched beside her. "Why did you come here?"

"I miss the baby, but I miss Amber, too. Isn't that strange when it's been over twenty years?"

"Give yourself a break, sis. Mom was trying to start her gallery and you took to Amber like a mother, like you were born to nurture. Sometimes, I think Amber's death hit you harder than it did Mom."

"I'm not so sure. I think Mom just knew better than me how to drive her grief underground."

"She morphed it into energy for that store."

"I remember," Laura murmured. She'd been only fourteen. Her little sister died and her mother became emotionally unavailable. Dad took his grief to another woman. Noah had understood Laura's anguish, but he'd been an active sixteen-year-old with a lot of friends and out of the house every day, leaving her with no one to whom she could turn.

Amber had drowned in a swimming pool and Laura's family had disintegrated. Laura had been trying to put a family together for herself ever since.

She didn't need a degree in psychology to understand fully what drove her. She wanted a *whole* family.

"Laura, I need to warn you," Noah said. "Nick Jordan's in town. I saw him on Main this morning."

"Thanks. I appreciate the warning, but he came into the bakery. We had a talk."

"I wouldn't mind having a talk with him." Noah's voice hardened and his hands curled into fists, curious given he was a lover, not a fighter.

"I did something crazy, Noah."

"What?"

"I told Nick Jordan he owed me a baby."

"Laura?" Noah asked quietly, with a mixture of dread and warning in his tone. "What did you mean by that?"

"I propositioned him. Told him we needed to have sex." She laughed, but there was no humor in it.

"Sis…"

"It's okay. He didn't take me up on it." She pulled a few tufts of too-long grass from around Amber's headstone. "I was feeling desperate. Vin called off our engagement, so there'll be no more babies with him."

He touched her hair. "You have rotten luck with men."

"I sure know how to pick them, don't I?"

A frown furrowed Noah's brow. "I'm worried about you."

"There's no need. It was temporary insanity. I won't do anything rash."

"You sure?"

"Positive. I know what I want, Noah, *and* what I *don't* want."

He stood. "I have to get back."

"Did you close the store to come over here?"

Noah shrugged.

"Meaning yes." She fingered the grass she'd pulled up. "Are you busy later? Want to have supper together?"

He looked disappointed. "Wish I could, sis. Tommy and I are leaving for Pike's Peak. We're rock climbing tomorrow."

She nodded. "Thanks for checking on me."

He touched her arm. "I'm having trouble not worrying about you."

"I'm fine."

"Really?"

"Really. You know I'm capable. I'm independent. I'm a survivor."

"Yeah," he said. "You have been all of those things in the past, but you're living through a hell of a lot right now. You know that stress list? The ten worst things that can happen? You've lost a baby and your fiancé. It's serious stuff, sis."

She forced a smile. "I'm good, Noah. Really. Go."

He kissed the top of her head. "Don't forget Mom's birthday on Monday."

"Thanks for the reminder." She had forgotten. Ever since the miscarriage, she'd been forgetting a lot of things. Her life seemed to be unraveling like a ball of fraying yarn.

"I'll make a reservation for dinner at the steak house for seven. Sound good to you?"

"Sounds good, Noah. Thanks."

She said her goodbyes and stood to walk to Dad's grave. Her relationship with him had grown complicated, complex, after Amber's death. They'd never quite made it back to the loving relationship they'd had before then, and Laura cursed herself every day for not having made peace with her father before he died.

CHAPTER FOUR

"Do you want to go inside the old homestead?" Nick asked Emily.

"Yeah!"

She ran up onto the veranda. He stepped around her and tested the front door. Unlocked.

For the first time in four years, Nick set foot into the house he'd grown up in. He'd come home for Mom's funeral. Before then, it had been nine years since he'd been in this house.

It hadn't changed. That angered Nick. If it had to still be here, couldn't it at least have a new look? What had Gabe done while he'd lived here? Preserved it? Coated it in formaldehyde to remind him of how hard their life had been? Gabe had always been a masochist of sorts.

He hadn't renovated at all, hadn't made additions to make the bedrooms larger, hadn't changed the structure to reflect the times and current styles.

He'd left the place clean. Spotless. Not a trace of a dust bunny or fur ball hid in the corners. Military training did that to a man, Nick guessed.

"Dad?" Emily said from behind him. "Can you move inside so I can see?"

No. But he did. He swallowed his distaste and stepped through the doorway.

"Wow, this is cool." Emily nudged her way around him.

Cool? Not by a long shot.

Over the years, as he'd become more secure in his wealth, he'd tried to give his mother things, even a new house. She'd refused, almost as though she didn't believe she deserved more than what she had here. He'd tried to pay for repairs, upgrades. Always the same answer. "Things are fine as they are."

Had she kept this house as a shrine to Dad? But it didn't feel like one. It felt, simply, like a small old house.

All Mom had taken from him had been flowers on special days and chocolates ordered and delivered from Europe. And trips to stay with him and Marsha and Emily, since he'd had no desire to step into this town again. She'd seemed to enjoy those visits. He'd treasured them.

He stood lost in anger and confusion and fear. Fear? Why? He had nothing to fear here. It was just an old house. Nothing more.

There were things that had happened here that he didn't understand, though, vague memories that confounded him, angry words that bounced around in a room in his mind that he kept locked, and that he never entered. Why dig up the past?

The living room sat empty, stripped of all its old furniture by Gabe. Everything had been cleared but Nick's room.

Still that frisson of fear confused him.

He stepped toward the fireplace, the stones and mantel blackened by years of use. He used to lie in front of the hearth when he was a child. If he were ill, his mother would bring him special treats. More often than not, though, she would be at work and he would be left in Gabe's care. Then, Nick would get healthy things. Chicken soup. Homemade, yes, and Gabe did a good job of turning himself into a credible cook, but to this day, Nick could not drink the stuff.

He'd wanted his mother and her affection. He'd far preferred her coddling to Gabe's practical solutions.

"Because of the way you talked about it, Dad, I thought this would be a really awful house."

"It isn't any great shakes. It was really run-down when we

were kids. Gabe did stuff since then. Fixed the roof, painted. Only the basics. I would have renovated. Gutted it. Enlarged it."

"Even without furniture it feels cozy."

Cozy? Claustrophobic, more like. "It does?"

"Yeah. You just can't see it 'cause you're used to our big place."

The kitchen was pitifully small. They had barely fit a table and four chairs into it. When the whole family was seated at the table, no one could open the fridge to get anything.

He looked down at his daughter. "And you wonder why I have such a big dining room. Now you know."

She turned in a circle, studying the kitchen, the hallway to the bedrooms and one bathroom, and the living room she thought was cozy and he thought was confining, and said, "Now I get it, Dad. You live in such a big house because the one you grew up in was so small."

"I wanted you to have more than I did."

"I do, Dad. I have you."

He swallowed hard. Sweet Emily. After all of his resistance, he was so glad she was here with him today.

"I mean, material goods," he said. "I wanted you to feel like you had comfort and room to breathe."

She wrapped her arms around him and tipped her head back so she could see his face. "I totally understand you now."

His sinuses hurt. His little girl was too wise and too loving toward a guy like him who chewed up business opponents as if they were M&M's.

She pulled away and he missed her warmth, felt a draft as though a ghost had stepped between them.

"Show me where you used to sleep. Which room was yours?"

"Don't—" But she was already running down the hall.

He followed her, his feet dragging because he didn't want to see…that nothing had changed. Gabe had kept it all exactly the way it had been when Nick had left to live in Seattle. More accurately, Mom had left it that way, almost as a shrine, and then Gabe hadn't changed it later when he'd returned from Afghanistan.

The single bed looked small now. The bookshelves were covered with all of his childhood and adolescent books, along with his basketball awards.

His old metal toy trunk sat in the corner where he'd left it.

All of it, every last item that marked the stages of his childhood, was covered with a layer of dust. Forgotten. Abandoned.

Gabe had kept the house clean, but not this room.

Rene had been after him for weeks to deal with his stuff.

"Either clear it out or I'm putting everything in storage. We gotta move on this."

If the weather held and there weren't any late Colorado snowstorms, they wanted to demolish the house so they could start digging the foundation of the hotel the second the land thawed.

He was here now. He might as well clear it out today.

He studied the room. When they were young, Gabe had tried to celebrate every little thing, every pennant or badge any of them had won. Had tried to cheer his younger brothers up.

Once Nick had grown up enough to attend school, though, he'd come to understand that the town hadn't adored him as his mother had. At home, he'd been special. Outside of this house? He'd been just another ordinary kid and that had been the cruelest trick life had played on him.

"Wow," Emily breathed. "You used to play basketball? Look at all of your trophies."

She stood in front of a wall of photos beside his bed. "Look at you and your brothers. You were about my age now. Wow. Surreal."

Farther along was the room Gabe had shared with Tyler. When they were kids, there'd been bunk beds. When Nick had returned for Mom's funeral, a double bed had already replaced those boyish ones.

"So whose bedroom was this? Gabe's or Tyler's?"

"Both."

Emily wrinkled her nose. "Really? Your bedroom was bigger even though there was only one of you?"

He'd never noticed. It had honest to God never registered that Gabe and Tyler had had less than he'd had.

Looking at their small bedroom now, Nick wondered why Mom had worked things out so unfairly.

Emily wandered to the back of the house.

"That was my mother's bedroom. Apparently," he said, "Gabe turned it into an office after she died."

"Can we visit her grave while we're here?"

God, that would be hard. "Yes."

"Can we go through the stuff in your room?"

He nodded.

Gabe had left flattened boxes and packing supplies in the small storage room at the back that used to hold emergency supplies for when they had blackouts. With Colorado's winter storms, they'd been regular. Nick dragged a couple of boxes back to his room.

"Dad, look!" From the windowsill, Emily picked up a tiny figurine of a woman wearing a long dress and with a lamb crooked in one arm. "It's so pretty. Is it really old?"

"Yes. It used to be my mom's, her favorite thing in the whole world." He took it from her. His sinuses ached again. Gabe must have left it in here for him. Okay, so maybe his brother wasn't a complete prick.

Nick handed it back to Emily. God, he missed his mother.

"Here," he said. "Keep it."

"Really, Dad? Thanks." She handled it reverently. "Look! A photo album."

Photos. He hadn't expected Gabe to leave him any.

"Oooh, let's look at them." Emily grabbed an album and

threw herself onto the bed, where light shining through the window formed a halo around her. She could have been a young version of his mother sitting darning the endless reams of socks he and his brothers put holes in.

Where they had inherited their dad's chocolate eyes and nearly black hair, Emily had inherited Mom's mahogany hair and those blue eyes with the striking hazel ring.

But Mom's prettiness had been beaten out of her by two jobs and her grief after Dad died, which she tried to muffle late at night so her boys wouldn't hear her. But they did.

We did.

It had driven Gabe, the oldest, to take care of her and his younger brothers.

It had driven Tyler into law enforcement, to protect any scrap that was good about this life.

It had driven Nick to run and not come back.

But none of that had touched Emily, and he didn't want it to now.

"Was this Grandpa?" She held a photograph of his father standing in brilliant sunlight on top of Mount Everest with a grin on his face. No wonder he'd been happy. The ascent had been a success, an incredible accomplishment.

The descent, however, had killed him.

He merely nodded, unable to speak. He'd been only five when Dad died, but so much tension had swirled through the house after his death, along with the grief. It had sent his mother into a tailspin that had taken her months to pull out of, but she had—eventually—and then she'd come to him.

"You're my last baby, my special baby."

"I'm not a baby," he'd protested, but he'd liked how tightly she'd held him.

"No, you're not. You're my little man." She'd kissed his head and whispered, "I love you," and he'd never felt more secure.

No one had spoken about the tension. There were things

Nick was sure he didn't know, those things that scared him, unaccountably, and he wasn't sure he ever needed to know any of it.

"How did he die?" Emily asked.

"On Mount Everest. When he was climbing back down from the summit, he'd come across a man who'd tried the climb without oxygen and was dying. All the other climbers were ignoring him, but Dad thought he could save him. Instead, they both died."

"Why?"

"Because that top portion of Everest is so hard. The air is thin. Even with a supply of oxygen it's hard to do anything, walk, even breathe, let alone try to drag someone else back down the mountain with you."

Nick's emotions toward his dad had been ambivalent ever since. He'd missed the big, fun man who used to toss him into the air and catch him before he fell, but he'd also been angry. Look what his death had done to Mom and his three sons. He'd left them with nothing more than the house he'd inherited from his father.

Mom had gone to work at two jobs to feed three hungry, growing boys and Gabe had turned into pseudo-dad.

Nick had a lot to sort through here. Emily could help him. Maybe it would be a good project to share with her—a father/ daughter project. The thought excited him. It might be the only way for him to get through this without breaking down into maudlin self-pity and grief.

He unfolded the boxes and taped their bottoms.

"Let's start here." He knelt on the floor in front of the old trunk. As a child, he'd never noticed how frayed the fabric covering was, or how dented the metal at the corners. When he had looked at it, he had seen it as his treasure box.

"We didn't have money when I was growing up, but my mom used to buy me a little something every week or so."

"Wow, look at all these old cars."

"Matchbox miniatures. Cars from movies. Look, here's the Batmobile."

He pulled out another tiny car. "James Bond's Aston Martin DB5. A perfect little replica."

Emily took James out of the driver's seat. "He's so tiny."

"It's a wonder I never lost him." He looked through the chest for more.

"I owned a lot of Matchbox vehicles. Buses. Motorcycles."

He picked up a car with large wheels. "Look! When Hot Wheels came on the market, Mom started to buy me those. They were exact replicas of muscle cars and hot rods."

He and Emily raced them on the bare floor.

He'd spent hours with his cars, would never go anywhere without one in each pocket. So many toys, and yet each one had been a treasure to him.

"You and your brothers must have had so much fun playing with these."

"What?" Nick asked. "My brothers?"

"Yeah. They must have loved these, too."

"They didn't belong to my brothers."

"Dad, are you saying you never played with them?"

"We played some stuff. Snowball fights. They taught me how to toss a ball around."

"No. I mean, you never let them play with these?" She pointed to the toy box.

"They were mine."

"I don't understand."

How could he explain? The way she looked at him he knew she thought he'd been selfish. "We owned so little. This room and these cars, these toys, were my universe. I had nothing else." In town, no one paid him any attention. He wore his brothers' hand-me-downs. He ate macaroni and cheese until it came out of his ears. But here in this room? He was the pirate of a great and worthy ship and he owned treasure.

No. His brothers were not allowed in here. It was his private paradise and he wasn't about to let them in to muck it up.

"Dad, you always said you lived in poverty."

"We did. We were hungry a lot of the time."

"But you have all these cars. A whole trunk full."

He'd never questioned why Mom spent money on these, why they had to scrimp for food and clothing, but Nick had these toys. Matchbox and Hot Wheels cars weren't cheap. He'd just believed that they were his due. He felt disquieted now wondering if his brothers had somehow been cheated for his benefit. If so, why didn't they hate him?

"Can I meet Gabe and Tyler while I'm here?" Emily asked.

Where had that come from out of the blue? "Maybe."

"Does that mean no?"

She was ruining their "together" time. "Let it go, Emily. Isn't it enough that you're here with me and I've shown you where I grew up?"

"Sure," she said, but he knew he'd disappointed her. "I need to use the bathroom."

"There might not be toilet paper."

"I have tissues in my pocket."

She returned a minute later, but something had changed. She was subdued.

They looked at more of Nick's things, but Emily's heart wasn't in it as it had been before.

He heard a vehicle turn into the driveway and come to a stop with a screeching of tires.

Curious, he went to see who it was.

Gabe stepped into the house. Nick hadn't seen him since the man had come to him in the winter desperate for Callie's address. Nick had given it to him only after Gabe had agreed to sell his third of the Jordan land to him.

"What are you doing here?" Nick asked.

From behind him, his daughter said, "I called him."

"When?"

"In the washroom."

When had she learned to be devious? Where? It was small consolation that she looked remorseful. She was also defiant. "I wanted to meet him. He's my uncle."

Gabe opened his arms. Emily ran into them.

They laughed and hugged and Nick wanted to rip them apart. She shouldn't be as happy to see the man as she was.

She's my *daughter*.

Nick knew he was being petty, but Gabe brought out the worst in him. It had started long before the man hadn't come home from Afghanistan to attend his mother's funeral. Until a few months ago, Nick hadn't known Gabe had been wounded at the time, but the seeds of his anger with this brother had been sown a long, long time ago—almost from the day their father died and Gabe took it upon himself to become a strict disciplinarian.

A sound on the veranda drew Nick's attention. Callie MacKintosh stepped into the room, looking bright and colorful and vibrant.

"Hello, Nick," she said with a smile, as though there were no hard feelings between them. Well, he had hard feelings, by God.

"Callie," Emily squealed and traded Gabe's arms for hers.

All of five-four and nothing more, redheaded and pixieish, Callie radiated health and happiness. She'd never looked like that when she'd worked for Nick. She'd been exceedingly competent, but had looked tired and harassed.

Once again, St. Gabe had come to the rescue. Everybody loved Gabe.

They look like a family.

Thunderstruck, he forced himself not to react, not to lash out. Emily had a right to know her uncle Gabe and she had a right to see her friend Callie.

She chattered to both Gabe and Callie, and the joy on Emily's face undermined his need to pull her away from these people and keep her for himself, to take her back to Seattle and lock her in their home.

"Dad, Callie invited me to stay with them tonight!"

What? But she'd wanted to spend time with *him*.

"I can meet the dogs. Gabe said he'll teach me all about dogsledding." Emily looked younger than her twelve years, like an excited little girl. "Can I sleep over at their place?"

How could Nick say no? She was crushing him into the dirt, trading him in for Gabe, but how could he tell his little girl no?

"Yes," he said, as though the word had been wrenched from his lips. Emily ran to him and threw her arms around his neck. He wanted to hold on tightly and not let go.

Gabe watched him carefully. Nick's senses, on high alert from the trip down memory lane in this godforsaken house, detected understanding. Or worse, compassion.

He shuttered his own expression. He didn't need anything from Gabe.

Emily kissed his cheek. "Uncle Gabe can take me to the B and B to get my knapsack."

"Have a good time, sweetheart." With an effort, he smiled. "Don't bring home any dogs or puppies."

"Aw, how did you guess?" Emily asked, but she was joking. Before she left, she turned back and studied him, frowning. "Will you be okay, Dad?"

He nodded, his throat full and closing up on him. No, he wouldn't be all right. He didn't want to spend the night alone. He wanted her back already. In Seattle, in his office, he was real, successful. Here in Accord, he was...

That was the problem. Who was he? That little boy who had grown up with so little? Who'd been ashamed of his hand-me-downs and his unending hunger?

They turned and walked to the car and Nick again had that sense of them looking like a family.

Ever since Dad's death, he hadn't felt like part of the family. Not really. Had Mom done that by treating him differently than she had his brothers?

There was no denying the bond between Gabe and Ty.

Emmy got into the backseat of Gabe's truck and waved.

Don't go.

His daughter had just blown him off. What did he expect? How many times in her life had he called to cancel outings he'd booked with her because something had come up at work?

Payback was a bitch.

He looked around the small house, eerily convinced that the ghosts of his dead ancestors walked these rooms. He couldn't stand to be here alone.

Seconds later, he closed the front door and fled to his car.

Coward.

You bet.

LAURA WANDERED DOWN the rows of headstones until she came to her father's grave and stared down at his headstone. He'd never understood that, when he had gone to another woman, he hadn't betrayed only Mom. He'd betrayed his daughter, too. A breach of faith and ethics affected everyone. She'd always thought him so strong, so perfect, so…Daddy. The man he became after Amber's death had been a stranger.

She heard a footfall behind her and turned. Nick Jordan stood with a bouquet of flowers in his hand. She thanked the heavens he didn't have his daughter with him.

"Are you okay?" he asked.

Her nod felt brittle.

"You don't look all right."

Neither did he. She couldn't put her finger on what was wrong with him, on what had changed since earlier today in her bakery, but some of his urbanity, his confidence, had been tarnished. He looked tired and, while he stared down at a grave, sad.

He leaned forward and placed the flowers beside a head-stone two plots down.

"Your mother's grave?" she asked.

He nodded.

Laura hadn't realized that her father and his mother were buried so close together. She knew that Gabe visited the cemetery every couple of weeks, presumably to leave flowers on her grave, but Laura had avoided coming here those days. Easy enough to do. Until recently, Gabe had run his life to a strict timetable.

"I'll leave," she said. "I won't intrude."

"Don't go," he said and, for a second, sounded desperate. "I intruded on you."

Ever since losing the baby, Laura had been immobilized by a strange lassitude that hit her at the most inconvenient times, and she stood frozen, undecided. Fate was messing with her head and she didn't know where strong, decisive Laura had gone. These days, she needed comfort, affection—love—and couldn't find it.

Nick ran his fingers through his hair—an odd gesture for him. He looked nervous, and so alone.

"I'm at loose ends," he said. "My daughter is staying with Gabe and I have no plans for the evening. Would you—?"

"Yes?"

"Do you want to have supper together?" He must have seen her alarm because he raised a hand, palm out. "This isn't a date. I don't relish eating alone in my old hometown and you look like you could use company, too."

He was right. She could. But Nick's company? That could be dangerous.

But she hadn't felt this alone since Amber died.

Mom was emotionally unavailable. Laura would have to figure out why eventually, but not today. First, she needed to get past her own blue funk.

Her two best friends were on a cruise they'd booked months

ago when Laura was pregnant and thought she'd have a baby to raise.

Nick held out his hand to her. A peace offering of sorts, she guessed.

She stared at his long fingers for moments on end, the temptation strong. She couldn't be alone tonight. She just couldn't.

She took his hand.

God help her.

CHAPTER FIVE

TYLER JORDAN HURRIED down Main Street toward Tammy Trudeau's gift shop. He glanced at his watch. Five-fifty-five. He might catch her.

If not for Lester Hughes stopping him to rail against the boys buzzing his doorbell every night then running away, Ty would have made it here on time.

He told Lester to ignore the boys, that getting a rise out of him was reason enough for them to keep doing it. Lester liked to complain, though. So he did. And Ty listened. And Ty was late.

Honest to God, sometimes his job was more about settling disputes than fighting crime. As sheriff of the county in which Accord sat, he should be grateful that crime was as low as it was.

During the week, Tammy worked as a schoolteacher, but sometimes on weekends helped out her employees in the shop she owned.

Ty stared in through the large front window. Tammy sat behind the counter. It looked as though she was working on her books. Alone. Good.

When he opened the front door she glanced up. He watched her grow quiet, still, and knew that she didn't want to see him. It hurt. She used to brighten up like a Christmas tree when he entered a room, but that was before Winona had come to town. Then the shit had hit the fan and Tyler didn't know how to change things back to the way they used to be.

She didn't say anything, just continued to watch him with

that soberness that was breaking his heart. He wanted his happy Tammy back.

"Hey," he said, standing inside the door with his hands in his jacket pockets. He needed to touch her so bad.

She didn't answer, leaving him hanging like a kite in the breeze with its string cut, lost and drifting farther and farther away.

She sat, eyeing him, as mute as he was. He'd seen her around town in the past four months, but never up close. Even those brief glimpses had shattered him. He wanted her back.

"Hi," he said, his voice a rough croak. He cleared his throat and stepped close to the counter.

For the briefest moment her expression softened, but it didn't last.

He'd screwed up about as badly as a man could. In their four years together, he'd been faithful to Tammy. If his dreams turned sexual, they were always about her. If he went anywhere socially, he took Tammy. He'd done worse than screwing around, though. He'd betrayed her in the most fundamental way, lying through omission.

"Thought you might be closing up."

She checked her watch. "I guess I lost track of time."

It wasn't like Tammy to not be on the ball.

Mauve shadows darkened the delicate skin below her eyes. A stunner with her pretty wavy blond hair and bright blue eyes, she seemed listless. He'd done that to her.

"What are you doing here?" she asked.

"Nick's in town."

She raised one eyebrow with the unspoken question, *What does that have to do with me?*

"His daughter is here. She's visiting Gabe and Callie. I've never met her, so they're having me over for dinner."

"Sounds lovely." Still, that raised eyebrow seemed to suggest, *And this concerns me how?*

"I want you to come with me."

Her eyes widened. "You're kidding."

"Tammy—" He tapped his fist on the counter. "You were a member of the Jordan family for four years. Everyone misses you."

"Everyone?" Meaning him?

A breath gusted out of him. "Like you wouldn't believe."

"And Winona?"

"She's gone back home. She left mid-January. She was only here for a week." This was a small town. Tammy had to have known to the day and minute when Winona left.

"I know she left town, Ty. Did she also leave your heart?"

"She hasn't been in my heart in years."

Thirteen years ago, while away at school in California, he'd had a meteoric affair with a stunning woman, Winona Clark, that had crashed and burned when she threw him over for another man. Ty had gone into a tailspin that only time and his work in law enforcement here in Accord had pulled him out of.

Then Tammy had come along. Six years ago, she'd moved into town to take over the gift shop her great-aunt had left to her and to become a teacher.

Ty had taken one look at her and had wanted her. She was a dead ringer for Winona.

Unfortunately, he'd never told her that. In early January, she'd found out. And that had been that. In her eyes, he'd only loved her as a substitute for Winona.

"Tammy, I don't know how many more ways I can say I'm sorry."

"It doesn't matter anymore that you only dated me because I look like her. What does matter—"

"I only *started* dating you because of that." He tried to set the record straight, but she talked right over him.

"—is that you never once told me you loved me. My guess is you never got over that woman. I deserve more than to be second best."

"Trust me, Tammy, you aren't." Lord no, she was the furthest thing from second best. "I don't love Winona. I don't care for her at all."

"But you only just discovered that in January. I think you always held out a crazy hope that she'd come back to you."

He couldn't deny the truth of that. He'd harbored hopes and dreams. He just hadn't realized it until Winona walked through his door after thirteen years.

"In the meantime, you were making do with me."

"I wasn't making do. I cared about you. I still care. I love you."

"Too little too late, Ty." Her voice sounded husky.

"Do you have a cold?" He stepped forward. At least she hadn't kicked him out.

"A sore throat."

"You been working too hard?"

She shook her head. "Haven't you heard?"

Her flat tone sent a chill rippling up his back—one of his witchy feelings he always got before something went wrong. Like when he'd sensed as a kid that Dad wasn't coming back home. Like when he'd known that Gabe had been injured in Afghanistan. Like when he'd known three months ago that something big and maybe bad was about to happen, right before a young girl came knocking on his door and said, "Hi. I'm Ruby. I'm your daughter."

He'd never known about her. Winona hadn't told him he was a father. He'd missed Ruby's childhood and that hurt.

Winona came back into his life to pick up her daughter, and Ty had lost Tammy when she realized how much she looked like his former lover.

"Haven't I heard what?" he finally asked, even though he was afraid of the answer.

"I left teaching, Ty."

She'd stunned him. "But you're the best teacher for miles around. Why would you quit? You love it."

"You really don't know? This is a small town and news travels fast. I thought maybe it had reached you."

"Tammy, I don't know what the hell you're talking about. Get to the point."

"Okay. This is the point." She stood up from the stool she was sitting on and stepped around the counter. She put one hand on her stomach, as though to protect it. From what? From him? Why would she need to…protect…her belly?

"Oh, Lord. Are you—?"

"Yes, I am."

But how? He always used a condom. Always, except that one time…. Enlightenment hit with the force of a sledge-hammer. The weekend of the storm. Ruby had arrived on his doorstep, the daughter he'd never known about. The shock had been profound.

Their lovemaking had been frantic that weekend, for Tammy because she sensed that life was going to change in a big way for the two of them, and for Ty because he knew that the girl's mother would soon follow to track her down. He'd known how hurt Tammy was going to be when she realized that he'd started dating her because she was a dead ringer for Winona, the woman he'd lost all those years ago.

Their sex that weekend, trapped indoors by the storm, had been panic-driven and he'd broken one of his own rules. He'd forgotten to use a condom one night.

Apparently, one night was all it took.

His mind got past the shock and moved on to wonder. Lord. She carried his baby.

He stepped close and she let him. He placed his big hand on her stomach. There was barely a bump.

Carefully, he took her small jaw in his hand, tipped her head up so her neck was long and elegant and he could look into her eyes, and placed his lips on hers. She watched him.

With the second kiss, she closed her eyes and he felt an exhalation of her breath, as if she were giving in to something.

He wrapped his arm across her shoulders and moved his other hand to rest on his babe again.

"For sure?" he asked, his voice threaded with the wonder that was flooding him.

"For sure. In six months, I'm having a baby."

"You mean *we*."

"No, Ty. I mean *I*."

His hand convulsed. "Tammy." His voice took on a warning tone, but she ignored it and stepped out of his embrace. She slipped away from him like water running through his fingers, like all of life seemed to be doing lately.

"What are you talking about? This is my baby, too."

"All of those times I wanted to talk about getting married, about starting a family, you cut me off. You didn't want to discuss it."

"I know, but I've changed. Now that I know about Ruby, I can't get enough of her."

"How is she?" she asked grudgingly, but he knew she really wanted to know. When they had spent that long snowed-in weekend at his ranch, she'd fallen for Ruby every bit as hard as he had. He knew Tammy had real affection for her.

"She's great. She's going to stay with me all summer. We use Skype all the time. She's writing a school report about bison and I'm helping her with it." He couldn't keep the enthusiasm out of his voice. He felt like a kid who had just received the best Christmas present on earth.

Tammy smiled, but it was tinged with sadness.

"I *love* being a father," he said. "I want to have more babies. I want to make them with you."

"And Winona?"

"She's in my past. There's nothing there now."

"Are you sure?"

He thought of the phone call they'd shared last night, and some of the things Winona had said.

"We belong together, Ty."

"You didn't think so thirteen years ago."

"I think so now."

"I'm not rich, Winona. You can't live like you used to with Kevin." She'd thrown him over to marry a man with better prospects. Kevin had been a lawyer with a good law firm.

He took too long thinking about that conversation.

"I've got my answer." Tammy stepped back behind the counter, using it as a barrier between them.

"Tammy, no. Don't do this."

"When you figure out who you love—yes, Ty, love—I won't settle for less, you come back and we'll talk, but not before then."

Ty left, slamming the door behind him.

Sometimes he felt so helpless, so out of control with women. Winona had manipulated and used him all of those years ago. She'd been trying to manipulate him all winter since she'd come back into his life. The harder he pushed her away, the harder she came on to him.

He'd learned his lesson with her, though.

He didn't want her.

He wanted Tammy.

How did he go about getting Tammy back? Who could he ask for advice?

These days he spent too much time alone and it brought back memories of other times in his life when he'd felt that way.

Shortly after Dad's death, Gabe and Ty had all but ceased to exist for Mom. She slid into a blue funk that lasted months. Ty might be the only one of the brothers who guessed, even at such a young age, the source of Mom's slide into depression. It had definitely been more than grief.

As soon as she came out of her depression and realized there would be no more babies, five-year-old Nick had become her favored son. She'd pampered him. Ty had been only seven at the time. He remembered that awful feeling of loss. First he'd lost Dad to death and then Mom to depression and then to Nick. Years later he lost Gabe to the army. Gabe had been gone for too many years, escaping a betrayal by his fiancée. It was immature of Ty to remember all of that old stuff from childhood now, but some things stuck with a man over the years.

Gabe was home and married and never leaving Accord again. That was a good thing. He'd told Ty that Nick was in town.

Could he ask either of them for advice?

Gabe? His older brother wasn't likely to know. He'd almost lost Callie because of stupidity.

Nick? Ty could honestly say he didn't know his younger brother well enough to go to him with problems in the area of romance. Besides, hadn't his marriage failed a few years ago?

He could ask one of his buddies, but wasn't sure they had women figured out any better than he had, even though most of them were married and had children.

Children. Plural. Like him. First Ruby. And now Tammy was pregnant. His breath caught. Tammy was having his baby. He sighed and then shook himself back to reality. She didn't want him to be part of the baby's life, or of her life.

Tammy had another think coming if she thought he would stay away. He'd missed his first child's early years. No way was another woman keeping another child away from him.

He plowed through his reports for the day then headed over to Gabe's.

Nick's daughter was a pretty, talkative, sweet young teenager. Nick had done a good job, which surprised Ty. In some ways, their mom had screwed up Nick's psyche more than she had with Ty and Gabe.

Ty doubted Nick realized it, but when Mom had coddled him, had given him everything he wanted when he wanted it, she had done him no favors. Ty doubted Nick understood the concept of delayed gratification.

Somehow, though, he'd done well with Emily.

Ty opened his arms and she slipped into his embrace.

He sighed. Family felt so good.

Why had he denied himself all of those years after he'd met Tammy? Why hadn't he committed heart and soul to her? Because Winona had screwed him over so badly. No, it went further back than that. Because Dad and Mom's relationship had been anything but stellar, had been riddled with fights about money and Dad's climbing.

There had been that one nuclear argument the night before Dad left to climb Everest.

Ty had hidden under the covers in his bed, way earlier than bedtime, but he'd been trying to hide from the words that caromed around the small house like poisonous arrows.

"If you leave this time, don't bother coming back," Mom had yelled. "I mean it."

Dad hadn't come back. He'd died on Everest. Mom had gone into her depression.

Ty still hadn't figured out why that one argument had screwed him up so badly that he hadn't been able to marry Tammy. He'd better figure it out soon, though.

He wasn't missing anything this time, as he had with Ruby. Not one thing. He planned to be there through the pregnancy. He planned to be there at the birth. He planned to be there for the rest of the child's life.

He planned to be there for Tammy.

If she couldn't accept that, well…she would have to.

It was happening, with or without Tammy's cooperation.

He was tired of being pushed around by women.

As of this evening, he was his own man making decisions *he* wanted to make.

LAURA ENTERED THE B AND B with Nick, unsure why she was here.

He'd caught her in a weak moment. He'd looked every bit as alone as she'd felt.

What did they have in common? What on earth did they have to talk about? How would they fill an entire evening?

There wasn't a chance in hell they would ever be spending time together, that there was a future for them. So why waste this evening?

Because she was lonely for someone she couldn't replace, her baby daughter. Because, ideally, Nick would offer loving arms and brief oblivion.

Since he'd only offered dinner, she would take it. It was either that, or her too-quiet apartment.

A consummate professional, the owner and chef, Kristi Mortimer, seated them beside the fireplace in the gorgeous old-fashioned dining room, without the hint of a raised eyebrow to comment on Laura and Nick being in the same room, let alone dining together.

The whole town knew what had happened between them all of those years ago, and of how it had ended her engagement to Gabe.

"I know this isn't up to your city standards," Laura said after Kristi had left to get them a bottle of white wine on which Nick and Laura had agreed, "but Kristi performs miracles with both local and imported ingredients."

She proved it almost immediately when she returned with the wine, but also with a small pot of excellent smoked trout spread with homemade crackers.

"Remember Kristi's cousin, Jeff Stone?" Laura asked. "He catches the trout every year and smokes it for Kristi."

Laura loved food. There was a good chance she was going to have trouble with her weight someday, but life was meant to be enjoyed and savored.

"So your daughter is with Gabe this evening?"

"With Gabe and Callie, yeah."

She didn't need a crystal ball to know she'd struck a nerve.

"You obviously don't want her to be with them. Why didn't you insist she spend the evening with you?"

"She was too excited. She hadn't seen Callie all winter and she'd never met Gabe. I couldn't say no."

Laura's knife clattered to the table. "She never met Gabe? How old is she?"

He sensed the censure in her voice. "Twelve."

"In twelve years she's never met her uncle?"

"She didn't come here for my mother's funeral. I thought it would be too hard on her."

"What about all the other years? Why didn't you come back to visit? I know you loved your mother."

Except for that, she would have thought Nick was incapable of love.

He shrugged.

"What was it that happened when you were a kid that made you so angry with Gabe?"

"Never mind, Laura."

"What made you so bitter about this town?"

"Give it a rest."

"I'm just trying to understand you."

He threw his napkin onto the table. "If you follow this line of questioning, this meal is over."

She thought of her dark apartment, of the hours stretching ahead of her, leaving her too much time to grieve for her lost baby and her failed engagement.

"Fine," she said. "Let's talk about other things."

Kristi brought entrées, steak for Nick and chicken marsala for Laura.

"Why did you come to town this weekend?"

Nick explained about the problem with the Native Americans.

Good. A neutral topic.

While he spoke, he surprised her with a glimpse into the businessman he was. He enjoyed the challenge of business, even the problems that arose. Another surprise? He didn't intend to annihilate his opponents' concerns. He planned to find a solution that would work for both of them.

She had to admire that.

Nick sipped his wine slowly, seemed to savor it. "Where did you get all of that music you were playing in the café today? Is it a local radio station? I don't remember hearing commercials."

"You didn't. It wasn't the radio. It's music from my own collection."

"You have eclectic taste."

"I seem to." She smiled. "Vin says—"

"Vin?"

"My fiancé."

"You're getting married? Why can't he give you a baby?"

"We're no longer engaged."

"You just called him your fiancé."

"Force of habit. He broke up with me today."

His jaw flexed. "I'm sorry to hear it. No wonder you were upset in the kitchen."

"It was more than that."

"What else was it?"

"Five months ago, I had a miscarriage. I was broken up about it. Vin was relieved. I thought we could try again. Today, he decided he didn't want to. He no longer even wants to marry me."

He set his cutlery carefully onto his empty plate and took one of her hands in his.

Her gaze flew to his.

"I'm sorry," he said. "I had no idea. No wonder you were so upset when you saw me."

"Yes. It was worse when you came to town in January, though. The grief of losing the baby was new and raw. It hurt to see you, but even more, it hurt to see Gabe. I hadn't seen either of you in years." Her pulse pounded. She wondered if he could feel it where one of his fingers sat on her wrist. His hand was warm, heavy, reassuring. This. This was what she'd needed, what she'd tried to find elsewhere. How odd that she found it with Nick Jordan, of all people.

Kristi approached to clear the table and Nick let go of Laura's hand, breaking the warmth of the moment. She missed the contact.

"What did Vin say about your music?" he asked.

"He thought it was weird. He wondered why I didn't listen to the hits on the radio."

"I'm glad you don't. I enjoyed what I heard today."

Kristi brought coffee and homemade chocolate Grand Marnier truffles.

They talked about music, about how much of their taste overlapped.

She bit into a truffle and caught him watching her tongue as it collected chocolate from her lips.

She stared at his refined hands, at his long fingers and the way he held his coffee cup. She was used to Vin's calloused construction worker hands.

Nick's would feel so different.

There it was. That same old attraction. So many years later, there was still that pull that was so hard to control. Why? What was it about Nick?

Plus ça change, plus c'est la même chose. She'd been studying French. Loved it. Adored it. Wanted to visit Paris someday so she could use it.

The more things change, the more they stay the same.

No. It wouldn't be the same as all those years ago. She was older and wiser. She might feel attraction toward Nick, but she wouldn't act on it. Absolutely not.

He'd stopped talking and she glanced up to find him watching her. He knew what she'd been thinking.

Nick wouldn't let her share the tab, went a little Neanderthal, actually. Feeling mellower than she had earlier, and less without hope, she didn't mind. He'd been a gracious dining companion. He'd grown up well.

Who would have thought she could share a civilized evening with the enemy?

He insisted on walking her home.

"Nick, it's only across the street. I live in the apartment above the bakery."

"So I'll walk you that far."

The night had turned chilly, but the skies were clear and the stars were out. This end of Main was empty. Farther down, where there were several bars, people were having fun, but here in the retail section all was quiet.

They walked across the street. When a raccoon crossed their path, Nick took her hand and steered her clear.

At the far end of a narrow alley and around the back of Sweet Temptations was the fire escape that led to her apartment.

"Why aren't there stairs from inside the bakery?"

"I don't really want them. I like that my home and workspace are separate. I like stepping outside to go home."

"Well," he said, looking down at her.

"Well," she said and stared at him.

CHAPTER SIX

HE MEANT TO say good-night and leave, really, after one kiss. Just one small kiss. Her full lips tasted of chocolate and coffee. Sweet. Lush. Warm.

He meant to leave it at that.

So why was she in his arms and kissing him like a starving woman, and he returning it with fervor, every bit as starving? Just as alone. Craving passion.

All evening, he'd been civilized, aware that he would be the last person Laura Cameron would want touching her, but there had been an attraction, a temptation.

He'd wanted this contact tonight with another human, with Laura, his affections tinder-dry and her touch a flint.

She took his hand and scrambled upstairs with him close behind, ready to burst with need and desire.

Once inside her apartment, she was in his arms again, because he couldn't wait for her, couldn't wait for the conflagration he knew was about to ignite.

He tasted her again, drawn in by her contrasts, her lips and tongue like wine and butter, at once mellow and sharp, and oh so heady.

Taking control, he pushed her coat from her shoulders to the floor.

He unbuttoned her dress and ran his hands over her breasts. Even confined by her bra they were full and ripe and womanly. His hands arced across the soft skin of her abdomen and waist and around to her back to cup her generous behind and pull her against him. He strained against his zipper, hungry for release.

Breathing hard, Laura took his hand and led him through a dark room to a bedroom. She lit a match and touched it to a trio of candles and a stick of incense in a holder. Her eyes shone when she pressed a button on a small stereo and Dr. John's rasp filled the room. "Makin' Whoopee."

He laughed and dragged her into his arms like oxygen into his lungs.

Her bedroom suited her. Warm colors tumbled like acrobats across her duvet, reds and purples and oranges. Fine gauze draped from the ceiling in swaths of color like swooping cockatiels.

She'd turned a plain room into a sensual paradise.

Taking his eyes from her briefly, he pulled his wallet out of his back pocket, removed a condom from it and tossed it onto a small table beside the bed.

Prepared.

Laura turned up the volume until the driving drums and horns filled the room, drowning out sense and reason. Her eyes shone. She unbuttoned the rest of her dress and shrugged out of it, the move so sexy Nick nearly swallowed his tongue.

Candlelight flowed over her lavish curves like melted butter. A scrap of lace between her round thighs hid treasures he wanted to plunder with his fingers and tongue.

Sandalwood, rich and thick and redolent with heady promise, scented the air.

His blood beat to the pounding of the drums.

He hauled her into his arms and took her mouth, biting her lips, sweeping her with his tongue, sucking on hers as though it were cinnamon candy—hot, spicy, juicy.

His fingers dived into her luxuriant hair, took fistfuls of it and angled her mouth where he wanted it. Her nails scraped his neck and he shivered.

Her tongue played with his, her fingers grabbed at his belt, annihilated the zipper of his pants and wrapped around him.

He couldn't breathe.

"Laura," he moaned, her name a benediction and a curse. Sweet Laura.

He popped her bra open and her breasts spilled into his hands in their ripened glory. He pulled back to feast on her beauty. Her nipples peaked in dark aureoles centered in pendulous goddess breasts. Not perky, not sweet, but full, mature and perfect.

He kissed and bit and sucked them then trailed his lips to her stomach, kissed and bit the fullness there, then licked farther down, skimming off her panties with his teeth. She leaned against the dresser, her head back and her legs spread wide—nothing shy about Laura. He drank in the sight of her, her chestnut curls barely hiding pink wet folds of unashamed arousal. He tasted her, sucked her and caught her when her knees went weak.

He turned her around. While he paid homage to her glorious ass, she leaned her arms against the wall and hummed low.

He kissed every tiny bone of her spine then nipped the back of her neck. She shivered and turned.

"Come to me," she said, reaching for him, her voice husky, as though her throat ached with unlocked secrets. "Give me…"

She took him in hand again, squeezing and urging him to meet her, falling back onto the bed and taking him with her.

He plunged into her and her lustrous body wept around him, hummed with energy and sexuality.

He pulled out then plunged again.

"Magnifique," she whispered, and he'd never heard anything sexier.

He rose to kneel on the bed between her legs, driving into her, and a satisfied laugh burst from deep in her throat.

God, she was uninhibited and hot, driving him to go deeper still, harder.

He took her hand and bit her fingers, one by one, starting hard then gentling. He sucked on the inside of her elbow and the soft flesh of her underarm.

Honest and earthy and loud, she cried out.

Wrapping his arms across the back of her waist, he leaned forward and sucked her breasts, first one and then the other. He hardened further inside of her.

Grinding into her—she wanted nothing gentle, demanded more—he urged her until she hung from the side of the bed, her body arching and as supple as a willow branch.

She let her arms fall over her head where her fingertips brushed the floor. Her strong legs gripped his back and she met him thrust for thrust.

His fingers grasped her thighs. Still, he moved, deeper and deeper, and her body accepted his as though made for him.

The room grew warm and fragrant with Laura. The scent of her sex mingled with the incense. In the flickering candlelight, she looked like Woman, surrounding, taking, swallowing him until all there existed was Laura.

He touched the perfect aroused nub of her sex and she cried out. Crooned. Purred. Her muscles contracted around him and he came with her.

He shuddered, continued to come, hissed and held her still when she tried to move.

When he got his breathing back, he pulled her up into his arms and fell onto his back, taking her lush body on top of his, panting as though he'd run a marathon.

He smiled, slowly. The only other time in his life when sex had felt so good had been with Laura.

Her hair fell across his face, soft and fine like spiderwebs. Her body still held him, her lips moist against his groin. He softened and slipped out of her.

She sighed, long and sweet, as though peace were settling through her.

Tenderness flooded him.

He laughed and took her face in his hands, kissed her and laughed again, happier than he'd been in years. She kissed his laughing mouth and then pressed her hands into the mattress and arose onto her arms to look down at him, her smile satisfied and smug.

Her lips shone in the candlelight. Her breasts hung like ripe fruit, tempting him, and he took a nipple into his mouth.

She stiffened. Not pleasure.

Something felt wrong. Had he hurt her?

He pulled away to look at her.

She stared at something beside the bed. Her expression changed, joy flitted away replaced by concern, worry. Horror.

He turned to see what had caught her attention and got a kick in the gut.

His condom sat on the bedside table. Unopened. Unused.

He'd lost control. He *never* lost control with a woman, had never once in his life. Before tonight. Before Laura and her tempting body. *She'd* made him lose control.

You owe me. Was she really that driven, that selfish and underhanded? *Today is the perfect day.* She was ovulating.

The look he turned on her could freeze hell. "You did this to get your baby."

She'd taken from him, had *stolen* from him. Robbed him of choice.

"No," she whispered. "No," she yelled. "No, no, no. Not like this. Not now. Not with you."

He grasped her arms and squeezed. "How could you do this to me?"

She fought out of his hold and jumped from the bed. He chased her down the hall.

"You can't get away that easily."

In the bathroom, she turned the shower on full blast and stepped inside.

"What are you doing?" She was splashing water into herself. She soaped up her hands and shoved her fingers into her channel. The room filled with steam.

"Trying to get rid of your semen." She sounded desperate, looked a little sick.

"Why?" he asked, suspicion high. What the hell was going on? "You wanted a baby. You asked *me* for a baby." He was just starting to get to know his daughter and now there might be a baby?

Water streamed over her head. Her hair hung in wet strings around her face. She stared at him, shattered. Broken. "That was temporary madness. My fiancé had just broken up with me. I was desperate."

He reached behind her and turned off the water.

"Are you crying?"

She shook her head. "I don't cry."

"You're a real piece of work." And the best damn actress he'd ever come across.

"*Me?* Why did you ask me to dinner? To seduce me? To see if you could do it again like you'd done once before? To make a fool out of me again?"

"You were giving me those little lost girl looks in the cemetery. I felt sorry for you."

She turned on him, her face flattened into shock. Disgust. "That was a mercy screw?"

He stalked back to the bedroom and gathered his clothes, dressing in the room that twenty minutes ago had felt like a sensual paradise, the sexiest room on the planet. His hands shook and he fumbled, but managed to get the job done.

He left without another word, without another glance in her direction, and crossed the street to the B and B where he showered in the hottest water he could stand.

He slept fitfully and by morning had settled on a plan.

Skipping breakfast, he pulled his rental car up in front of the bakery. He walked around to the back and took the stairs to her apartment two at a time.

She opened the door just as he raised his fist to bang on it.

Shrugging into a jacket, she asked, "What do you want?" Graceless and humorless, but still gorgeous as hell. Shadows marred her eyes, but did he care? No. Why should she have had trouble sleeping? She wasn't being dragged into parenthood against her will. She was getting what she wanted. A baby.

"I'm taking you to the hospital for a morning-after pill." He should have taken her last night, but he'd been too angry to think straight.

"There's no need," she said. "I'm going to the clinic. It's closer and staffed on Sundays."

He didn't trust her. "I'll go with you."

"Why?"

"To make sure that's what you're doing."

"I don't want this baby any more than you do."

"Yeah, right." *You owe me a baby.* "Last night was all about getting pregnant. You're ovulating, remember?" At the bottom of the stairs, when she would have walked to her car parked behind the café, he took her arm and steered her toward Main Street.

"I'll drive." His tone brooked no objection and he got none.

She yanked her arm out of his hold, but approached the passenger side of the car. "You're a bully, you know that?"

"Too bad. You did one nasty number on me last night."

She settled into the seat without a word and remained silent while he drove.

At the clinic, they gave her the prescription, with Nick sitting in the doctor's office right beside her to make sure she asked for the right thing. He took her to the drugstore to fill the scrip. He bought her a bottle of water and watched her take the pill. Done. There wasn't any more he could do.

CHAPTER SEVEN

ON SUNDAY AT NOON, Olivia parked her Escalade in front of Aiden's house. The driveway was so overgrown she almost missed the turnoff. A quarter of a mile in, it opened to a charming glade in the middle of which stood a barely civilized, rough-hewn log house.

Last summer, he'd shown her artwork for her to sell in her gallery, but they'd been in his garden. She assumed that since it was a cool day, she would be invited inside this time.

The front door opened and there he was, big and muscular in his jeans and white shirt with the sleeves rolled up and bare feet, the most masculine man she'd ever met.

"Come in," he called, and his deep voice sent shivers down her spine.

She got out of the car and approached. So, she was to be invited inside.

As she walked the pathway to the front door, his attention seemed to be focused on her legs and then her hips, and last, her lips, but that couldn't be. She was imagining it.

Her curiosity piqued about all things Aiden, she followed him down a hallway too quickly for her to get much more than the briefest impressions of rooms as they passed. She did notice, though, that it looked a heck of a lot more refined than the outside.

They stepped into the kitchen and Olivia stared, stunned. If the outside of the house had been primitive, the kitchen was glorious, massive and made for someone passionate about food.

It smelled of garlic and seafood. She noticed a bowl of shrimp waiting to be tossed into a pan.

Aiden stepped behind her, startling her, and she jumped. "What—?"

"I'm just taking your jacket."

Her jacket? So this would take a while.

"Make yourself at home." His breath whispered over her hair.

How could she possibly relax with the man prowling near her with a knowing look in his eye and a smile hovering around his mouth?

"I'm disturbing your lunch." She stood beside the counter feeling as awkward as a schoolgirl.

"I invited you to lunch."

"No, Aiden. You asked me over to see your recent work."

"It's noon," he said as though it explained everything. "Why would I invite you here at noon if I didn't plan to feed you?"

"You didn't make it clear. You enjoy making me uncomfortable, don't you?"

He'd been about to open a bottle of wine but put the opener back onto the counter. She'd startled him.

"Uncomfortable?" He strode to her. "No. I want you to feel at home here." He placed his palm against her cheek and his big hand covered the side of her head. Calluses scraped her skin, sending a jolt of desire to her stomach.

She didn't know what to do with him. Was he making passes at her? He'd said he had work to show her. Was that why she was here? Or was it more?

God, she didn't know. The last time she'd flirted with a man had been in high school and that boy had become her husband. Tomorrow she turned fifty-eight. In all those long years, there'd been no lovers other than her husband. She didn't know how to read signs. Didn't know what was there and what wasn't. Besides, men went for younger women, *not* older women.

He returned to the stove as though nothing had happened.

She was imagining things.

He tossed the shrimp in a wok with butter—tons of glorious butter—and garlic and white wine. When they were cooked, he drained linguine and spread it onto two plates then covered it with the shrimp and sprinkled on parsley to finish.

He motioned for her to follow him. The dining room was little more than a corner of the living room with windows on both sides.

A basket of crusty bread sat beside a small crock of more butter.

So simple and the man had thrown it together as though it were as easy as breathing.

She took a bite of shrimp. Delicious. Aiden had depth and skills of which she hadn't been aware.

He handed her the basket of bread and she took the smallest slice. When he offered her butter, she shook her head. It was hard enough to stay trim without indulging.

Olivia glanced out the window and gasped. Aiden had been hard at work. The still dormant garden was full of pieces of artwork, both in stone and in metal.

The metalwork intrigued her. They were glorious, curvaceous, sparkling pieces, both rustic and elegant. Very like the man.

Some were coy and some blatantly sexual.

One item in particular appealed to her—a huge swooning petal with a melting stamen in its center so feminine in concept and so voluptuous in execution that Olivia was aroused just looking at it.

Aiden's sensibilities were growing, evolving. What would he come up with next? Quite simply, the man took her breath away on so many levels.

"Beautiful," she whispered.

"Keep eating. Your food is getting cold."

"I'm overwhelmed, Aiden. Your pieces are gorgeous."

"There's beauty all around us. We still have to eat."

She looked at him and laughed. "Says the man who creates art for days on end, but forgets to eat and to shave and who knows what else?"

He smiled and watched her steadily.

When his regard became uncomfortable, she gestured toward the metal pieces and said, "You've been taking chances."

"Aye. Life is about taking chances, trying new things. Isn't that right, Olivia?"

"Ye-es." She wasn't sure he was talking about art. Were they having the same conversation? Why did it feel as though Aiden had an agenda today that she wasn't getting?

"Eat, Olivia."

She took another few mouthfuls. She could feel the butter going straight to her hips.

"I'm full," she said. "It was wonderful. Thank you."

"You didn't eat enough to fill a hummingbird," he said, sounding disgusted. "You're watching your weight, aren't you?"

Stung by his criticism and by his tone, even though he was right, she picked up her fork and took a large mouthful of linguine and shrimp. Oh, so delicious. So buttery. So garlicky. She spread her tiny slice of bread with butter and ate it.

She didn't stop eating until her plate was empty.

"Satisfied?" she asked.

"The question is," he said, grinning, "are *you* satisfied?"

Oh, she was. So happy. In heaven. She laughed.

"I want those sculptures for my gallery. You need to have a showing."

Aiden nodded. "Say when."

"I want that one—" she pointed to the one that looked like a giant melting vaginal petal "—for my own."

"It's yours."

"I'll pay you whatever its retail value would be."

"I said, it's yours. I'm not charging you. If you want it, Olivia, then I'm giving it to you."

She got chills. That gorgeous, sexy, weeping petal was hers? It was going in her bedroom. "Oh. Thank you."

"Do me a favor."

"Anything."

"Model for me."

What? He'd stunned her. Left her speechless.

"What do you mean?"

"Exactly what I said. I need a model."

"I don't know what to say. Surely you can find someone in town younger than me who would be willing to pose for you? How about Laura? She's beautiful." *And looking for a man and is more your age than mine.* The thought of them together twisted the linguine in her tummy into a knot. *Oh, Olivia, jealousy of your own daughter does not become you. You're better than that.*

But she wasn't. She didn't want Laura anywhere near Aiden. She wanted him for herself.

"I don't want Laura," he said, and Olivia rejoiced. "I want someone mature."

"You mean someone old." The slightest bitterness clouded the statement.

"Don't change my words. I meant mature. I don't want a girl. I want a woman."

"Laura isn't a girl. She's a woman."

"I want you."

Before she could object, he said again, "Model for me."

"I don't know."

"Say yes."

"I don't—"

"Stop thinking. Say yes."

"O-okay. When?"

"Tomorrow."

On her fifty-eighth birthday.

"The gallery is closed on Mondays." He'd thought it through. "Do you want to see what I've done so far?"

He'd already started?

"Yes."

He took her to a solarium of windows that felt like part of the garden.

"The light in here is perfect. All natural."

He was right. It was stupendous. Sunshine poured through the windows and the ceiling, lighting a vertical piece of stone slightly taller than she was. He'd already carved a head with a face that looked remarkably like hers.

"How…?"

"From memory." He stood too close. She looked up at him, but couldn't see his face clearly without her reading glasses. Reading glasses, for heaven's sake. *He* didn't need reading glasses.

"You have a good memory."

"I observe people. I watch them when they don't know it."

Meaning that he'd been watching her when she wasn't looking. It should have felt creepy, but didn't. She was flattered.

"I need you here to get it right."

It was a large piece of stone. "Are you sculpting all of me?"

"Yes, full body."

"What do you want me to wear?"

"It doesn't matter."

"What?" He was out of his mind. "I won't model nude."

"I'm not asking you to. You'll be wearing a sheet wrapped around you that I'll provide."

"Oh. I see. Okay."

"Come after lunch. One o'clock. Is that all right with you?"

"Yes."

The rest of the conversation revolved around booking a

Saturday to launch his new work. She left soon after, but spent the rest of the day and night trying fruitlessly to get the man out of her mind.

AFTER NICK LEFT, Laura took refuge in her apartment.

She stared at the bed. Their lovemaking had been scorching. Stellar. Better than sex with anyone else. Ever.

That's how it was between her and Nick. At least last night, unlike on that first night years ago, there had been more than just sex. There had been warm conversation. Conviviality.

But it had meant nothing.

There would be no relationship. No baby. No family.

Nick hated her.

She hated him.

"This sucks," she cried out. "This isn't fair."

She jumped up from the bed and stood on it. She tore at the colorful gauze hanging from her ceiling, pulled it down, shredded it. Goddamn her overpowering attraction to the man and her own passion that had undone her last night as it had that one night years ago.

She carried her swooping gauze sheets out the back door and flew down the fire escape to the garbage can at the bottom of the stairs, where she stuffed the tatters of her heady unwise lust. She slammed the lid on top and climbed the stairs back to her apartment. Her rooms stood mute in quiet condemnation.

Plus ça change.

Nothing good ever came out of encounters with Nick Jordan.

She should have remembered that.

She called her mother. No answer.

"Mom, I need you," she whispered and called again. Still no answer.

Later that day, in her industrial kitchen downstairs, she pounded out cinnamon buns as though she was mass mar-

keting them, drinking water to hold off the nausea that the
pill had caused. She didn't want to vomit in case it screwed
up its effectiveness.

She kneaded yeast dough, formed loaves of bread and
rolled pastries, working until her arms and back burned.

Alone, long into the night, she worked.

Plus ça change, indeed.

NICK SPENT SUNDAY afternoon on the phone until he found a
professor, Arthur Hampson, who'd researched Western Indian affairs extensively and who was willing to advise Nick
on Monday.

Bedeviled by images from his Saturday-night lovemaking
with Laura and filled to the gills with rage, he threw himself
into clearing out his bedroom at the house, into packing up
the boxes of his life until the room was empty and Nick was,
once again, invisible.

Emily decided to spend another night with Gabe and Callie. Apparently, they were camping, for God's sake, since
Gabe's house wasn't ready. The foundation hadn't even been
built.

At loose ends on Sunday evening, he called Mort.

"We'll be staying here a few extra days. Just thought you
should know in case you dropped by the house."

"Okay." Mort sounded subdued. No wonder.

"Are you okay?"

"Good as c'n be." He slurred his words. Mort had probably been drinking all day, alone in his house.

Nick should be there for him. He and Emily should be
home with him, making him dinner, keeping him company.

Instead, Emily was off having a ball with other people
while Nick lay on his bed alone, staring at a strange ceiling
in a bed-and-breakfast, trying to reach out to a lonely old
man. What a pair he and Mort were.

What goes around comes around.

Nick had spent too much time on business and not enough on people and it was coming back to bite him on the butt.

Long after he hung up after finishing with Mort, he stared at the ceiling before sleep finally claimed him sometime in the middle of the night.

CHAPTER EIGHT

NICK SECURED A room in the small library for Monday afternoon.

Salem Pearce brought half a dozen elders with him, one man so old Nick thought they should have emergency responders stationed nearby. Just in case.

Soft-spoken and intelligent, Pearce seemed noncombative and open to solutions that might not be readily apparent. If Salem had come to the meeting with harsh or unreasonable demands, Nick would have tossed him out and torn down the house and built without a touch of conscience, but he liked that Pearce was strategic and subtle.

Not that Salem needed to know that. In business, it wasn't smart to give in too easily.

Nick had researched Salem on the internet. Heavily involved in his tribe's history, he devoted his days to bringing it to light and to life, and to educating the young of his tribe.

When asked, the professor had raved about Salem. If this project were going to work, so that Nick could still build his resort while honoring the native culture, he wanted to work with someone intelligent and reasonable.

While they waited for the library to get the key, Nick talked to Salem and took his measure.

"Tell me about what you're doing to preserve your culture."

"I've been making CDs. I talk to the elders and they teach me the language and I record it. They are the last who know the language. If my generation takes no steps to preserve it, it will disappear."

Nick tried to imagine losing his language. It would be gut-wrenching.

"What else?"

"I want to preserve women's art. Beading moccasins. Painting on tepees. Preparation of the food the elders grew up on."

"You're really into it, aren't you?" Nick asked, while the librarian approached from down the hallway and unlocked the door.

"Totally."

Admirable.

They seated themselves around a small conference table. Nick would have to make sure the resort housed good conference facilities to entice business people who wanted to hold meetings in the morning and then enjoy a round of golf in the afternoon.

"The challenge, as I see it," he said, broaching the heart of the problem, "is that there are no clearly marked burial grounds. There's no way to know where individual bodies were buried."

He turned to the elders. "Isn't that so?"

"Yes, that is so, but they are there. On that land."

Nick glanced at the historian, who said, "It's true. I've looked through what limited archives there are and a migratory route did, indeed, run straight across your land."

"Is there any way that you—" he gestured toward the professor "—and you—" he gestured toward the elders "—could confer and come up with a good guess exactly where that route ran?"

"What do you have in mind?" Salem asked.

"If it didn't actually cross where the house now stands, I can go ahead and build."

When Salem would have objected, Nick raised his hand. "I know that you won't want tourists running roughshod over burial sites, so I have an idea."

Salem smiled, a restrained slip of his lips, willing to listen but maybe taking things with a grain of salt. Native Americans had been burned in the past. "What's your idea?"

"There must be college students studying archaeology who would be happy to spend the summer on a dig in Colorado. I would fund the operation. The elders and the professor could make an educated guess where we could start. Every artifact or bone would be handed over to you."

"That would disturb our dead." Salem shifted in his seat. "I'm not comfortable with that. Where would we bury them?"

"If you can't find a place, we can come up with a solution together."

"Still, uprooting our ancestors…"

"There's more," Nick said. "I would be willing to build an education center on a piece of the land and devote it exclusively to Indian affairs."

"Okay, I'm intrigued. You have my interest."

"Enough to consider running it? I would pay a good salary."

Salem sat up straight. "Me?"

"Are you interested?"

He grinned, his teeth white against permanently tanned skin. "Hell, yes." Handsome devil.

"There will be a lot to work out, but I'll pay you, the elders and Professor Hampson a consultant's fee until we build."

Nick stood. "Professor, the second you and the elders have any idea where it's clear for me to build on the land, let me know. I've got a construction crew sitting around on my dime doing nothing. This delay is costing me a fortune."

He left the room, but Salem stopped him in the hallway.

"About the design of the building?"

Nick nodded.

"Could the architecture incorporate our heritage, our sensibilities, the things we used to use to decorate our clothing and tepees? Can the building harmonize with nature and honor the land as well as the people?"

"Fair questions," Nick said. "I'll call the architect to see if he can get down here this week. He can look at the land and talk to you before he starts. Later, he can fine-tune it so it fits the land and the history of your people."

Salem looked taken aback. "Why are you doing this?"

"Because I learned the hard way it doesn't always have to be all my way. Sometimes it pays to listen to other people." And sometimes you had to give to get.

This could be a win-win situation rather than a knock-down drag-out fight that could land in the courts and stay there for years.

He shook Salem's hand and walked away, secure that he'd found the right man for the job.

He was a good judge of character and Salem was a good man.

Back in his car, Nick called his architect and arranged for him to fly down the following day.

He rolled down the window and called out to Salem. "My architect is flying in tomorrow. Are you available to meet on the Jordan land on Wednesday?"

Salem smiled broadly. "Yeah."

"Good. 10:00 a.m. See you at the Jordan house then."

OLIVIA CAME OUT of one of Aiden's bedrooms where she had been changing and walked down the hallway to the garden room at the back of the house. Her knees were shaking. She couldn't seem to stop them. She'd tried.

Lord knew she was trying to be sophisticated about this. An artist wanted to sculpt her. It flattered her. It terrified her.

She wore only a white bedsheet and her bra and panties. The only person who ever saw her in so little, or less, was her doctor, and she wasn't the least bit attracted to *him*.

How was she to get through today without embarrassing herself? Without letting her hopeless infatuation with Aiden show?

She would have to do what she always did with him—act the prude, like an uptight, classy little prig.

John had always told her she had an innate elegance, but she turned it into something cold and brittle in her dealings with Aiden.

She had no choice.

When she entered the solarium, Aidan approached and placed his hands on top of hers where she had the sheet in a death grip against her chest.

"Easy," he whispered. "I'm not going to hurt you."

He urged her to the far end of the glass room where he'd draped a white backdrop from the ceiling and across the floor. She stepped from the carpet and onto the backdrop and found it warm on her bare soles, from the sun that poured in through the windows.

"Stand right here," he directed. "Let me drape this differently. Let go."

She eased her hold on the bedsheet. When it fell from one shoulder revealing her bra strap, Aiden made a sound that Olivia couldn't interpret.

Before she knew what he was about, he reached his hands into the back of the sheet and unhooked her bra.

"Take it off," he ordered.

No. Not at her age. She'd never been a big woman, but she had enough. She'd had a good figure, but even smaller breasts lost the fight with gravity over time.

"I'm fifty-eight years old," she said, appalled by how stuffy she sounded. *Today, I'm fifty-eight. I'm getting older by the minute.*

He stared for a long time. "You're beautiful."

"For my age, you mean." There was that bitterness again. Why, oh why, couldn't she grow old with grace and acceptance? Because she loved a much younger man.

"Don't," he said.

"Don't what?"

"Put words I don't mean into my mouth. You're a beautiful woman. When a man gives you a compliment, smile and say thank you."

She smiled, but it felt brittle enough to crack her cheeks. "Thank you."

"I'll turn my back," he said. "Take off the bra. I won't see anything."

Her fingers trembled but she managed to remove a frothy bit of lavender lace and tossed it onto a settee.

He turned back around and eased the sheet from one of her shoulders until he could pull one arm out and then the other. He hadn't wanted her bra straps to show. But did it really matter? He wasn't photographing her. He was sculpting her. So he could add or take away whatever he wanted.

Behind her now, he eased the fabric down her back. Farther. And then farther still. She pressed it against the tops of her breasts so it wouldn't slip down at the front. How low did he intend to go?

She found out when she felt his wet lips against the small of her back. She yelped and gripped the sheet while his big hands spanned her waist. She started to throb in all of the right places.

Oh, she hadn't felt this in such a long time.

Sunlight warmed her closed eyelids.

His fingers traveled her spine then around her waist and up until they brushed the bottoms of her breasts. She gasped and her eyes flew open. He was inside the sheet.

"Let go," he whispered in her ear, his warm breath feathering her neck and collarbone.

"What are you doing?"

"Loving you."

His fingers moved with authority under her hands and the sheet fell away. She caught it over her stomach and leaned her head back against his chest. He cupped her breasts, his calluses rough and abrasive and delicious against her nipples.

Then those calloused fingers slid down her stomach, moving quickly. Too quickly.

When he drew the sheet from her nerveless fingers and the warm sun caressed her skin, all of it, she gasped. Standing in a room drenched with light from floor-to-ceiling windows, her poor body had nowhere to hide. Aiden would see everything, every stretch mark that three children had inflicted upon her, every bump and groove of cellulite, every flaw.

"I can't do this," she cried and ran from the room, hoping that he wasn't watching her inelegant retreat. In the bedroom where she'd undressed, she grabbed her clothes and put them on, her hands shaking. Her bra was still in the other room.

She didn't care. He could keep it—a souvenir of her humiliation.

She stepped out of the room.

"Don't go," he said, striding down the hallway toward her. "Do you think I care about imperfection?"

"You're an artist. You look for beauty."

"When I saw you naked—" she cringed but he plowed on "—I saw *you,* Olivia. You! A mature, beautiful woman. I want to love you. We can do it in the dark. We can do it wherever, however, you want. I want you."

"I thought I was here to model, not to be mauled." Her voice shook, because his mauling had been so delicious.

"Is that how it felt?" he asked, staring down at her in both puzzlement and understanding. "Like I was pawing you?"

No! "Answer my question. Did you ask me here to model?"

"Yes."

"Then what was all that about?"

"You're an attractive woman, Olivia. I'm crazy about you. I want to make love to you."

To me! He wants to make love to me.

Hope arose, but not as quickly as fear. "I'm fifteen years older than you."

"What difference does that make?"

"Look at you! You're in your prime while I'm over-the-hill."

His expression hardened. "There's nothing over-the-hill about you."

She leaned back against the wall, because the strength of his personality weakened her knees. "What would people think?"

"I don't care. There's passion under that contained poised exterior of yours and I want to unlock it."

"Then what?"

"Does it matter what comes next? We're a pair of grown-ups. We should be able to love without worrying about age or what society will think. We should be able to burn up the sheets if we want to." He stepped close, the heat from his expressive body singeing her. "And we could, Olivia. You and me. We could."

His hazel eyes bored into her, deep into her quaking cowardly soul. Cowardly, yes, because she couldn't do this.

She stepped away from him.

It was easy enough for him to say age didn't matter when he looked like a god and had a body that wouldn't age for years to come.

When she drove away, she wrapped her shaky equilibrium in anger, because it was easier to do than to try to overcome her terror.

CHAPTER NINE

Nick was about to beard the lion in his den. He drove to the piece of land Gabe had bought with the money Nick had paid him for his share of the Jordan land.

He'd written up a contract that would allow his brothers a portion of the annual profits from the resort. His lawyers had thought he was nuts. So did he. He still refused to look closely at why he'd felt compelled to do it, especially considering how much he disliked Gabe.

Gabe and Callie hadn't started building yet, but a few trees had been taken down and land marked off for the foundation.

Nick wondered where he was supposed to find his daughter. There was no house. He got out of the car and stood still, listening. Somewhere in the woods there were people talking. He followed that sound.

Pockets of not-yet-melted snow coated the forest floor. In a small clearing, Gabe and Emily fed dogs—at least a couple of dozen of them—fastened to a thick rope that ranged the perimeter. The dogs saw him and barked.

Emily laughed and ran to him. "Dad!"

She flew into his arms and he caught her and grinned. God, he'd missed her. On Friday, he'd made the decision to spend more time with her and had even brought her to Accord, but then Gabe had whisked her away, and Nick had missed her with an ache that had caught him off guard.

He hugged her so hard she squealed. "I can't breathe."

"You ready to go?" he asked.

"Yeah, but I want you to meet the dogs first."

"I—" he forestalled, but she was already off and running.

Nick nodded at Gabe and Gabe nodded back, the two of them like a pair of wary dogs.

Emily introduced him to every single dog, all thirty of them. At the last one, she said, "Daisy doesn't like to be touched. Don't pet her."

"Okay." Nick had wanted a dog when he was a kid. Gabe had said no. His mom had supported Gabe on that, the one and only time she hadn't given in to Nick. Nick had hated Gabe for deciding what Nick could or couldn't own, as though he were Nick's father, for God's sake. He'd hated even more that his mom had sided with Gabe.

So why did Gabe now own thirty dogs? Obviously, he hadn't disliked them as Nick had assumed. Nick watched Gabe feed and interact with the dogs. He loved them.

Nick had known about the dogsledding business, but had thought of it as just that—a business. Now, watching Gabe, he understood that it was a labor of love.

Gabe had been watching Nick and approached.

"It was too much work to own one when we were kids." *What?* Was the man a freaking mind reader? Or was Nick that transparent? "Plus, we could barely afford food for us, let alone for an animal."

It made sense and went a small way toward mitigating Nick's resentment. In that area.

And yet, what about that trunk of toys and cars he owned? Mom had made sure there was money for that. The inconsistencies in his childhood and his memories confounded him.

"Dad, come here," Emily called. She led him to a large tent, maybe twenty-by-eighteen feet, dirty-white with guy wires extending into the trees.

She opened the front flap and stepped inside. "This is where I slept both nights. It's what prospectors used to live in when they were panning for gold."

Nick stared around the rugged interior. A rectangular iron

box with a pipe that went through the roof constituted a stove. Kerosene lanterns hung from the ceiling. Rolled-up sleeping bags lined the walls along with blankets, pots and pans, plastic storage containers, winter coats, rubber boots. Rudimentary. Basic.

So why was his daughter so excited?

Nick had provided her with the best—the *best*—that money could buy and this was what made her happy? *Cheated* didn't begin to describe how he felt.

"Let's go," he said.

He'd been too brusque. At his tone, her face flattened.

He softened his voice. "On the phone you said you wanted to see the Jordan land. Plus, we have reservations for dinner. We don't want to be late."

"Okay." She seemed somewhat mollified and picked up her knapsack.

They said goodbye to Gabe and drove to the Jordan place.

While they walked, Emily chatted about Gabe's dogsledding business. Nick had to admit that once you stopped looking at it purely as a business, it had its appeal.

"Uncle Gabe had amazing photographs and videos of the Iditarod." In March, he'd entered his first dogsledding race. He hadn't won, but had finished with he and his dogs all in one piece. Apparently, that was an accomplishment.

"Where was Callie today?"

"She's setting up a home for adults like her mom who have Alzheimer's and for senior citizens."

"A long-term-care facility?"

"Yeah. Her mom and a woman named Sophie are already living there. That's where we all showered."

Nick hadn't even thought about how Emily would clean herself at Gabe's. "You could have come to the B and B."

"I know, but I liked doing what they were doing. They'll keep using the showers at the nursing home until their house is built. Callie does a lot of stuff to get the place ready for residents. She's getting people and businesses to donate furniture. She's interviewing nurses, but there aren't a lot around here."

She should get the town to send some of their high school graduates to school to become nurses on the condition they return to Accord to work, as he'd done with the resort.

"Callie said she really liked your idea of sending kids to college, so she's trying to convince town council to pay for kids to study nursing."

Nick smiled. So, Callie had been thinking the same thing. He'd always thought she was a smart businesswoman.

They arrived at the old homestead. There were no protestors or construction workers around today. It looked forlorn and abandoned.

"Let's go," he said, leading her around the house and into the woods. Snow coated the ground in shady areas, hanging on by its fingertips until the bitter end of winter. It wouldn't be long now until it disappeared altogether.

"It's so pretty here, Dad. I can't believe you got to hang around in the country when you were a kid. What kinds of games did you and your brothers used to play?"

"We had snowball fights." He'd remembered that much already during his snowball fight with Emily. He would amend the memory now, though. More often than not, Gabe didn't join him and Tyler. Nick didn't know why.

"That's only one season. What else did you do?"

They had arrived at the only pond on the property. He caught a glimpse of a memory, struggled then managed to bring it into focus. Gabe, of all people, had taught him how to fish.

"We used to fish," he said.

"What did you catch?" Emily sounded wistful.

"Trout. Brookies because they were easiest, but I think Gabe caught rainbow trout in this pond." He glanced down at Emily, who stared at the water with such longing that Nick laughed. "Trout need cold water. The pond looks good, but it's fed by runoff from Luther. It's icy cold."

"Luther?"

"Our mountain."

"Can we walk to it?"

"Yep. We can walk up some of it, too. You need to climb to reach the top, though, with climbing gear. As far as I know, no one climbed it after Dad died."

They continued their walk until they came to a large clearing. "Judging by photos Callie sent to me, I'd guess this is where Gabe ran his dogsledding business."

"Wow, it's pretty. Look at how tall the trees are."

Sunlight poured through the tops of the trees ringing the clearing, sending streamers of gold to the needle-coated earth. Pinecones crunched beneath their feet.

"These are Rocky Mountain Douglas-firs. We used to have campouts in this clearing. Each of us had our own pup tent."

"Sounds like fun."

To Nick's surprise, yeah, it did. He remembered some good times camping. "One night it rained and we found out how leaky the tents were. We ran to the house and Mom dried us and put us into our beds. It turns out the tents were old hand-me-downs from someone who no longer wanted them."

"Still," Emily said, her voice wistful again. "It was an adventure."

"Yes, it was that." Had he kept her childhood too safe? Had he robbed her of adventure?

They reached the base of Luther in fifteen minutes, a good hike through the woods.

Twenty minutes later, they had managed to hike a trail partway up Luther. It was cooler up here and snow covered everything.

"Are you cold?" he asked.

"No. This is awesome. Wow, what a view."

"I'd forgotten about the view."

"Dad, I think you forget a lot of things."

"Why do you say that?"

"Because you're looking at everything like you've never seen it before."

Out of the mouths of babes.

He'd spent too much of his adult years trying to ignore his childhood, trying to squelch memories that had seemed all bad, and yet here he was with good memories trying to break through.

"Is that your land, too?"

Emily pointed to acres of flat farmland on Luther's far side.

"No. That belongs to Ron Porter. I'm in negotiations with him to buy. He's playing hardball. He knows his land would complement the downhill skiing. It would be great for cross-country-ski fans."

"Maybe he just wants to keep farming, Dad. You can't make people leave their land if they don't want to."

Nick blew a raspberry and Emily laughed. "Ron is past ready for retirement. He just wants to make a lot of money when he sells his land."

"He should. Just like you want to make money from all the people who'll come here. That's what people do. That's all they want. They want to make money."

Nick would have protested Emily's cynical tone, but he'd taught her that it was true. That's all he did. What else had she ever seen him do? Or aspire to? Or plan and plot about?

"Except Uncle Gabe," she amended. "He wants to do more. He wants to save the environment."

Saint freaking Gabe. Would Emily ever talk about her own father with that much admiration?

"Come on," he said, in a funk. "Let's drive to town. We're losing the light."

Dinner was steak and baked potatoes at a steak house across the street from Sweet Temptations.

Despite his best efforts, Nick couldn't stop staring at the

bakery. Someone was working in the back because light spilled from the kitchen through the doorway to the café. Occasionally, a shadow crossed.

Laura? Baking tomorrow's treats?

He didn't care.

"Dad?"

"Yes?"

"I asked you a question three times."

"Sorry. I was thinking about something."

Emily's glance flickered to the bakery and back to him, but something in his face must have warned her not to ask why he was preoccupied with it.

"What were you asking me?"

"How did your meeting with the Native Americans go?"

She was showing an interest in his business? She never had before. But then, it had never been real to her, or immediate, as it was here.

"I found a professor who's going to work with elders to determine exactly where the migration routes were. Do you remember that young man I spoke to on Saturday? The protestor?"

"The good-looking one? Yeah, I remember."

She was looking at men? At boys? And judging their looks? Was she old enough for that? *Emily, I lost your childhood and already you're showing signs of moving further along.*

"Anyway, his name is Salem Pearce. I asked him whether he wants a job once the resort is built."

He described his idea for honoring the dead and the local native heritage, and about building something on the land.

"Oh, wow, Dad, that's awesome. I *love* that idea." The admiration Nick had heard in her voice earlier for Gabe now rang for him and it warmed him to a ridiculous degree. "The clearing where Uncle Gabe used to keep his dogs and the tent would be an awesome spot for the building. The trees are so tall and, when it's quiet, it's like a cathedral."

Nick smiled warmly at his daughter. "Good idea, Emily." What other smart ideas did she have?

"Fancy meeting you two here."

Tyler approached their table.

Nick nodded. Emily jumped up to hug Ty. "You've met Ty?" he asked.

"He came to Gabe and Callie's for dinner on Saturday night."

"Dinner? There's no house."

"We had it around the campfire."

Ty laughed. "With heavy jackets on. We started early, but it got cool toward the end of the night."

"Are you here for dinner?" Nick asked, actually considering inviting him to join them.

"No. I saw you in the window when I passed."

He was in uniform. "You're working?"

"Yeah. I don't usually work evenings, but one of my deputies called in sick. I've been on the job since eight this morning. If the night stays quiet, I'll catch some *z's* on the cot in the cell."

"In the jail cell?" Emily asked.

Ty nodded and laughed. He'd always been the easygoing one, the peacekeeper between authoritarian Gabe and rebellious Nick.

"We've finished dinner, but do you want to join us for dessert?"

"I wouldn't mind."

They ordered apple pie and coffee.

Nick brought him up to speed on the Native American issue. Ty nodded his approval. "Doesn't sound like there'll be any trouble I'll be called out for once you start to build."

"Don't think so. The talks have been civilized." Nick finished his pie and asked, "What's your impression of Salem Pearce?"

"He's a real good kid. A man of his word. What's your impression?"

"Same. I told him I want him to run the Native center once it's up and running. In fact, I want him to get it going."

"Good choice. I've never had a speck of trouble with him." He glanced at Emily. "How long are you staying in town?"

"Probably just until the end of the week—just until I get this problem settled and construction headed in the right direction."

"Aw, Dad. It feels like we just got here."

"I know, but I left a lot of work behind and who knows what you're missing at school."

Before Emily could get a real pout going, Ty said, "I've been thinking. My daughter, Ruby, is coming to stay with me for six weeks in the summer, starting end of June."

Nick had heard about Ruby. It seemed the girl's mother had kept her existence a secret from Ty until the girl popped up on his doorstep in the middle of a blizzard in January.

"I'd like for Emily and Ruby to meet. After all, they're first cousins and the same age. As far as I know, Emily is Ruby's only cousin."

Emily squealed and pumped the air with her fist. "Yes! Say yes, Dad. Pleeeease."

Until this weekend, Nick hadn't known how much Emily craved an extended family. Marsha had been an only child so there were no cousins on that side. Now, there was Ruby.

He hadn't realized his girl had been starving for family, that he'd been depriving her of something valuable—another mark against him as a father.

How on earth could Nick say no? But that would leave him alone in Seattle when he had finally decided to spend more time with her.

She seemed to read his mind. "Can you take a holiday?" She turned to her uncle. "Can Dad stay with us, too?"

"Of course."

"That's not necessary. I can stay at the B and B."

"Why?" Ty asked.

Good question. Nick didn't have an answer.

"Come on, Nick. Get your head out of your a—" He glanced at Emily and flushed. "Sorry. I mean, we're family. I have bedrooms sitting empty. It's embarrassing to have my brother visit and not stay with me."

He hadn't realized Ty would feel that way.

"Okay, how about if Emily and I come for the Fourth of July? How about we arrive a couple of days before?"

Ty grinned. "Sounds like a plan. Ruby will be here by then. We'll have a barbecue at the ranch. I'll have Gabe and Callie over, too."

Ty stood and left but not without another bear hug for Emily.

"The architect and Salem and I are going to look over the land on Wednesday morning," Nick said to his daughter. "We'll discuss ideas for the museum. Want to come?"

"Yes!"

Nick smiled, so damn glad he'd brought his daughter with him to Accord.

When they got back to their top-floor suite at the B and B, Nick had Emily call her grandfather. She was on the phone with Mort for a good half an hour. Nick listened to her describe every dog to Mort, as well as every feature of the prospector's tent.

Nick also heard Mort's laugh on the other end of the phone. Emily's call had perked him up. Mort and Emily usually spoke every night. He must be missing his granddaughter.

When they returned to Seattle, Nick had to make a point of having Mort over for dinner, often.

LAURA WENT TO the house she had been raised in, two blocks behind Main, to pick up her mom for her birthday dinner.

Coming here was still hard more than twenty years after Amber's death.

Laura's teenage years had been difficult after that and nothing had brought her comfort until Gabe Jordan had shown her kindness. Missing her baby sister—and her mother and father's attention—she had lapped up Gabe's affection as though it were mother's milk, sunshine and gold all wrapped into one.

Throughout their friendship, though, there had been that mischievous, unruly, troubling attraction to a boy three years younger than her. Nick. Her boyfriend's brother.

She'd never forgotten Gabe's kindness and love. To this day, she couldn't forgive herself for betraying him, even though he had forgiven her and had moved on. She hoped he was happy.

She stepped into the house and called, "Mom, I'm here. Are you ready?"

"I'll be down in a minute."

Laura stepped in only as far as the living room, noting that the flowers she and Noah had ordered had arrived—hot-pink gladioli splayed in a fan from a low flat dish.

The style of the room was slightly dated, but elegant, perfect. Like her mother. Mom's favorite pieces of artwork from the gallery, the ones she bought for herself—she did get first dibs, after all, because she saw the work before anyone else did—hung on the walls, everything from abstract to landscape.

If Laura had eclectic taste in music, her mom did in art.

When Olivia finally came downstairs, dressed in a cream-and-peach two-piece suit, exquisitely designed and perfectly tailored, her eyes and nose were red.

She had obviously tried to hide it with makeup, but Laura knew she'd been crying.

"What's wrong?" she asked.

Olivia's cool, practiced smile couldn't hide her sorrow. "What makes you think something's wrong?"

Laura put a hand on her hip. "Mom. Come on. You've been crying."

Mom's hand shot to her cheek. "It shows?"

"It shows."

"I can't go out."

"Sure you can. Just give it a minute. We have time before the reservation. We have to wait for Noah, anyway." She gestured toward the tasteful arrangement of furniture for her mother to sit. "Do you want to talk about it?"

Olivia peered into the antique federal mirror in the hall. "I can't go out like this. We'll have to order in."

She turned to mount the stairs. "I'll change out of my suit."

Laura stopped her with a hand to her arm. "Mom, talk to me. What are you trying to avoid telling me?"

Olivia stared at her hand on the banister and seemed to hold her breath, then said, "I don't want to grow old. I don't want to celebrate another birthday."

"We don't have to go out, then," Laura said softly. "We can eat in."

Mom released her breath. "Good. Let's have pizza."

"Okay." Laura watched her mother go upstairs and wondered where all of this worry about aging had come from. Mom had never had a problem with it before.

Too bad. Laura had arrived a few minutes early because she'd wanted to talk to Mom about Saturday night's disaster. She needed a shoulder to cry on, but it obviously wouldn't be Olivia's.

On Wednesday morning, Nick pulled into the yard at the Jordan house with his architect, Mike Canning, in the front seat and Emily in the back.

Two cars were already there—a beat-up old junker and a

late-model Honda Civic. Nick imagined the junker belonged to Salem, but who owned the Civic?

Mike and Emily followed him to the veranda. He opened the unlocked door. No sense locking a house that had nothing in it.

Salem's voice rang out from the kitchen along with throaty feminine laughter that kicked Nick in the gut. What was Laura doing here?

"Salem?" he called.

The young man stepped out of the kitchen with Laura. He smiled. She didn't.

"I asked Laura to deliver some of her coffee and cinnamon buns. They're here in the kitchen. My treat."

"That was generous of you."

Salem watched Mike with interest.

Nick introduced the two of them. If it was rude to ignore Laura, so be it. She'd done a real number on him in trying to get pregnant without his permission. Sure, he understood revenge, but thirteen years later? That was a long time to hold on to old resentments.

It was petty beyond belief to act on them so many years later, but worse, to act in a way that would alter a man's life forever.

Mike stepped forward, held out his hand and introduced himself. Laura smiled and took it.

Emily said, "Hi."

"Sorry, I forgot," Nick said. "Salem, this is my daughter, Emily."

"Dad told me all about what you want to do. I love the idea. Can't wait to see what you and Mr. Canning come up with."

Salem smiled down at Emily and Nick saw something he couldn't quite put his finger on—a bonding, maybe? A communion of like minds?

Laura laughed at something Mike said, drawing his attention.

She walked over to Salem. "I have to get back to the bakery."

"Thanks for bringing the stuff. I'll come in later to settle the tab."

"Whenever. Don't worry about it."

She kissed him and hugged him and left.

Smiling, Salem turned to Nick, but the smile died on his face. "What?"

"You always hug and kiss the caterer?"

"She's my cousin."

She was? "Oh." He'd had no idea.

"You weren't friendly with her," Mike said.

Nick shrugged.

"Is there something I should know?"

"Why would you need to know anything?"

"I'm taking her out to dinner tonight."

"What?"

"I assume it's okay for me to eat while I'm here." Mike's tone had taken on an edge. "She's a beautiful woman. I wouldn't mind her company."

"Do what you want."

"I usually do."

Salem jumped into the breach. "Come into the kitchen. Let's eat then get out on the land."

They had coffee and cinnamon buns, both of which were excellent.

Mike and Emily raved about the buns.

"Dad, we so have to get more of these tomorrow."

"We'll be leaving tomorrow."

"O-kay. Why are you in a bad mood? You weren't before we got here."

"It's the house."

Mike watched him, his smile too knowing. He knew that Nick was having trouble dealing with Laura, even if he didn't know why.

"Let's get out of here." An itchiness pulsed in Nick's limbs as though he needed to run a marathon or go a round in a boxing ring. He needed to get away from Laura's cinnamon buns and out onto the land.

"Emily had a great idea for a good spot for the museum." He led them to the clearing where the morning sun slanted onto the forest floor.

Salem's face lit up. "Here?" he asked in his smooth soft voice. "She was right. It's perfect."

"It feels like we're in a church," she said. "A cathedral."

"That has nothing to do with native culture," he replied, "but I understand perfectly."

Mike roved the space. "This is beautiful. What do you think, Salem? Wood, brushed steel, plenty of glass so the beauty of the forest becomes a part of the interior space. Round corners. No sharp edges."

Salem couldn't stop smiling. "Yeah. How about making it tall, like the pines?"

"Three stories? Okay. How about a column of steel up the center to house an elevator and washrooms, but we'll cover it with wood so it blends into the forest."

"Reclaimed wood would be incredible."

Mike nodded. "I love it. How about self-sufficiency? Solar energy."

"Yeah. Make everything green. We need large empty spaces for showcasing the culture. It would be great if it was all glass. You know, have everything protected from the elements, but feel like you are outdoors. A full-size tepee in the lobby that we could light up at night would look awesome from both inside and outside."

Nick felt like a fifth wheel, as though looking in on lovers. He'd done his job. He'd paired the two best people to bring this off.

"Do you two want to come back to Accord to talk ideas? I've got the library conference room booked for the week."

"Good idea."

"Do you want to ride back with me, Mike?" Salem asked.

"Yeah. Let's stop at the B and B to get my drawing materials. I'm having ideas already. We can go through sketches together. Nick says you want to incorporate your culture into the design. Should be interesting."

They'd arrived at their cars.

"See you there," Nick called and started his rental. Emily climbed into the passenger seat.

Before they'd even turned onto the small highway into town, Emily said, "Dad?"

"Yes?"

"What's going on between you and the woman from the bakery? You didn't even introduce me to her."

He debated what to tell her.

"She lost a baby a few months ago and is angry that I have you."

"Why should I matter to her?"

"It isn't something I can discuss with you except to say that it's ancient history that neither of us seems to be able to get past."

"Okay."

She'd accepted the little he'd cared to tell her, but worried her bottom lip all the way into Accord.

NICK LOOKED FORWARD to another evening with Emily. There would only be one more and then it was back to Seattle and normal life.

He would have to make sure he shaped a new definition of normal. This week was too good, his time with Emily too precious to ever go back to the way things used to be.

Tonight, they were having supper at a family restaurant that catered to all ages, with food that ran to burgers, fries, chicken fingers and onion rings.

They had only just ordered when Nick glanced up at the opening front door.

Laura walked in with Mike. Of all the joints in town, they had to choose the same one as he and Emily? What were the chances?

A slow burn started in his gut. She'd sure fooled him. When he was young, he'd thought her ethical, moral.

When he'd seduced her—she'd been right about that; he believed she would have resisted her attraction to him if he hadn't pushed it that night—and had Gabe find them, she'd been truly devastated.

So, had she really changed so much over the years that she would use him to get pregnant? The temperature between them had been solar. Had she forced the sex that high that quickly? Or had she been as carried away as he?

Four days later, he was still angry with her and no closer to answers.

Neither of them saw Nick and Emily.

When the waitress brought their food, Nick found Emily watching him.

"Dad, what's wrong?"

"I can't talk about it. You're too young."

"I'm not a kid anymore. Besides, kids grow up really fast these days."

Too fast. How to tell a G-rated version? "Years ago, your uncle Gabe was engaged to Laura."

"The baker."

Nick nodded. "I was in college when I met your mom. We liked each other immediately and wanted to get married right away. She took me home with her to Seattle to meet her father."

"Grandpa Mort," Emily said, sucking her milk shake through a fat straw.

"Yes. Gabe found out I'd left school. To this day, I don't know how." He sipped his root beer. "He came to Seattle, found out I was at Grandpa's office tower and gave me hell in front of Grandpa and your mother. He embarrassed me. Took me back to school like I was a little kid."

"Uncle Gabe seems more cool than that. Why did he do it?"

"He had this swollen sense of responsibility for me and Tyler. After our father died, he took over the role."

"It must have been hard. I would miss you so much if you died."

His daughter would miss him. Her simple statement warmed a corner of his heart. "After Gabe left me at the school, I ran away again and returned to Accord."

He chewed a mouthful of burger, buying himself time, trying to figure out how to tell Emily what an ass he'd made of himself and of how he'd betrayed a family member.

"And?"

"And…" He swallowed a mouthful of his drink.

"Don't tell me," she said, her tone judgmental. "You slept with Laura."

Nick choked on root beer. He sputtered and coughed. When he could finally speak, he said, "You shouldn't be talking about things like that."

"I read. I watch TV. I go on the internet. Sex is everywhere, Dad. I could see where the story was going. You slept with Uncle Gabe's fiancée to get back at him."

"In a nutshell, yes."

"That was bad."

"Very bad. I'm not proud of it."

"She still hasn't forgiven you."

"No. I had thought for a very brief few hours that she had, but I was wrong. She was just biding her time until she stuck it to me."

"Stuck what to you?"

"She got her revenge."

"How?"

"*That* is definitely private."

"But—"

"Nope. No more talking about it."

Looking thoughtful, Emily chewed a fry. After swallowing, she said, "Well, I, for one, am really glad you met Mom and married her and had me."

Nick laughed. How could he not?

He caught Laura watching him. She'd finally realized he was there.

"Let's blow this pop stand."

Nick paid for dinner and they left for a walk on Main. Farther down, they found an ice cream parlor and had dessert there.

Nick, for another, was glad he'd married Marsha and fathered this brilliant child.

EMILY AND NICK were ready to leave on Thursday morning. Much of the work on the resort could be done long-distance. He left Salem and the elders and the professor working with Rene, who would report to Nick regularly on progress.

In the past few days, Nick had managed to organize a dig that would begin in May, through the Colorado Archaeological Society. They would coordinate with Salem, the elders and the professor.

As soon as they figured out where the migratory route was, Rene would dig the foundation for the resort.

All in all, as well as spending quality time with his daughter, he'd got a lot done this week, had tied up a lot of loose ends.

All but one. A *big* one.

He stormed into Sweet Temptations and approached the counter.

"Is Laura in the back?"

Tilly looked away from the customer she was dealing with and said, "No. She's gone for the day."

He left without thanking her. He knew he was being a

prick. Too bad. He was in a mood today, anxious to be gone already.

Just at the bottom of the fire escape stairs, a garbage can caught his eye. Colorful fabric hung out from under the lid on one side. It looked a lot like the fabric he'd seen swooping from the ceiling in Laura's bedroom.

He lifted the lid. The can was crammed with the stuff. Why?

He dropped the lid back onto the can and took the stairs two at a time.

Why would Laura tear down something she'd obviously spent a lot of time and imagination fashioning? Wait. Did it really matter to him?

Nope. It was no concern of his.

But a small niggling part of him still wondered what was going on.

She answered on the second knock. Surprise colored her cheeks.

"What do you want?" she asked, her tone hostile.

"This." He handed her his business card. "I've written my home email address on the back."

She turned it over and raised one eyebrow. "'Head honcho'?"

"Emily set it up for me."

"You should have introduced her to me."

He might have gotten angrier if she'd shouted, but her reproach was so subtle, and so true, that he deflated. "Yes. I should have. It was rude of me not to."

"She's very sweet. Pretty."

"She's like Marsha. Her mother."

She studied the card she held between her hands. "Why are you giving me this?"

"In case you need to contact me. In case…"

"In case I'm pregnant."

He nodded, one sharp strong jerk of his head. God help her if she was.

"I won't be."

"Good." He left without saying goodbye.

BACK IN SEATTLE, Nick and Emily took Mort out for dinner on Friday night.

"What have you been doing with your time?" Nick asked.

"Working."

Good Lord, did that mean Nick would have fires to put out when he returned to work on Monday? Possibly. Probably.

Mort must have read his thoughts because he said, "The company isn't completely lost without you, you know."

Nick felt his cheeks heat. He'd been running Mort's company for so long, and doing it so well, that he'd developed an ego. Nothing like having the owner of the company put him in his place.

"Tell me about Accord." Mort's demand was nuanced with envy and wistfulness.

Maybe Nick should have invited Mort to come with them. He hadn't thought of it. Opening up to Emily had been tough, though, and doing so with Mort would have been strange. They had been business partners for so long, and had spent so many of the great holiday celebrations their wives had planned over the years discussing business, that it was strange to think of him as a friend outside of business.

Emily told him everything that had happened while they had been in Accord for the week. She found an interested audience in Mort.

Maybe Nick should take him there with him the next time he went.

Naw. Rene was capable, and Nick could handle the business from here. There wouldn't be a next time.

But you promised both Emily and Ty that you would go back for the Fourth of July.

Nick sighed. He'd forgotten. He would be going back to Accord after all, but at least this time it would be for fun.

It wouldn't be to put out fires or solve problems.

NICK HAD MORT over to the house for dinner almost every night. He couldn't stop himself. The man needed people. It seemed that Nick and Emily were all he had left.

The drinking issue, though, came to a head one night.

Mort had been complaining about his wives, and swearing as badly as a trucker, throughout dinner. When Mort dropped the F bomb, Nick said, "Enough," and sent Emily to her room early.

"Mort," he said, "you're drunk as a skunk."

"So what? What's the point of staying sober?"

"How about your granddaughter?"

"Emily loves me just the way I am." Mort sounded stubborn and looked like a little boy.

"Maybe not after tonight."

"What are you talking about?"

"You've been cursing like a stevedore all evening. Why would she enjoy that?"

"Me?"

"Yes. You're so drunk you don't even realize you're doing it."

Mort settled into a blue funk. "Sorry," he mumbled.

"You'll be even sorrier if you don't quit drinking." Nick hated to take a hard line with Mort, but he suspected it might be the only way to help the man. To his surprise, he found he wanted to help.

"I want to see the smart, savvy, sharp man you used to be, not the maudlin cl—" He'd almost said *clown,* but that was too mean-spirited. He couldn't say it out loud, not to Mort's face. "You're an alcoholic. You need help."

"The hell I am. I don't need anyone's help. I—"

"You'll get help or you won't see Emily again." Nick said it quietly, but the threat thundered through the room.

Mort stared at him slack-jawed. "I love that girl," he whispered.

"I know. Use her as motivation to get better."

"I don't know if I can."

Compassion filled Nick. Mort's drunkenness was ugly, but underneath it all lay a good man.

"I've checked out AA meetings in Seattle," Nick said. "We can go tomorrow night."

"We?"

"Yes, we. I'll go with you."

Mort's lips worked and his chin trembled, as though he were controlling the urge to cry. "You must think me an old fool."

"A fool? No. Lost? Yes." Nick led Mort to the front door. "You've done a lot for me, Mort. A couple of weeks ago, you stopped me from losing my daughter. I owe you a debt."

"I don't want your indebtedness."

"How about my friendship?"

Again Mort's chin trembled. It took a moment, but then he said, "What time should I be ready tomorrow?"

"Six-thirty. I'll pick you up."

Nick drove Mort home in his car and then took a taxi back to the house.

It remained to be seen what would happen with Mort, even with Nick's help.

Nick ended up accompanying Mort to more AA meetings than he'd originally thought he would have to. In time, Mort came around, but between work and the time Nick carved out to spend with Emily and the stressful nights spent trying to keep Mort sober, Nick began to feel worn-out.

He considered it a labor of love, but it took its toll.

Throughout it all, despite Emily and Mort's company, Nick

developed a loneliness that eased only when he slept. It eased in those hours because they were filled with dreams of Laura.

He awoke angry and frustrated. He didn't want to think of her, didn't want to dream about how she looked in her naked glory.

He didn't want to remember how she felt, or smelled, or kissed, or came to orgasm with a glorious triumphant cry.

Yet, even so, every night he fell into bed exhausted, but filled with hope—because he knew he would dream of her.

CHAPTER TEN

Nick Jordan <headhoncho@hmail.com>
30 June 12:35 PM

The rabbit died.
Laura

Laura Cameron <sweettreats@accordmail.com>
Re: The rabbit died.
30 June 1:17 PM

What the hell does that mean?
N

Nick Jordan <headhoncho@hmail.com>
Re: The rabbit died.
30 June 2:42 PM

I'm pregnant.
L

CHAPTER ELEVEN

"MOM, I DON'T understand why you're so angry about my being pregnant," Laura said. "You weren't this angry last time."

They stood in the middle of the airy Palette, surrounded by enough beautiful artwork to take Laura's breath away. She wasn't looking at it now, though. She was trying to figure out her mother.

She was tired of Mom's mood swings, angry one moment, depressed the next, but damned if Laura could get to the bottom of it. She'd tried. She really had, but Mom wasn't opening up.

"You had Vin to support you last time," Olivia said. "You don't now."

"Yes, Vin was so supportive he ran away."

"You know what I mean. If you hadn't lost the baby Vin wouldn't have left."

"Probably not." And Laura was only now realizing how unhappy they both would have been had they stayed together because of the baby.

"Who's the father?"

This wasn't the first time Mom had asked, but Laura didn't want her to know. *Don't you think it's ironic to criticize your mom for keeping secrets when you won't open up to her?*

She knew what Mom would think, how disappointed she would be that Laura had had sex with Nick Jordan after what he'd done to her thirteen years ago.

"The father isn't around" was all she would share. "He's out of the picture. I'll raise this baby on my own."

"What did you do? Pick up someone at a bar? I expect better from you, Laura."

Laura gasped. Her own mother was insinuating that she was easy. A slow boil churned in her stomach. She was losing patience with her mother.

"There's no need to insult me, Mom. You know I don't pick up men in bars. I don't have one-night stands."

What exactly would you call what happened between you and Nick?

Insanity. Utter insanity.

Mom tossed the packing from a vase toward the back of the room, making a mess. She never used to unpack in the showroom of her gallery, only in the back. In the main space, things had to be just so. Now here was Mom throwing around cardboard and packing peanuts. There was a heck of a lot more going on here than Laura could wrestle her way through.

"If you refuse to get help from the father, then you've made your own bed. You can lie in it." Olivia set up the vase on a narrow pedestal where it caught light from the window. "Don't come crying to me to babysit when the going gets tough."

"Mom!" Laura couldn't believe what she was hearing. She'd hoped Mom would be available sometimes to help, but she would never presume to rely on her. Mom's criticism stung. "What exactly is your problem? And don't tell me it has anything to do with who the father of this baby might or might not be. What's going on in your personal life?"

She stepped close to Olivia so she couldn't disappear into the back room as she'd been doing every time Laura asked a tough question.

She grasped her mother's shoulders. "Mom," she said quietly, "what is it?"

Olivia threw a box onto the floor and yelled, "I don't want to be a grandmother, okay?"

The air in the silent gallery seethed with words that could break a heart.

"Okay." Laura stepped away from her. "I won't ask you to babysit. I won't bring the baby around. You'll never have to ever see her. I didn't realize you disliked children so much."

Olivia sighed. "I don't dislike children. I won't dislike my grandchild." She looked tired, the sheer skin beneath her eyes bruised. Mom wasn't sleeping. She slumped into a chair and said, "I don't want to be old enough to have a grandchild."

So, they were back to the age issue.

Laura touched her shoulder. "You don't look old enough to be a grandmother, Mom. You've kept yourself in shape. You take care of your skin. You've got great style. You look wonderful. Why is your age bothering you all of a sudden?"

Olivia shrugged. "It just is."

"I'm not sure why it's bothering you so much, but if you want to talk about it, we can go out for lunch."

Olivia patted her hand. "No. I don't want to talk about it. I really don't."

"Okay." Laura stepped toward the door. "You know where to find me if you need me."

She crossed the street and unlocked the empty space beside the bakery, shaken by the depth of her mother's feelings and about as alone as she'd ever felt in her life.

Both of Nick's parents were dead and Mom was the only surviving one on Laura's side—and she wanted to have nothing to do with being a grandparent.

Laura's child would have no grandparents.

Noah was always off on one adventure after another.

What a mess Laura had made of things. Her baby wasn't even going to have an extended family, let alone a father.

She'd been alone in her life before when Amber had died, and this was so much the same.

She stepped into her new storefront and closed the door behind her, leaning back against the door and molding her palms to her belly. The baby wouldn't show for a while yet, but she couldn't help her fascination with what her body was going through. Or her fear.

She'd lost one baby. She couldn't stand to lose another.

This wasn't how she wanted to do this. She'd wanted a husband, as she'd grown tired of telling well-meaning friends with their "Rah, rah, you can do this without a man" support.

Yes, she could.

Did she want to?

No.

She wouldn't take on a man to make her dream come true, though.

She wouldn't take on Nick Jordan.

Wandering farther into the shop, she opened a bottle of sparkling water, sipped it then set it on an old counter. It settled the vestiges of morning sickness that lingered.

She'd bought this retail space months ago, excited about expanding her café. As it was, there wasn't enough seating for the traffic that came through her bakery. She needed a larger café. Business was that good.

These days, this empty store seemed to be the only place she found solace. Nick's presence in her apartment that one night, and its disastrous consequences, had tainted the warm, sensual cave she'd created for herself.

Despite knowing she'd chosen the worst possible time to sink money into expansion, albeit unwittingly, she craved this space for the validation that things were working in one area of her life. Not just working, thriving. Succeeding beyond her wildest dreams.

How could she have known when she bought this all of those months ago how things would have changed?

At the time, she and Vin were getting married. She'd thought she would have a life partner to help her through the coming business challenges. Then their birth control had failed and she'd been thrilled and not the least bit intimidated. Vin would help her through.

Only he hadn't. He'd been freaked out by the pregnancy.

"What did you expect?" she'd asked. "We'd both agreed that we would have children."

"Not so soon."

"When, Vin? When we were in our forties?"

Both she and Vin had been fooling themselves. He'd never been father material. But he had been a lot of fun, a good bed partner and someone to talk to. She missed him more than she'd thought she would.

Now she was pregnant again, this time entirely through her own fault. She'd become so lost in the moment with Nick, in the passion he'd set off in her like fireworks, she hadn't paid attention to birth control. Now her baby would pay for her mistake.

She pulled the curtains open and let morning sunlight flood the shop. She would have to get rid of the dusty old things. The ancient counters would have to come out.

The walls needed washing and a fresh coat of paint. The former owners had closed up their floral shop to retire. Good thing. Their designs had become dated.

Accord had made itself over into a town tourists would want to visit and money was starting to come in. They needed to keep the momentum moving forward. The little floral shop had been a holdout, refusing to change, to update.

Laura opened the blueprint her architect from Denver had shipped to her yesterday. She loved the woman's design, carrying it with her around the room as she paced off where things would go.

Excitement flowed through her veins.

Her next step was to call in contractors for quotes.

The wall between the kitchen and the café next door would have to come down at some point, but not too early into the renovation. She needed to be able to serve customers. She'd get the contractor to do as much else as possible first.

She'd have to work twice as hard with the expansion, and now with a baby in tow.

She would have to hire day care, or a nanny, expenses that would have been mitigated by a husband's paycheck.

She patted her belly.

"We can do this, little one." If her voice sounded wobbly and more than a little uncertain, who could blame her? "We'll get through this. Just you and me."

"Talking to yourself?"

She spun about.

Nick Jordan stood in the doorway, as handsome as on the day she'd first noticed him in high school, the boy three years younger than her who drew her attention away from his older brother Gabe. The boy who'd started to change and grow up and was no longer just Gabe's pesky younger brother.

His expression was as thunderous as on the day he'd left town. More so, now that he knew about the baby.

As though to protect her child, she threaded her fingers across her abdomen. The motion drew his eyes.

"I'm not going to hurt you." He stepped into the room and shut the door.

He could destroy her in so many ways. He could kill her with a look. He could devastate her with a carefully targeted word.

She'd always been vulnerable to Nick. She just hadn't understood how deeply until now.

You picked a fine time to figure it out, Laura. You're a couple of months too late.

Hindsight wasn't all it was cut out to be. It didn't give a girl much protection from certain men.

"I had you investigated." Of all of the things she might have imagined him saying, that wasn't it.

"Why?"

"Because you hadn't been honest with me. You tricked me into sleeping with you."

"You have to be kidding. You mean when I was sitting in the graveyard minding my own business? You mean when *you* invited me to dinner?"

He ignored her. "You picked up a new mortgage with this place."

"I'm expanding."

"Did you think if you said you were having my baby, I would give you money? I would keep you afloat?"

She could see how he might be cynical. She'd told him he owed her.

"I don't need to be kept afloat. My bakery is going gangbusters. I don't need money." Well, child support would sure come in handy, but she could pay her own mortgage. "I need help with time, with people who will spend time with my infant so I can work and earn my *own* living."

"Is it mine?" he asked.

"Excuse me?" Had she misunderstood him? He couldn't mean...

"Is the baby mine?"

She held her temper in check, but barely. He was the second person today to question her morals. "How can you even ask?" Her voice sounded mean.

"You took the morning-after pill. I watched you."

"You also heard the doctor tell us it wasn't one hundred percent. Who else would the father be?"

"Mike Canning."

She was across the room and slapping his face before she knew her own intention. Her hand stung. Her pulse pounded in her throat and drowned out all reason.

"Get out of here."

He raised a placating hand, even while his cheek turned red with the imprint of her palm and fingers. "I'm sorry. You were with him. I thought—"

"You thought I would screw anybody to get a baby. Is that really what you think of me, Nick Jordan?"

He stared at her, his expression stone and flint. "You like sex."

"So what? A woman can't? If she does, she's a floozy?" She leaned close. "*You* like sex. Does that mean you'll sleep with anyone who offers?"

He didn't respond, but her barb hit home. He looked as though he regretted his statement.

"I had the same boyfriend for five years," Laura said. "A man I thought I was going to marry. After I got pregnant, he would no longer sleep with me. I was pregnant for four months and then lost the baby. Five months later, I spent one night with you. I went out with Mike because I was lonely. I didn't sleep with him. There have been no other lovers."

She strode to the door and yanked it open. "Get out of here, you bastard, and don't come anywhere near me or *my* baby again."

"I'm sorry. I—"

"Get out!"

She slammed the door behind him and leaned her arms against it, breathing hard. How could he think that she would, that she could, that she was *capable* of foisting someone else's baby on him? How could he think that her character was that low?

How could he think that she slept around so easily? Because she was passionate? Because she enjoyed sex? She had a right to! That didn't mean she was easy. Or devious.

She'd never struck a person in her life, didn't believe violence was any way to fix a problem.

But he'd thought—

She could strangle him.

NICK STOOD ON Main Street feeling, well, if he were going to be honest about it, as though he'd killed something small and helpless.

Only Laura Cameron was not helpless.

He rubbed his still-smarting cheek. It had been an honest question. He'd used to think that Laura was honest, but he didn't know anymore.

She'd tricked him into giving her a baby. He still couldn't figure out how he'd so lost control with her that he'd forgotten about the condom. The woman was a witch.

She said she didn't want his money and that she could take care of herself. Judging by how successful the bakery was, it was probably true.

So why did he feel as if he'd killed something small and not quite formed? It took him a while to figure it out through the twists and turns of what might be imagined and what might be real. When she'd told him he owed her a baby and then had managed to make him forget to use a condom, she'd broken his trust.

By accusing her of fooling around with Mike and then trying to fob off Mike's baby on him, he'd broken her trust.

"What's up?" Ty stood on the sidewalk in front of him. "You look like someone killed your kitten."

"Something like that. I just screwed up with Laura."

"Yeah? How?"

"She's having my baby."

Ty gaped at Nick. "When? How?"

"On that Saturday night when you had dinner with Gabe and Callie?"

"When I met Emily? You were here getting it off with Laura? I didn't know you two had been in touch over the years."

"We haven't. I saw her at the bakery and then later at the graveyard."

Ty leaned against the storefront and tucked his thumbs into his pockets. "And cemeteries being so sexy, y'all figured it would be fun to go a round together again for old times' sake?"

"No. We didn't plan anything. It just happened."

"And you didn't use protection?"

"I told you." Nick scowled. "It just happened."

"That's an excuse for teenagers, not for smart successful people like the two of you."

"I know. I can't explain what happens between me and Laura. It never ends happily."

"So what happened today that has you so blue?"

"I asked if the baby was mine."

Ty's jaw dropped. "Who else's would it be? Laura doesn't sleep around."

"The week I was here, I flew in my architect, Mike Canning. He went out with her one night."

"And you accused her of sleeping with him a couple of days after sleeping with you?"

Nick nodded.

"Jesus, Nick, for a smart businessman you sure can be clueless. If Laura says the baby is yours, then it's yours. She's a good woman. She doesn't fool around with every Joe that wanders through town."

"I know that now," Nick snapped. He scrubbed his hands over his face, wanting to forget this whole business, willing it to disappear for a while. "I'm heading back out to the ranch. You need a lift?"

"I've got my truck here. I need to talk to someone and then I'll head out. You want steaks for dinner?"

"Sure. I'll pick them up."

"If you go to the market, get corn on the cob, too. Then consider getting down on your knees and asking Laura to forgive you."

TY ENTERED TAMMY's gift shop and waited for his eyes to adjust. The sun was blazing full blast today.

Looked as though the day after tomorrow was going to be a good day for a barbecue.

Ty was tired of pussyfooting around. He wanted life ordered and settled and figured out. The Fourth of July seemed like as good a time as any to fix his family.

Or die trying.

Some people weren't going to like what he had planned.

Tough shit. He was tired of being a nice guy.

Tammy came out from the back with her arms full of items to put on display.

She looked good. Damn good. She'd obviously been taking care of herself.

"Ty." She hesitated when she saw him then straightened her spine, which made her hard round belly stick out. Lord. His baby was in there. He planned to marry Tammy before the child arrived. Not that she was helping much in that area.

That changed today.

"I'm having a barbecue in two days. I want you there."

She set the vases she held onto the counter. "I have plans, thanks." Her voice never used to sound so crisp, or so hard. She used to have a throaty laugh he liked to trigger when they had sex.

He wanted sex with Tammy again. He wanted love with her.

He wanted to make her laugh again.

"Please come. It's important to me, Tammy. I want—" How best for a man without poetry in his soul to convince her? Maybe he didn't need it. Maybe honesty was enough.

"I want to have sex with you again."

Her beautiful bright blue gaze shot to his. She opened her mouth to object. He didn't give her a chance.

"I want to make love to you from sundown to sunup."

Her mouth fell open, ever so slightly.

"I want to French kiss you anytime we can, anywhere we can find privacy. You know how to kiss better than any woman I've ever known. *Any* woman."

He wouldn't reference Winona any further than that. He didn't want her between them ever again, in any way.

"I want you to laugh again. A lot. With me."

He stepped closer. "I want you in my home again. I want my home to be yours and our baby's."

He took her hand and drew her from around the counter and against him. He kissed her, giving her no time to step away, seducing her with his lips and tongue.

When he pulled back, they were breathing hard. "That's what I'm talking about."

He settled his cowboy hat onto his head.

"Come, Tammy. One o'clock."

He left the shop, barely restraining himself from taking her into the back room and loving the daylights out of her, convincing her with his body what he didn't seem to have the right words for—that they belonged together.

There wasn't much else he could say. She would be at the barbecue, or she wouldn't.

NICK FOUND HIMSELF looking forward to dinner with Ty, but he wasn't easy with it. He'd never had a problem with Ty. That didn't mean any peaceful coexistence with him would last.

The next couple of weeks were fraught with pitfalls as long as he hung so close to family.

Nick didn't do family well, didn't know how to be a family with his brothers. He'd always felt apart from them.

He couldn't escape the feeling, though, that it was time to change that, that it was time for him to put in an effort. Starting to make that effort with Ty was far, far easier than contemplating making a change with Gabe. His relationship with Ty had never been as complex as the one with Gabe.

To make matters even more strange, Nick had brought Mort along with him, with Ty's permission. Mort seemed to take to the ranch like a duck to water. As far as Nick knew, Mort had never been on a ranch before.

When he and Emily left Seattle, he hadn't been able to do it without Mort—and Nick hadn't minded.

In the past, he'd been rabid about keeping his business and personal lives separate, as much as he could under the circumstances, but somehow in the past couple of months, he'd thrown that concept to the wind. It had become apparent that Mort needed him and Emily.

So, he'd taken Mort under his wing. After all, he was family.

What was family? Was it merely shared history? Did shared memories make a family? Was it more? What and how was it? What did he have to do to make it more?

He didn't have a clue.

He would rather have stayed in the B and B. If things got tough, Nick could pull away from his brothers and close the door of his hotel room. As it stood, if anything went wrong on July Fourth, Nick had nowhere to go but to leave and head back to Seattle, which would let both Emily and Mort down.

He didn't want to. Honest to God, he didn't want anything to go wrong, didn't want to have to leave, didn't want to lose with Emily what they'd been slowly, tentatively, building.

He heard voices on the veranda and then the two girls entered the house, chatting as though they'd always been friends. Mort stepped in behind them, with color high in his cheeks. Unless Nick missed his guess, that had nothing to do with alcohol and everything to do with being out of the city, away from work and in the company of a pair of bright preteens.

When she spotted him coming downstairs, Emily said, "Dad, have you seen the bison yet? They're amazing. They're huge."

"Yeah, Uncle Nick," Ruby said. "They've lost their winter fur and still they're huge."

Uncle Nick. He hadn't thought to work it out—Ruby was Ty's daughter, which meant that Nick was an uncle. He was collecting family. His relationship with his daughter was blossoming and he'd sat with Ty earlier and had a beer and conversation that had been downright civilized. And now he had a niece.

And in two days, Gabe and Callie would come over for a barbecue. How would that go?

Throughout dinner, Emily and Ruby talked nonstop about the bison and the paper Ruby wrote about them.

After they'd cleared the table and washed up, Nick turned to Ty and said, "You're lucky you're involved in something that Ruby can relate to."

"You are, too," Ty responded. "I had a great talk with Emily when you were out earlier. She loves what you're doing with the Native American Heritage Center. Couldn't stop talking about it."

"Really?"

"Yeah, really." Ty got them a couple of beers and they headed out to sit on the veranda.

"Mort," Nick called. "You want to join us?"

"Don't mind if I do."

When Ty offered him his beer, Mort stared for a long time then said, "You mind if I help myself to some of that lemonade I saw in the fridge?"

"Mi casa es su casa," Ty replied.

Nick's heart moved, so damn happy that Mort was making smart decisions.

When Mort returned with his lemonade and they'd all settled into comfy chairs on Ty's veranda, Ty said, "Emily's crazy about you, Nick."

"I don't know why. I spent her childhood years at work."

"Maybe now's the time to back off on work."

"I've been trying. We spend more time together. It's good."

"Company can do a lot more without you than it does now," Mort said. "And me, too. You've done your job well.

The company's wildly successful. Well-organized. Spend time with your daughter. Spend more time here."

"This coming from a workaholic?" Nick asked.

Mort chuffed out a laugh. "Yeah, from a man who's seen his mistakes too late. You've got time to fix yours."

Nick would have argued, but the heat of his defensiveness waned the more he spent time with his daughter.

Mort was right. It wasn't too late for Nick.

A pickup truck veered off the highway and onto Ty's long driveway, kicking up a plume of dust.

"Know whose truck that is?" Nick asked.

"Might be Davis Fuller's."

"Know why he's here?"

"Haven't a clue."

Davis pulled up in front of the veranda and stepped out. "Hey."

Davis had been Nick's high school gym teacher and basketball coach. He'd aged some, but hadn't gone so soft that he couldn't shoot hoops any longer. Or not that Nick noticed.

He stood and shook Davis's hand.

"How've you been, Davis? It's been a long time."

"Good to see you, Nick. Glad you're in town."

Ty offered him a beer and Davis nodded.

Ty returned from the kitchen with a cold one. "What's on your mind?" he asked after Davis had taken a long draw on the beer.

"How long are you staying, Nick? I got a problem and you can fix it for me."

"Me? Here in Accord?"

"Yep. I need a coach for a bunch of boys in a summer basketball camp."

Nick's skin shifted. His nerves lurched. "You're not asking me, are you?"

"It's only for a couple of days. I committed to coaching

them, but just got a call from my mom. My dad's had a heart attack."

"Aw, hey, Davis, sorry to hear it," Nick said.

"Thanks. He's okay, but gave us a real scare."

"What does it have to do with me and coaching?"

"I'm leaving in the morning for Wyoming to see him and to support my mom. She's getting on. She's stressed."

He finished his beer and handed the can to Ty. "I need you to cover for me. I've got no one else, Nick."

Nick opened his mouth to object, but Davis raised a hand to forestall him.

"You were the best b-ball player I ever coached, Nick. Bar none. You were smart. You were quick. You knew the game inside out. Your strategy was flawless."

Basketball. His legs hummed just thinking about getting onto a court and running the length of it in a handful of strides. He'd loved the game. But…

"I'm not in the shape I was in high school."

"Who is?" Davis laughed. "You don't have to play. Just teach. Please, Nick. I'm in a bind."

Nick turned to Ty. "I'd have to leave Emily with you and Ruby."

"That's fine. I'm off for a couple of weeks to spend time with Ruby. It'd be no hardship to get to know Emily better."

"I can help with that," Mort said.

"So?" Davis asked. "Is it a yes?"

Nick nodded and grinned. "Looks like it."

Davis returned his grin and shook his hand. "Good to have you aboard. Wait until you see some of these kids. Real promise. Can you come over to my place? I'll go over the schedule with you."

Nick handed Ty his empty and followed. "Want me to take my own car so you don't have to drive me back later?"

"I'd appreciate it. I still gotta pack tonight. I'm over on side road 42. Follow me there."

Nick didn't return until nearly eleven, his head crammed full with kids' names and game and practice schedules. A fire simmered in his belly that felt an awful lot like excitement, like the thrill he used to get the night before a game.

The girls and Mort were in bed, but he found Ty at the kitchen table using a laptop. Ty glanced up. "You look like a different man."

"What do you mean?"

"I mean, you look alive. Happy."

"I'd forgotten how much I'd missed b-ball. All I did was talk about it tonight, didn't even pick up a ball, and got excited anyway."

"Looks good on you, bro."

NICK STARTED COACHING the following morning. Trial by fire.

He met the boys, discussed some of Davis's strategies, then put them through drills. He joined them in those drills. His legs and arms tired quickly, but man oh man, it was fun. His body hummed. *Buzzed.*

It was better than sex.

He thought of Laura. Okay, not that good.

When had he last had fun?

The snowball fight with Emily.

He should get her out on a court.

On a whim, he detoured to the nearest town with a sports store and bought a basketball hoop for Ty's yard. It would be delivered tomorrow.

When he got home, he found Mort and the girls waiting for him on the veranda.

"What's up?" he asked.

"Can you drive us to Uncle Gabe's?" Emily asked. "I want to show Ruby and Grandpa Mort the dogs."

More exposure to Gabe. And to Callie. What difference did it make? He'd be seeing them tomorrow anyway.

"Sure. Let me shower, then we'll leave."

An hour later, they were on Gabe's property making friends with the dogs, and Mort was in the prospector's tent pestering Gabe for details about the business.

Facts and figures flowed from Gabe's lips, all of the information that Nick had needed so desperately in January, when he'd sent Callie here to spy on Gabe, to find out whether they could somehow sabotage the business to get Gabe to sell. In the end, it hadn't been necessary.

All Nick had basically had to do was hand Callie over to Gabe. The two had fallen in love. From what Nick had been able to tell the couple of times he'd seen them together, they were deeply in love. And Nick was jealous.

He had no idea how "deeply in love" felt, but it sure looked good.

"Do you want to visit the home?" Callie asked Emily and Ruby.

"Yes! Can we, Dad?"

In for a penny, in for a pound. "Sure," he said, and they set off in two vehicles.

Twenty minutes later, they arrived at the nursing home.

"There are only a few residents at the moment," Callie explained when they entered. "We haven't finished fundraising and staffing, so we haven't filled it yet."

They stepped into the solarium and Mort spotted Callie's mother, Johanna. He'd met her shortly after Callie started working for the company. She'd come to her first Christmas party as Callie's "date."

Johanna looked confused when Mort addressed her by name, but that didn't stop him. He knew about her early-onset Alzheimer's—Callie's mother was only fifty-five. He sat beside her and chatted with her as though they were old friends, until Johanna relaxed and began to enjoy herself.

Mort questioned Callie about the business side of the home. There was nothing wrong with Mort's mind. He had lost none of the sharp intellect that had built a successful business out of a few modest bank loans.

If Nick kept an open mind, he could still learn from Mort.

He caught Emily's smile and they laughed, because it felt good to see Grandpa Sanderson enjoying himself.

Watching Mort, seeing how much he was enjoying himself in Accord, Nick's heart filled with satisfaction that he was helping a man who had done so much for him and whom, he'd only realized recently, he loved.

CHAPTER TWELVE

ON JULY THE THIRD, Ty entered Sweet Temptations. He needed to see Laura now that he knew she was pregnant with Nick's baby. He could have talked to her yesterday when he'd finished with Tammy, but after Nick's confession about how idiotic he'd been with her, Ty figured giving Laura a day to cool down couldn't hurt.

"Hey, Tilly. Is Laura around?"

"She's upstairs."

He left the café and mounted the fire escape out back. In the shade of her deck, he took off his cowboy hat and ran his fingers through his hair. Sure was a hot one.

Laura answered after his first knock. When she saw him, she raised her brows. He figured he was guilty just by being a Jordan.

"Ty, what can I do for you?"

"I came to invite you to a barbecue at my house tomorrow."

"Aren't Nick and his daughter staying with you?"

There was nothing wrong with Accord's small-town gossip mill.

"Yes, and Gabe and Callie will be there, too."

"Why would you invite me?"

He pointed, swiftly and briefly, to her stomach. "That's my niece or nephew you're carrying."

Laura's frown was thunderous, but not one iota of it was directed toward Ty. Thank goodness. The woman looked fierce. "Not according to Nick."

"Nick's an idiot. He told me what he said to you yesterday. He's having second thoughts."

"So he should."

"I'm not arguing with you. He needs a smack upside the head."

Laura blushed. So that *had* been a palm print Ty had seen on Nick's face yesterday. He grinned. Nick had had it coming.

She leaned against the doorjamb. "Your barbecue won't be much of a holiday celebration with both Nick and me there at the same time."

"It's a big ranch." She didn't smile at his joke. "You're carrying family. I want you there."

"I don't—"

"Do you have other plans?"

"No. Mom hasn't planned anything this year." She sounded bitter and Ty wondered what was going on there. "I've been too tired to organize anything. Noah's using his time off to rock climb in Yellowstone."

"Then come," Ty urged. "For God's sake, don't stay home alone."

"Ty, you're crazy to even think of this."

"I'm looking for peace in my family."

"And this is how you're going to get it? By inviting enemies to dine at the same table?"

"Maybe it's time for you two to stop being enemies."

"And me and Gabe?"

Ty ran the brim of his hat through his fingers. "I thought you two had worked things out."

"I don't know his wife, though. Will she resent having Gabe's former fiancée present?"

"I don't think anything gets Callie down these days. Just heard she's pregnant. The woman seems to be flying high."

"I don't know, Ty. It's a crazy idea."

"I know," Ty said quietly. "Please come, Laura."

Something in his plea must have gotten across to her. She nodded and Ty walked away satisfied. "Come over about one."

He strode down Main to the post office to pick up fireworks he'd ordered for the Fourth.

There might be fireworks of a few different varieties tomorrow, but he had to give his family a shot at getting things right.

LAURA HAD NO idea exactly what Tyler Jordan expected of her, or why he thought she should be at his celebration today, but she'd said she would attend, so she would.

She also had no idea why she was taking such care with her dress. After all, it was only a summer barbecue. That was all. So why had she discarded four dresses so far?

Why did her room look as if a cyclone had spun through her closet? Why was every pair of sandals she owned out on the floor?

Why was she so nervous?

Because today had the possibility to become a disaster.

Unable to avoid it any longer, she drove to Ty's ranch and got out of her car. He'd been blessed with a beautiful day, sunny and clear. No rain for the fireworks tonight, if there were any.

The veranda had been inexpertly festooned with red, white and blue cotton swags. She wondered whether Ty had tried to do it himself, or if Nick's and Ty's daughters had done it.

They were shooting hoops when she drove up.

When she stepped out of her car, they stopped and stared, then ran over, a pair of good-looking girls, like their fathers.

"I'm Emily. Dad didn't introduce us before. It was rude."

"I'm Ruby. Are you here for my dad's barbecue?"

"I'm Laura. I used to be friends with your fathers. In high school."

Satisfied, they nodded and turned back to their basketball. Laura strode around to the back of the house, where red, white and blue decorated everything with more enthusiasm than precision. She smiled. It had definitely been done by the girls.

The scent of charred meats filled the air.

No one noticed her.

She had the chance to observe.

Ty stood beside the barbecue looking grimly determined to make a success of the day.

Tammy Trudeau stood on the opposite side of the yard talking to Callie MacKintosh, the woman Gabe had married.

Laura wondered whether Tammy had noticed the looks Ty sent her way when he thought no one was looking, and whether she could tell his heart was in his eyes. She wondered whether Ty was even aware of how often he glanced at Tammy.

Something had to give there, soon. Tammy was about six months pregnant, her stomach a hard ball on her petite frame. Laura would probably start to look like a water buffalo at about six or seven months and would start to spread in all directions, not just forward.

Small price to pay to have a child.

Gradually everyone stopped talking and that's when she knew she'd been spotted.

Nick turned to stare at Ty and Ty stared right back with a mulish jut of his jaw.

Gabe turned immediately to his wife with a raised brow. *Are you okay?* She returned his look, shrugged and raised her own eyebrow. *I'm fine. Are you good?*

The tenderness between them hurt to watch. It should have been hers. Water under the bridge. Regrets would do her no good today.

Laura stepped away from the shadows of the house and into the center of the yard.

"I was invited," she said, addressing everyone. "Ty, would you care to explain why?"

"Glad to." He put down the barbecue utensil he held in his

hand and crossed his arms over his chest, his body language clearly conveying that he had no regrets about bringing them all together. "I'm tired of my family fighting. I'm tired of old resentments that were never dealt with and never healed."

He pointed to Callie then to Tammy and then to Laura. "We have three cousins who are going to be born only a few months apart."

He pointed to Ruby and Emily, who stood behind Laura. "These girls deserved to know each other all of their lives. Instead, they were hidden from each other."

He looked at Nick and Gabe. "I want a whole family. No more secrets. No more feuding. I've learned that family is a rare and precious thing. We've got family that we're wasting. Let's get along."

When no one moved or spoke, Ty went on, "What Nick did all those years ago was wrong. Dead wrong. He betrayed you, Gabe. I understand that." Ty looked at Gabe and Laura followed his glance. No problem there. Happy with his wife and baby on the way, he was content to let go of old problems. It was written all over his face. "You seem to have moved on. But you, Nick," he looked at his brother, "if you continue to wallow in anger and resentment, you're going to create a re-ality that stands to ruin a poor kid's life. You might want to consider getting along with both Gabe *and* Laura."

Gabe glanced at Laura and then at Ty. "*What* are you talking about? They're going to ruin what kid's life?"

Ty turned to Laura, slack-jawed, suddenly realizing that he might have been the only one besides Nick who knew that Laura was pregnant with Nick's baby. He cursed and said, "I'm sorry."

He scrubbed one hand down his face. "I wanted to bring the family together. I should have been more careful. Made sure everyone knew. I'm so sorry."

"No problem, Ty. Everyone would have known eventually, anyway." She glared at Nick, daring him to object. When he didn't, she said, "Ty's talking about the baby I'm having with Nick."

A bomb could have gone off and no one would have noticed.

Gabe was the first to react. He approached Laura and opened his arms. She walked into them, so grateful that there wasn't a speck of censure on his face, only acceptance.

"Congratulations," he whispered in her ear. "I know you've been wanting a baby for a long time." Years ago, when they were still engaged, he'd known she had wanted children and had wanted to start their family early, too.

She pulled away. "Thank you." She smiled at him, so blessedly relieved that their tough times were over for good.

She turned to find his wife beside her. They'd seen each other in town and in the bakery, including once when Callie had tried to fish information out of her about Gabe. Laura had thought that it had been about getting Gabe to sell, but now she wondered how much had been purely curiosity about the man with whom she had been falling in love.

"Congratulations," Callie said.

Laura put out her hand to shake, but Callie waved it away and hugged her. "We're having cousins. We're family."

The next thing Laura knew, she was seated on a park bench with Tammy and Callie and they were sipping non-alcoholic drinks and chatting about pregnancy and morning sickness. Laura even mentioned her fear of another miscarriage. Tammy and Callie were sympathetic and supportive. What a blessed relief to talk to women who actually listened.

"DAD, HOW COULD YOU?"

Nick turned to find Emily standing behind him, her expression rife with outrage and hurt and, if he wasn't wrong, fear.

"You heard what Laura said?"

"Yeah. She's nuts. Right?"

"It was an accident, Emily. I never meant to have a baby with Laura." Wasn't that a fine example he was setting for his daughter? He wasn't much better than a randy teenager getting his girlfriend in trouble.

"You mean, it's true?" Her lower lip wobbled. "It's really true?"

Nick heaved a sigh that felt as if it came from the depths of his soul. "It's really true and, for once, your dad doesn't know what to do. How to fix this."

"Are you going to marry her?"

"No."

Emily relaxed, marginally. "Are you going to live with the baby?"

"No."

"So, you'll still live in our house in Seattle with me?"

Nick cursed Laura and the baby from here to eternity. He wasn't losing his daughter because Laura wanted a baby and decided that he should be the one to give it to her. "Come here, honey. I love you and nobody on earth will ever change that."

She rushed into his open arms and buried her face against his chest, burrowing in like a small wounded animal. He felt her shoulders tremble.

"Stop doing that," he said.

"What?"

"Crying."

"I'm only crying a little bit," she mumbled.

"Well, stop it." His own lips felt wobbly. "You're breaking my heart."

"So that baby won't change things?" The fear in her voice overwhelmed her earlier anger.

"Between us? No."

"Good. I love you, Dad."

"I love you, too, sweetie."

After a quick squeeze, she ran off.

"You got yourself a real problem."

Nick turned at the sound of Mort's voice. "No fooling," he answered.

"What happened?"

"With Laura?"

Mort nodded.

"The usual," Nick replied. "Man is in town alone because his daughter decides to stay with her uncle and friend. Man is lonely and attracted to beautiful woman. She's lonely, too. They end up in bed together. Unfortunately, they leave the condom on the bedside table. Unopened and unused."

Mort studied Laura. "She's beautiful. Stunning. I don't blame you for being tempted. Brave of her to come today. She seems strong. Good."

"She is."

"What does she do in Accord?"

"She owns the bakery in town. It's highly successful, a real going concern. She's the one who makes those cinnamon rolls I picked up the other day."

"The ones that were ambrosial?" Mort whistled. "You need to marry that woman."

Nick set his jaw. He wasn't getting married and he wasn't getting to know the baby.

He looked around for Ty and saw him at the barbecue with Gabe. The man was getting a piece of his mind for inviting Laura here today.

SHADOWS SETTLED OVER the three women and Laura looked up. Emily and Ruby stood watching them.

Emily spoke up. "You're really going to have a baby with my dad?"

Laura felt herself blush. Yes, she had made the foolish mistake of sleeping with him to start with and then had compounded it by not using birth control. She nodded.

"He's not going to marry you." The girl's tone held a world of spite.

Laura bit her lip so she wouldn't respond in kind. She wasn't the only one who'd made a mistake that night. Her father had screwed up, too. It wouldn't do to tell this child so, though. "I know. I'm raising the baby alone."

"But Uncle Ty says we all have to get along so Ruby and I can get to know our cousins. I don't want to get to know that cousin." She crossed her arms, jutted one hip and gestured with her head toward Laura's still-flat stomach. "I want to get to know Callie's baby and Tammy's baby, but not yours."

"Emily!" Callie tried to take the girl's arm, but Emily side-stepped out of arm's reach.

"This is my baby," Laura said. "Mine and mine alone. I'm not forcing it on anyone else, especially not you or your father."

Under those odd blue-hazel eyes was a keen intelligence that was overlaid at the moment with unhappiness and anger. Emily turned to Ruby. "I have to be alone for a little while. Okay?"

Ruby shrugged. "Okay."

Laura watched Emily go, knowing that she had made yet another enemy just because of being pregnant. Her indignation urged her to give the girl a piece of her mind, to tell her to take her spite elsewhere, but Laura wasn't twelve years old and trying to keep her father all to herself. Nick hadn't done a very good job of raising his daughter if she'd grown up to be so spiteful.

Or maybe it was just the shock that made her so mean.

Either way, Laura was glad that Nick Jordan wouldn't be raising her child.

TAMMY HAD BEEN waiting for an opportunity like this. She couldn't let it pass.

"Ruby? While Emily's busy, take a walk with me."

She stood and wandered to the bison corral, hoping that Ruby would follow.

She leaned her forearms on the top of the fence and bison slowly shuffled over, the biggest one, Hirsute, in the lead. Hirsute was her favorite, used to be her buddy when she stayed here on weekends with Ty.

That was before Ruby had shown up at the beginning of a blizzard and the three of them had been trapped in the ranch house for a weekend.

Near the end of that forced confinement, Ruby had shown Tammy a photograph of her mother. Tammy wanted to know why. She'd just been too shocked at the time to wonder about Ruby's motives.

Tammy had taught school for a dozen years, young teenagers, until this past spring. She knew kids. She wouldn't have thought that Ruby had a manipulative bone in her body.

But she could be wrong.

She wanted to know for sure.

She felt Ruby draw near and pet the animals. She also thought she sensed fear in the girl.

"Why did you show me that photograph of you and your mother?" Tammy knew that Ruby would pick up on exactly what she was talking about and what she was asking.

Ruby touched Hirsute's forehead. "I wanted you to see how much you looked like my mom."

"Why?"

"Because I wanted you to see that my dad still loved my mom. He must have. Otherwise, why would he go out with someone who looked so much like her?"

"Why did I need to know that? I could have lived the rest of my life without that."

"Because I wanted them to get together again so we could be a real family."

She sounded miserable, as though she were on the edge of tears.

Tammy understood Ruby's reason, but the shock had

been unbearable for Tammy, and the ensuing break from Ty painful.

"And how is that going? Do you think Ty is still in love with your mom?"

Ruby's lower lip trembled. "No. Dad doesn't like talking to her. He doesn't even like her at all."

Tammy's happiness shouldn't come at someone else's expense, but God, it felt amazing. Vindicating. Take that, Winona! She'd heard a lot about Winona through the grapevine and not much of it had been good.

"Did I hurt your feelings?" Ruby asked.

"Yes, you did."

"I'm really sorry. I liked you a lot, but I really wanted my mom and dad together."

"That's okay. The truth would have come to light eventually. Maybe there was no easy way for me to learn that I looked so much like your mother."

"So, like, I'm going to have a little brother or sister?"

Tammy nodded. "How do you feel about it?"

"I think it's awesome. Dad says he'll send me for a St. John Ambulance first aid and babysitting course so I'll be able to babysit if you guys want to go out."

Tammy tried to frown, but couldn't. Easygoing Ty was taking charge, making sure everything would go his way, and it didn't bother her as much as it should.

NICK STOOD AT the grill with Gabe and Ty.

"Having fun with your meddling?" he asked Ty, tension pouring from him in waves. "Do you know how badly you hurt Emily?"

"*I* didn't, Nick. *You* got Laura pregnant. Obviously, you hadn't told Emily about the baby. Why not?"

"I hadn't found the right moment."

"Big mistake." Nick wasn't sure which one of his brothers said that, but, God, what an understatement.

He turned on Ty. "Are you nuts, bringing us all here together? You knew there'd be trouble."

"I'm sane for the first time in years." He flipped a couple of burgers too hard and one of them fell apart. Bits of ground beef slipped through the grill. The fire flared. Ty spritzed it with a water bottle. "We don't have an extended family. We don't have cousins or grandparents or aunts and uncles. We've only got each other. It's stupid that we haven't worked harder to hold on to what we have."

Nick felt Ty's chastisement to the soles of his shoes, but even so… "You had no right to meddle. Laura and I will work out something."

"That's what I'm afraid of," Ty countered.

"What do you mean?"

"You're madder than hell and Laura will pay the price."

"You like to get even with people," Gabe said. "To get revenge. You're mad at Laura for getting pregnant. It takes two to tango, buddy. You were there, too."

"I know that." Nick's patience was wearing thin. "You don't know the whole story. She told me I owed her a baby. Then she made sure she got pregnant."

"Did she rope you to a bed and have her way with you?" Gabe asked.

"No!"

"So she didn't force you to have sex," Ty said.

"No." He sounded as grumpy as a two-year-old.

"Did she lie about being on the pill or somehow prevent you from using birth control?" Gabe asked. "Condoms are cheap and easy."

"I know. I had a condom. I just…lost control in the heat of the moment."

"Did you hear that, Gabe? The mighty Nick Jordan lost control. I gotta mark that on the calendar. It needs to go down in the history books."

Nick didn't understand Ty's sarcasm, but for the first time

wondered how it must have felt to Gabe and Ty to have Mom coddle him so much. Could Ty have been jealous? Was he still carrying traces of it around?

"I wonder if Laura knows how much power she has over you." Ty flipped another burger too hard. "So are you as angry with yourself as you are with her?"

Culpability had always been hard to admit. In business, it was lethal. But Nick had to give Ty credit for trying to right old wrongs and for wanting to put the past to rest.

"Yes," he conceded. "I'm angry with myself, too. Furious."

"How are you and Laura going to work this out?" Ty asked. "Long-distance parenting?"

He'd already done that with Emily, hadn't he? Not literally, but in essence. He might as well have worked on the moon instead of in the same city for all the good he'd done her as a father. Was that what he wanted to happen with his second child? But he hadn't wanted a second child. Laura was getting what she wanted. Let her handle it. "I haven't figured out the details yet."

"You're a whiz as a businessman, but you screw up where everything else is concerned."

Nick's dander rose. "I do my best."

"Sometimes that's not good enough." Ty stared across the yard to the women huddled together talking.

"Are things any better with Tammy?" Nick asked, turning the tables on his brother. The night before, Ty had filled him in on the story with Tammy, Winona and Ruby. Talk about a soap opera.

"Not yet."

Nick turned to stare at Ty. He'd never heard his easygoing brother sound so determined. He exchanged a glance with Gabe that said *who knew Ty had it in him?*

"I'm making sure things will turn out." Ty annihilated another burger.

"Give me that." Gabe snatched the utensil from Ty and

took over the grill. "We didn't have the best example in our parents, but we can make things work as adults." He glanced over at Callie. "Even if it does take us a few years to finally figure ourselves out and make it happen. Don't quit working on Tammy, Ty."

He turned the girls' hot dogs. "Nick, make things work with Laura. It took me years to realize it, but you two belong together."

"Me and Laura?" Nick stared at Gabe as though he'd lost a few marbles. "Are you nuts? All we do when we get together is make a mess of things." *We fly too high, too hot, too fast.* Nick had one failed marriage under his belt. In fact, he'd never had a single successful lasting relationship with a woman, but even he knew that marriage had to be based on more than just mind-blowing sex.

The girls were talking to the women now. Emily separated from the group and entered the stable.

Nick started to follow her, but Ty touched his arm. "Looks like she wants to be alone. She has a lot to think about."

"Can she get hurt in there? Will the horses bite or kick her?"

"Relax, city boy. The horses know her and like her."

"Here comes Laura," Gabe said.

Nick had been concentrating on holding himself back from running after Emily to make sure she was all right. He turned to find Laura striding across the lawn toward him.

"Excuse me," he said, approaching her, taking her arm and steering her around to the far side of the house so they could have this out privately.

"Were you coming over to give me shit?"

"No. I want to clarify a few things."

"Like what?"

"I did not sleep around. This baby is yours."

A sigh gusted out of Nick. "I know. I'm sorry." He deeply

regretted being so rash in his assumptions. On a level deeper than his anger, he knew how good Laura was.

She looked skeptical, as though she didn't believe anything that came out of his mouth.

"I apologize," he said. "I do believe the baby is mine."

"Apology accepted." She stepped away from him, almost as though she didn't trust herself to get too close. "Second, I didn't seduce you to get this baby. This isn't how I wanted things. I wanted a whole family. I wanted a father who would be available."

He still wasn't sure about the seduction part. *You owe me a baby. I'm ovulating.* About being a father, though, he had plenty to say. "I can't—"

She raised her hand to stop him. "I don't expect you to be here for the baby. I know you, Nick. I know you follow no one's agenda but your own."

"I—"

Again she raised her hand. "Stop doing that," he said. "It's irritating the hell out of me."

She ignored him and plowed on. Talk about someone following her own agenda.

"I said no to your money earlier, but I'm amending that now." Surprise, surprise. He'd been chased more than once for his money.

"I will expect child support from you. I need to pay for day care while I work. We *both* lost control that night. I'm willing to raise the baby on my own, but you should pay something."

It takes two to tango. Nick stared straight ahead. "I'll have my lawyer contact you with a fair settlement."

She walked away.

Well, that bit of cold business had been fun. *Cold* wasn't a word he would have ever thought to use with regard to Laura, but she'd just about scarred him with her dry ice.

This was turning out to be one hell of a celebration.

Thank you, Ty.

Emily skidded around the corner of the house with Ruby.

"Dad, will you teach us how to play basketball with the new hoop?"

He smiled. Good old Emily. His gem. She'd recovered.

"Sure."

"See?" Emily spoke to Ruby and they headed toward the front of the house. "I told you he'd say yes."

"How was I supposed to know? He seemed like he was in a bad mood."

Yeah, he had been. Life wasn't going as it should. The mistakes he was making these days were irreparable. Babies couldn't be put back where they came from. You couldn't pretend they didn't exist. Once a baby was made, there was no turning back.

The thought of having another one left him shaky and sick. He'd entered into fatherhood so cavalierly the first time around. Marsha had wanted a baby and he'd said yes. What did he care? He had a business to run for her father. That was all that mattered to him. Only now did he realize the responsibility parenthood was. Only when he'd almost lost his daughter did he understand how much she meant to him.

It wasn't a job contract that had a clear start and finish. The job of parenting never ended. Once you started down that road, the responsibility never stopped.

AT DUSK, TY BUILT a bonfire in a sand pit and they toasted marshmallows and made s'mores and did all of the hokey family things that Emily thrived on.

His girl looked happy and that made Nick smile.

He glanced at Laura; in fact, he'd done too much of that today. The firelight shot her chestnut hair with red. Her top slid off one shoulder. He knew her skin was covered with freckles there. He wanted to bite them.

She laughed at something Callie said and Nick's libido shot through the roof.

He fought the urge to swoop in, to pick her up and carry her into the woods and have his way with her, to push her against a tree, to have her wrap her strong arms and legs around him while he screwed her lovely body and the both of them into oblivion.

She laughed again and he wanted to kiss the huskiness in it, wanted to swallow it whole and carry it with him.

Laura did this to him—tied him into knots so convoluted and tight that he barely managed to control himself.

OLIVIA WATCHED THE fireworks that the town put on every summer in a small park with a bust of Ian Accord at its center. Ian, a railroad baron, had founded Accord in the late 1800s. His large Victorian home had eventually become the Accord B and B.

She hadn't felt like celebrating today, but had wandered over as soon as dusk fell, excited despite herself to see the spectacle.

A rough hand grabbed her arm and, before she could do more than let out a startled cry swallowed by the boom of the fireworks, pulled her behind a tree. In the darkness, a head descended and lips covered hers.

She had never kissed Aiden McQuorrie, but she knew him. Knew his scent and his heat and the way his body felt.

He kissed her with authority and passion and she gave in, to him and to her desires, for just a few brief, tempting moments.

His big hand cupped her head and his lips spoke a wonderful language. His tongue sang a marvelous tune.

With his body, he pressed her against the tree and his knee moved between her legs, starting an ache there.

Aiden. My darling.

She'd dreamed about this. Reality was so much better.

He pulled away and whispered in her ear, his breath fanning her hair, "This is us. In the dark, we are not old or young or rich or poor. We are only ourselves, sweetheart."

The temptation to give in overwhelmed her and she pulled his lips to hers for more.

She couldn't get enough, didn't think she would ever get her fill, but ended the kiss anyway.

Here, in the darkness, in the heat of a summer's night, she understood Aiden, but tomorrow morning, in the light of day, she would still be fifteen years older than him, living in a small town where everyone knew everyone else's business.

She relinquished his lips slowly, biting and licking to draw into herself the last drop of his essence. "I have to go."

"No. I won't let you."

She smiled, sadly, because despite Aiden's ferocity, he would do what she wanted. She stepped away from him and left, rushing so she could get into the safety of her home before she broke down.

CHAPTER THIRTEEN

Nick walked into Sweet Temptations on Tuesday morning, wishing like hell there was another bakery in town.

The professor and the elders had painstakingly researched migratory routes and had determined the house was clear. Nick could build.

They were breaking ground tomorrow morning and, to celebrate, he wanted to arrange to have coffee and goodies delivered for the entire crew.

The shop was busy, as usual, so he joined the lineup. Might as well get a coffee and a treat for himself while he was here.

Roy Orbison's "Crying" finished up just as he stepped inside and Neil Young's "Helpless" started.

The lineup was ten deep and the service slow. Tilly was training a new girl who was apparently getting some of the orders wrong.

Laura should have been on the counter helping as he'd seen her do before. Where was she? Things moved along quickly when she served.

She was smart to consider expansion, but she would be stepping into a new level of service. She would need a full staff, maybe even waitresses.

Nick's blood started to burble like the engine of a fine car. He loved business, every type and every aspect of it. The fundamentals were the same no matter how small or large the business.

While he waited, another song came on that he didn't

know. It sounded like k.d. lang singing something about a heart caving in and willpower being gone.

What was with all the sad music? Might as well take an IV, fill it with tears and mainline it.

When he finally got to the front of the line, he demanded, "What's going on with the music?"

Tilly looked glum. "Ask the boss."

"The place is packed. Why isn't she out front helping?"

"Ask her."

"I need to discuss catering. I'm going to head back. Okay?"

Tilly nodded and served the next customer, ignoring him when he stepped around the counter and into the back. He couldn't help but contrast the atmosphere to that of a couple of months ago.

In the kitchen, he saw a layer cake on the floor, upside down, where it had landed with a big splat. Icing covered the floor.

He called, "Laura?"

"Back here." She sounded as if she had a cold.

He found her in a small office with her head in her hands. When she looked up, he could tell she'd been crying.

"Oh, crap, it's you," she said. "Why do you always catch me in my worst moments? I do laugh. I do have fun. I am eminently capable and efficient."

"Did something happen to the baby?" A spark inside of him tugged at his heartstrings. For Laura's sake, he didn't want her to lose this baby, and wasn't that a weird revelation when he didn't want the baby to exist at all, when it scared the bejesus out of him. "Or is the problem that cake on the floor in the kitchen?"

"The baby's fine. The problem is the cake. I dropped it."

"I noticed. It's not the end of the world."

"It is when I'm too tired to make another one."

"Was it a special order?"

Her tired nod was a barely perceptible movement. "For a birthday party tonight."

"When's the party?"

"Seven o'clock."

"Make another one."

"Easy for you to say." She rubbed her hands over her face. "I'm just working up the energy to start again."

"Do you always get this upset over a mistake?"

"My hormones are going nuts. Usually I bounce back from things, but you know pregnant women. How we can get."

No. He didn't. He tried to remember Marsha pregnant, but couldn't. Mort had worked the daylights out of him at the beginning. Nick had even missed Emily's birth.

"So I'm guessing women get blue during pregnancy?"

"It happens."

"Is that why the music is so painfully sad out front?"

"It is?" She looked surprised.

"You need to change it before your customers slit their wrists."

A laugh chuffed out of her. "That bad, huh?"

Nick smiled, grudgingly. Laura was the most attractive woman he knew, but she didn't look exactly like a beauty queen when she cried. Not many women did. He smiled to himself. She probably wouldn't want to know that, so he didn't tell her.

Despite his anger with her and before he could think better of it, he asked, "Have you had lunch yet?"

"No."

"You want to go out somewhere?"

"I probably shouldn't. I've been crying."

Given that her nose was red, yeah, she shouldn't go out.

"How about if I ask Tilly to put something together for us and we eat it in here?"

He walked back to the door leading to the café and shook his head. The lineup was as long as when he'd entered.

He returned to Laura.

"It will take forever to get through the lineup. We'd better go out."

"We can go upstairs and I can whip up some pasta and vegetables."

"Sounds good."

She didn't move, still sat in the same spot and stared at the wall. He'd never seen her like this. He'd never seen her without energy to spare, without a laugh in her voice.

Except when she was angry with him, which, of course, was always.

Her eyes looked like two golden caramels in a pair of bruises. "Are you sleeping?"

"It's normal to be tired in the first trimester, especially with morning sickness. It should get better in the second and then flag again in the third."

He hadn't thought about what it would be doing to her body, had only worried about how it would inconvenience him.

"I get up in the middle of the night to bake," she said. "By the time the place opens, I've already been hard at work for six hours. Normally that's not a problem, but this baby makes me want to sleep for hours on end."

She touched her belly. "I'm afraid to work too hard. I don't want to lose her. Maybe that's why I lost the last baby."

He didn't like this version of Laura. He wanted the capable, feisty woman back. "Come on." He held out his hand to her.

"What?"

"We're going to bake another cake."

"We?"

"Yep. Tell me what to do."

In the kitchen, she stared at the cake on the floor.

"Go," he said, gently grasping her shoulders and turning her toward the counter. "Get your ingredients together while I clean this up."

While he cleaned, she buttered cake pans and dusted them with flour then started measuring ingredients. When he finished cleaning the floor, he fetched cooking items for her.

At last, she got the cake into the oven and baked it, then turned it out onto cooling racks.

She went out to ask Tilly to ice it later and deliver it to the birthday party.

"The activity was good for you," Nick said. "You look better." A lot better. She looked good enough to have for lunch. He reined himself in. That wasn't going to happen again between them.

"Thanks for your help. I didn't feel so alone." It looked as if it cost some of her pride to admit that. Her stomach grumbled. "I'm going upstairs for lunch. Join me."

He was hungry, but upstairs? Alone with Laura in her apartment?

She stopped a foot away from him, clear-eyed now. "No sex. We absolutely cannot have sex. It screws us up. I'm just offering lunch."

"No sex," he said, even though his body vehemently disagreed.

He followed her up her stairs and into her apartment.

While she threw garlic, greens and vegetables into a wok, Nick sat on a stool at the kitchen counter.

"You mind if I give you some advice about the bakery?"

She turned warily. "It's successful. I know I look like a mess these days, but I know baking and I know how to run a café."

"Yes, you do. The baked goods are out of this world. I can see that the café is a raging success, but you've got Tilly down there training someone and the customers waiting too long to get served."

Laura nodded. "I'm usually out there to help her but the pregnancy has been draining my energy."

"You need to either get back on that counter or hire more staff."

"It's going to be hard to stay on the counter much until this fatigue passes."

"Then you need to train a bunch of people."

"You're right."

Just talking about all of that work made her look tired again, dead on her feet, as though a stiff wind would knock her down. If he knew anything at all about cooking, he'd make her sit down and he would finish making lunch for her.

She took already cooked pasta out of the fridge and tossed it with the sautéed veggies.

"This will have to do." She plonked it onto the counter, along with plates and forks. "Do you mind if we sit at the counter?"

"Do I mind? My intention wasn't to put you to work. I wanted to do something for *you*. I would have taken you out to lunch."

"I'm too tired."

She smiled and sat down. A sigh slipped out of her.

They ate in a surprisingly companionable silence. Maybe Ty's idea of forcing them to spend time together on the Fourth hadn't been so bad, even if the tension that day had soared with the temperature. They needed to get along. Inside of Laura's body was a tiny creature forming slowly. Tiny and real and intimidating.

After lunch, Nick rinsed the dishes and made her a cup of tea.

They moved to the living room.

"Show me your music collection. We need to get something upbeat onto those speakers downstairs before your customers start running from the café in tears."

She pointed to a CD collection that sat beside a computer on a small desk.

"I use my CDs and I have a bunch of music already on the

computer that I bought from iTunes." She started to rise but he waved her down. "You can burn whatever you want onto a CD and take it downstairs with you."

He scanned row upon row of music, mesmerized by the selection, and by how closely some of it mirrored his own.

"What's Caro Emerald like?"

"Fun. Sexy."

"Okay, we'll start with her. What does she do that's up-beat?"

"'Dr. Wanna Do' and 'That Man.'"

"Who else is upbeat?"

"Imelda May. Rockabilly. Try 'Johnny Got a Boom Boom' and 'Train Kept A Rollin'.'"

"Who else?"

"Anastacia. 'Paid My Dues.'"

"How about a male artist?"

"Jonny Lang plays the blues, but his guitar work is sub-lime. He makes me happy."

With a fistful of CDs, he sat at her computer and brought up her iTunes.

They discussed music for an hour and had barely scratched the surface of what they had in common.

When he finished, Nick took a compilation CD out of the computer to take downstairs to Tilly.

He stood to find Laura sound asleep on the sofa with her head resting on one hand and her elbow on the arm of the chesterfield.

She couldn't be comfortable.

He touched her shoulder. "You need to get into bed."

"I'm fine here."

"No, you're not. You need to sleep properly."

When she refused to move, he lifted her into his arms and carried her to the bedroom, where he laid her on the bed.

"Neanderthal," she said.

He laughed.

She looked so sexy, so womanly, that he had to fight to not lie down with her and make love to her.

"No," she said, awareness in her eyes. "We can't ever go down that road again, Nick."

"You're already pregnant."

"We're too hard on each other. We fight as hard as we make love."

She was right. Considering what a cool head he had for business, he spent too much time turned inside out when he was with Laura, as though she peeled back his skin and left him exposed.

But they made love like masters.

He pulled a cover over her and walked out before he could use his hands, and everything else in his arsenal, to convince her to let him stay.

Downstairs, he handed the CD to Tilly. "Put this on the CD player."

She looked at it suspiciously. "What's on it?"

"Something a hell of a lot more upbeat than what's on right now."

"Thank God." She grabbed it and took it to the corner. A second later, Caro Emerald came on and she smiled.

There were still a lot of customers in the café. "You want some help?" Nick asked.

"What can you do?"

"I don't know. Give me something."

"You won't like it."

"What do you need?"

"Keira and I have to keep serving customers but dirty dishes are piling up on the tables."

Nick Jordan, successful businessman and multimillionaire, bused for the rest of the afternoon and washed dishes. If his colleagues could only see him now.

He returned to Ty's ranch feeling as if he'd done something useful, as though he'd helped out a friend in need.

Was Laura a friend?

He didn't know. His feelings for her were so polarized, clanging like fire alarms between poles, sometimes angry, most times lustful, and occasionally, like today, in sweet harmony. He didn't know which end was up.

He did know that he'd never talked about music with another woman as he had with Laura today.

THE FOLLOWING MORNING, Nick had basketball coaching duties. He'd bought shoes and workout clothes and wanted to actually get out onto the court with the boys.

Ruby, Emily and Mort had come along to watch. Neither of the girls knew the first thing about basketball, but every day came outside with him to shoot hoops and pick up pointers.

Since finding out about the baby, Emily had been dogging his heels. He couldn't hug her enough or reassure her enough of his love, of how stable and unending it was. She doubted.

He'd put that doubt there. He spent endless minutes of his days trying to eradicate it.

On their way to the high school, they stopped at Sweet Temptations for drinks and doughnuts. Emily might not like Laura, but she loved her cinnamon buns.

Laura was behind the counter serving. Two women Nick had never seen there before served efficiently beside her, while Tilly took orders and handled cash.

When she saw him, Laura motioned to come to the end of the counter.

"Thank you for yesterday," she said, smiling, looking as strangely at ease with him as he felt with her. "I really needed it. I slept right through until three this morning."

"Good. You look better." The bruises under her eyes were gone. "There was a reason I came in yesterday. We're breaking ground today and I wanted to celebrate. Could you put something together for the workers for tomorrow morning? Thermoses of coffee and sweet treats?"

"Sure. How about if I make a few trays of bars tonight? Brownies and lemon squares and Rocky Road bars. Does that sound good?"

"It sounds great. Perfect. There are about eighteen men out there."

An odd thought occurred to him. "If you slept through the afternoon and evening yesterday, how did you manage to hire two women and train them so fast?"

"At one point this morning, the lineup was so long I called out that I needed new employees. Both of these women came forward and agreed to start right away."

"You hired them just like that? For all you know, they might rob you blind."

"No. I know them both well. I didn't leave town like you did. I know everyone. They're middle-aged farm women who've been serving food all of their lives. They're taking to this like ducks to water and they get to make money for themselves. I don't know why I didn't think of it sooner."

Nick smiled.

They stared at each other, Nick unsure what to think of this strange new harmony between them. The baby issue would always be a barrier to true harmony, and how they were going to work it out, but the harsh edge of their animosity was gone.

Ty was one smart guy. He'd started this ball rolling by putting them together on the Fourth and basically telling them to grow up and solve their differences.

Good on him. He hoped things were working out with Tammy.

Now it was up to Nick to not screw up, to keep things on an even footing with Laura.

Next, he guessed the smart thing to do would be to mend his relationship with Gabe.

Gabe was going to be a tough nut to crack, not because of Gabe, but because of Nick and those strange old feelings and memories that bothered him at times.

"You okay?" Laura asked.

He'd been staring at her without saying a word.

"I'm good. Fine," he said, at a loss to say more. "I'll pay Tilly for today's goodies and for whatever tomorrow's catering will cost."

They got to the gym and Nick changed while the girls sat in the stands.

Nick came out a moment later and dribbled a ball up and down the court, running on rusty legs. He'd spent too many hours sitting at a desk. His life had been saturated with nothing but work for so long, he'd forgotten there was more to life than business.

He might be rusty, but his body had moves that seemed to be ingrained in his arms and legs. For twenty minutes, he ran and shot hoops, his body thrilled with the pure joy of movement and rhythm.

Music with Laura the other day and this afternoon, basketball. This holiday in Accord had its merits.

The kids he'd met the other day started to arrive.

Salem Pearce walked in.

"Something wrong at the work site?" Nick asked.

"Nope. I'm here to play basketball."

"But you've already graduated."

"I know, but this isn't a school league. It's a summer camp. They need me."

"Why didn't I meet you the other day with the other boys?"

"I had a funeral. One of the elders died."

"Sorry to hear it, man."

"Thanks. He had a good long life, so the funeral was more a celebration."

Nick tossed him a ball and said, "Let's see what you've got."

He put the whole team through drills, and when it looked as though they'd reached their limit, he put them through more. "This might be a summer camp," he said, "but there will be games against other teams and I want this one to win."

He divided them into two teams, but one of the boys had to leave early.

"Sorry. My tooth aches. I have a dental appointment."

Which meant that since there were only ten boys enrolled in the camp, and there were five per team in basketball, Nick would have to fill the kid's spot.

"Let's play," he yelled and tossed the ball onto the court.

Hours later, he drove the girls home, his body humming, his hamstrings sore.

He spotted a pharmacy in town and pulled into a parking space. He planned to soak his sore muscles when he got to Ty's, otherwise they'd seize up and he'd be useless tomorrow. Tomorrow afternoon, he had to coach again.

He turned to Mort in the passenger seat. "You need anything?"

"Nope. I'm good. Can we stop at the home for a little while before we head back?"

"Sure thing."

The owner of the shop was an older guy Nick only barely remembered.

"Nick Jordan, what can I do for you?"

"You can point me in the direction of the Epsom salts."

"Heard you were coaching basketball. My youngest is taking that camp."

"Oh? What's his name?"

"Al Lethbridge Junior."

"He's a good player."

Al's chest swelled with pride.

"He plans to take one of those Culinary Arts courses you're offering. You're doing good things for this community, Nick. I'm glad Al will be coming home to work."

He was? There was self-interest involved on Nick's part. He'd wanted the town on his side when he built the resort.

He also wanted good workers who would commit to a couple of years, so his workforce for those first few years would be stable.

He just hadn't really thought of how much it would mean to their parents to have them close to home.

He bought his Epsom salts and returned to the car.

The girls had been talking but stopped when he climbed into the passenger seat. When he started to drive home, he noticed in his rearview mirror they were texting on their phones. Kids!

"You know, while you're together in Accord," he said, "it would be a better use of your time to talk to each other rather than texting friends on your phones."

"We aren't texting friends. We're texting each other."

"You're sitting beside each other *texting* instead of *talking?*"

"Yeah."

"Why not just talk?"

Emily didn't answer. Nick glanced in his mirror. The girls were exchanging what seemed to be significant glances.

"You don't want me to hear what you're talking about."

Beside him Mort chuckled. Presumably, he knew what was going on.

"It's nothing personal, Dad."

"You're talking about boys, aren't you?"

"Your dad's smart," he heard Ruby whisper.

The only boys they'd seen in town were the boys playing basketball today.

"You're talking about the basketball players."

They didn't respond.

"So, who's the cutest?"

"Salem Pearce," Ruby blurted. "Totally!"

She slammed her hand over her mouth because Nick had caught her off guard.

A second later, the girls started to giggle, Mort laughed

and didn't stop until they turned into the driveway of the nursing home.

Nick's sense of well-being shot through the roof.

He only had one week of vacation left in Accord. Already he was sorry it was going to be so short.

Wasn't that a kicker for a workaholic like him?

Callie greeted them and led them to the sunroom.

Mort sat down with Johanna, who didn't recognize him. As he had done a few days ago, Mort talked until she relaxed and laughed with him.

"He's really good for her." Callie stood beside Nick, watching. "I never knew he could be so patient."

"Me either. It's good to see. Accord seems to agree with him."

He stared down at Callie. His feelings toward her had changed. None of his old resentment and anger had emerged. Somehow, where his relationship with Callie was concerned, Nick's one night with Laura had blown whatever feelings he still held for Callie out of the water.

That night had changed him fundamentally.

THE FOLLOWING MORNING, Nick got up, showered and had breakfast.

He found Ruby and Emily at the kitchen table. "Where's Ty?"

"Doing chores with the bison," Ruby answered.

"What are you two up to today?"

They looked at each other and shrugged.

"I'm driving out to the work site after breakfast. Do you want to come?"

"Yeah!" Emily said. She turned to Ruby. "I'll show you where Salem is putting the Native American museum."

"Okay."

"Emily, run and ask your gramps if he wants to come."

An hour later, they drove over with Nick's stomach doing

somersaults. The last time he'd been here, the house had still been standing. He hadn't come back to see it demolished.

They turned into the driveway and Nick stared at the big empty space where a house used to be, where his childhood used to reside.

His breath came too quickly.

He hadn't expected to feel this loss, this emptiness.

Laura's car was already here.

While Mort and the girls ran to see what she'd brought today, Nick walked to the hole in the ground that had been his childhood. He stared into the hollow chasm, grieving for a time when things had been good.

Those years with his mother had been wonderful, but if he wanted to find a time when the whole family had been happy, he had to look further into the past, to the time before Dad's death. He'd been so young then. He didn't have memories, only a general feeling of well-being. Something awful had happened then that Nick wasn't sure was *directly* related to Dad's death. He couldn't put his finger on it, though.

Emily had helped him to remember some of the good times he'd had with his brothers after that, but whispers of memories that weren't so good still lingered.

He couldn't pinpoint them, just saw a general darkness, but knew that he would need to figure it out at some point.

The time after his father's death had been so dark and so empty. Mom hadn't been there for him for long months on end. When she'd finally overcome her sorrow, she'd taken to him wholeheartedly, and life had become sunny again. He'd associated darkness and loneliness with his dad. Then Gabe had taken over that role and had probably been so afraid of screwing up that he'd gone overboard in protecting his younger brothers.

Nick had chafed against the restraints, especially given how much Mom spoiled him.

No wonder he'd carried so much negative emotion around

Gabe all those many years. He'd associated him with Dad, and with that dark, dark time in his life.

If Nick could bring himself to look at the whole thing objectively, when all was said and done, Gabe had done an exemplary job of practically raising his two younger brothers.

Fundamental beliefs shifted inside of him, like tectonic plates in the ocean, and he felt a tidal wave of gratitude toward Gabe unlike anything he'd felt toward him in his life.

He let go of resentment, finally, breathing it out and, to replace it, breathing in the healing energy of the land around him.

The workers swarmed Laura's car, catching his attention.

She laughed at something one of them said and his mood lifted even higher. She did that to him, even when he didn't want her to.

"You look like you're feeling better today," he said when she approached.

"Pregnancy is like that. Some days are good and some, not so good. Today, it feels great to be out of the bakery and in the sunshine."

"What did you bring?"

He bit into the lemon square she handed to him and nearly moaned in pleasure. Man, the woman could bake.

She noticed his eyes drifting to the big hole in the ground.

"It's strange that it's gone, isn't it?"

Yes, it was strange. That big hole, that empty space, turned his memories into dreams that disappeared with the light of day.

What did you expect? You'd wanted to obliterate the past.

Yeah, but I didn't know it would hurt like this.

Tough, pal. You can't have it both ways.

For a man who didn't like to look at himself too closely, he sure spent a lot of time doing exactly that here in Accord.

CHAPTER FOURTEEN

THE FOLLOWING TUESDAY AFTERNOON, Laura got a call from Salem Pearce.

"We've been playing all morning and it's two o'clock and coach is still pushing us." He sounded winded. "We're starving. Nick said he'll pay for lunch. Can you bring over a bunch of sandwiches and cold drinks?"

"Sure. You want dessert, too? I've got cookies."

"Yeah! There are ten players, coach and Emily, Ruby and Mort."

"Got it. See you soon."

She turned to the two women she'd hired, Gayle and Norma. The Gems, she called them, because they could do no wrong. They made her life so much easier.

"We need sandwiches for—" she glanced at the notes she'd taken "—fourteen people. Ten of them are hungry teenage boys."

The Gems laughed and immediately started slicing and buttering bread and pulling cold cuts out of the fridge.

"Tilly, can you pack a couple of dozen cookies? I'll get cold drinks."

Fifteen minutes later, Laura packed her car and drove to the high school.

Planning to get help carrying in the food, she entered the gym and stopped just inside the door.

Nick and Salem were facing off, running from one end of the court to the other. Tall men, their long legs ate up the length of the court in a few strides.

Nick dribbled the ball toward the net, rose in a long twisting arc and dropped the ball in, turning the sport into a graceful ballet.

She remembered how often Gabe had wanted to attend Nick's games and how she'd never objected. She used to sit holding one man's hand while she lusted after the beautiful athlete that Nick was on the court.

Salem laughed, grabbed the ball and dribbled to the other end of the court, Nick hot on his heels and jumping to block the ball as Salem made a shot toward the basket.

Nick Jordan. Poetry in motion.

The attraction she felt for the man exploded inside of her, wouldn't be denied.

Why did he have to come back to Accord? Why did he have to decide to build here? Why did he wreak havoc with all of her best intentions? Where this man was concerned, her brain was mush, and her body a quivering mess.

His daughter approached from the stands.

"What are you doing here?" she asked, her tone unfriendly. Rude.

Lusting after your father.

"I'm delivering lunch. If you want any, learn how to be polite." She didn't need the kid's sass. Her life was stressful enough at the moment.

Salem ran over. When she asked for his help to carry in the food, her smile felt shaky.

Nick ran past her to help. She caught a whiff of sweat and it didn't bother her one bit. The man was too real, too tempting and too *here*. Why hadn't he stayed away, like a former lover ought?

AFTER EVERYONE ATE and the garbage was piled into boxes for Laura to dispose of, she sat down on a bleacher and watched the rest of the practice.

Nick's boss came and sat beside her.

"That was a great feast," he said.

Laura laughed. "It was only sandwiches."

"I've eaten in the best restaurants, but I haven't enjoyed any of those meals as much as I enjoyed this one."

About to make a smart crack, Laura halted. He was serious. She smiled. "Thank you."

He tapped her arm. "It's the love you put into your food and your business that makes it successful."

"I do love the work," she conceded.

"Do you love Nick?"

The question threw her. "I—" She didn't know how to answer it, especially not when it was being asked by a stranger.

"He's a man worth loving, if only the right woman would."

Laura cocked her head and studied Mort. "He used to be married to your daughter. Why would you try to promote a romance for him with another woman?"

"Because I believe in acting on what is right, and a romance, a future, between the two of you would be right."

"But—"

He didn't wait to hear her objections, but squeezed her arm and went back to sit with the girls, leaving Laura with dreams and wishful thinking.

She shook herself back to reality. No way was anything more happening with Nick. He didn't want the baby she was carrying.

These days, they were more than civil with each other, and some of their conversations had been downright excellent, but Laura and her baby were a package deal that Nick Jordan just didn't want.

AFTER PRACTICE, NICK LEFT the change room in fresh clothes. He usually didn't shower here, but he had today. It had been a long practice.

When Laura had shown up with lunch, he'd tried to ignore her. Ha! Might as well try to ignore the sun, or oxygen.

His cell phone rang.

He checked caller ID. Davis Fuller.

"What's up, Davis?"

"Nick, I've got a problem here. My dad's going to need long-term care and my mom has to go into a home. I'm scrambling to find places for them. I need to put her house to rights and get it on the market. When are you heading back to Seattle?"

"Tomorrow."

"Damn. Is there any way you can postpone? I'm going to be here another three, four weeks. Are you your own boss? Is your vacation flexible?"

Nick thought about everything that would be waiting for him back at the office.

Salem slapped him on the back as he passed on his way to his car.

The camaraderie with these boys, the fun of the sport, the pleasure of waking up to do this every second day, had changed him.

He actually resented that he had to go back to work. Wasn't that a kicker? What was happening to him here in this town? Had it changed so much since his childhood? Were the cosmetic changes on Main Street more than skin deep?

"Let me see what I can work out and I'll get back to you."

"Thanks, Nick."

"Emily," he called.

She came running from the stands. "What's wrong?"

"You want to stay here for another three or four weeks?"

She broke out into a broad grin. "Really? Yeah!" Her smile slipped. "But where will you be?"

"Here with you. Davis needs me to coach b-ball for another few weeks. I won't have as much time to spend with you as these past two weeks, though. I'm going to set up an office in the B and B, I'll get Rachel to come to town, and

I'll have a lot of work to catch up on, but I'll still be at Ty's in the evenings."

"Okay." Her joy was tempered by distrust. She was afraid that once Rachel arrived with her father's work, he would have zero time with her. Nick knew that was exactly what he'd done to her before.

But not this time.

She told Ruby what was happening and they laughed and high-fived.

Mort came over and shook his hand. "Good coaching, and good idea to stay on longer."

They walked to the sheriff's office, where Nick found Ty doing paperwork.

"How would you feel about me, Mort and Emily staying with you longer than originally planned?"

"It would be great." He smiled at Ruby. "Ruby was blue this morning because Emily was leaving tomorrow. Weren't you, honey? So, what's up, Nick?"

Nick outlined what was happening and how he planned to bring his work to Accord, so he could stay longer and coach.

After he left Ty's office, he called Rachel and asked her to come to Accord along with whatever needed his immediate attention. "The earlier tomorrow, the better."

He stopped at the B and B and arranged to rent the top floor. The small suite would serve as an office and the second bedroom as Rachel's to sleep in.

Emily was silent as they walked to the car. He wrapped his fingers around the back of her neck and squeezed.

"I'll still be here for you. I promise."

THE SUMMER LEAGUE's first game was held in Accord in the high school auditorium a week later, on Tuesday evening.

To Nick's surprise, the stands were packed with parents and friends. Standing room only.

Laura came in and sat in the front row, looking about as beautiful as a Madonna.

Lord, did the woman take beauty pills?

Was he the only one who saw what a stunner she was?

When she saw him watching her, she sent him a thumbs-up. That one afternoon spent talking about and listening to music had been a truce of sorts. When he saw her in town, there wasn't the animosity there had been, and that was a good thing. She needed to stay calm for the baby.

What animosity there was came from Emily. No matter how much he tried to convince her that the baby wouldn't change their relationship, she remained sulky about it. He didn't blame her. Mistakes were hard to fix. He and Emily had been mending bridges, but Nick still had a long way to go.

He turned his attention to the game. It started with a bang, with the opposing team scoring a three from behind the three-point line in the first couple of minutes.

The home team rallied and the game became a nail-biter. Nick yelled and cajoled from the sidelines. Salem, his star player, shot the winning basket with a slam dunk.

The crowd went wild.

Nick ran onto the court and the players converged in the middle and piled onto each other.

No business deal, no building completion, no contract signed, had ever felt as good as this. He'd forgotten about the high of a sports win.

The team gathered at the Springs Family restaurant afterward for milk shakes and burgers and fries. Most of the parents and spectators were there, too.

Nick couldn't sit still. He wandered the restaurant, shaking hands with parents and talking up the players. The sense of pleasure, of being part of a community, was something he'd never experienced here as a kid. Why not?

He thought about it. Usually he avoided introspection, hadn't really had much time for it in his life, but since returning to Accord he found he could no longer avoid the issues he'd lived with in childhood.

In fact, he didn't want to.

Above all else these days, he wanted the truth.

Could a town change? He didn't think so. Individuals changed, not entire towns.

Was he friendlier now than when he was a kid? Maybe. Probably. Yes, definitely.

If truth was so important to him then he had to admit his responsibility in how the town had seen him. It had stemmed from how he'd seen himself.

Because of the hand-me-downs he'd worn and the terrible feeling of being normal to the townspeople when he was so special at home, he'd carried a chip on his shoulder the size of the Grand Canyon.

He'd caused many of his problems in town when he was a kid. He was sure of it.

He spotted Gabe and Callie squeezed into a table in the corner. Nick walked over. He needed confirmation, needed to know that he was on the right track.

"Great game," Gabe said.

"That was more exciting than professional sports," Callie added.

"It's certainly more immediate," Nick agreed. "Gabe, I need to ask you something."

"Sure."

"Was I a bit of a prick when we were kids?"

Gabe almost laughed, but caught himself. "You sure you want me to answer that honestly?"

Nick laughed. "I think you just did, didn't you?"

"You sure you want to go down this road?" Gabe dropped his napkin onto his empty plate.

Gabe's tone worried Nick, but he nodded anyway. "Yeah. There are a lot of things I didn't understand when I was a kid that I want to know about now. I had a chip on my shoulder, didn't I?"

"Yeah. You carried it everywhere you went, because we were poor. It made you combative when you were small and then later, in high school, standoffish."

What Nick had been thinking was true. He'd never understood that he'd brought his problems onto himself.

"The only time you seemed to get past that," Gabe continued, "was when you played basketball."

Yeah, he remembered everything feeling good when he played. The world would melt away and there was only running, reaching, striving for those magical baskets.

"Thanks," he said simply. "I appreciate your honesty, Gabe."

"Anytime."

Nick walked away, unsure what to do with what he'd just learned about himself, how to right old wrongs or to become a better man, but certain that self-awareness was worth something.

CHAPTER FIFTEEN

In August, Laura entered her second trimester and her energy returned in spades.

She hired a contractor to start work on the shop next door and, thanks to the new staff in the café, had plenty of time to spend in her new space once she finished her baking and cleaning up for the day.

She immersed herself in the work, reveled in the noise, the mess, the "it gets worse before it gets better" state of renovations and the joy of making something new out of something tired.

When they started removing old plaster, the workers ordered her to get out. They were right. The last thing she needed was to expose herself and the baby to plaster dust.

They were stripping the far wall down to brick and leaving it bare, a look Laura had always loved. Excitement bubbled up inside of her like a pot of her finest Colombian on the brew.

"Can't wait to see it when it's finished. You guys stop in later for cold drinks and sandwiches. I'll tell Tilly it's all on the house."

One of the men made a comment she didn't quite catch, but by his friendly leer, she guessed he'd been making a pass. Even four months along in her pregnancy, she still got her fair share of male attention. After the months of morning sickness and feeling like an old hag, her heart did a happy skip and tumble.

She'd stopped wearing pants because she couldn't get the top buttons done up anymore. Dresses made a lot more sense.

Someday soon, though, she was going to have to buy maternity clothes.

She laughed, closed the door, stepped onto Main Street... and bumped into a hard male chest.

She glanced up. Nick Jordan.

NICK HELD HIS ARMS away from his body so Laura wouldn't spill either his coffee in one hand or the chocolate éclair in a serviette in the other, but he couldn't stop her from piling headlong into him.

She looked up at him, her expression momentarily unguarded, a smile in her clear hazel eyes, laughter on her lovely lips.

She sparkled, everything that he'd seen wrong with her—the weepiness, the fatigue, the regret—gone, all of it, every last ounce, replaced by energy, happiness, joy.

Dear God she was gorgeous, more alive than any woman he'd ever known. And so tempting.

She stepped away, almost shyly. "Sorry. I wasn't paying attention to where I was going."

"It's okay." It looked as though she wanted to say more, but didn't. He wanted to stay here with her for a while, to hold her close for a second, to drink in that joy that had her twinkling like a glowworm. He cast about for something to say. Anything.

"The café's going well. The ladies are working out. It didn't take me long to get this." He showed her what he'd just picked up.

She smiled. "I always say, you want a job done right, hand it over to a middle-aged woman."

"How are the renovations going?"

"Great! Want to see?"

She opened the door without waiting for his response, like a child showing off a toy.

Dust flew toward them and Nick wrapped the arm that held the éclair around her waist and hauled her back outside.

She waved a hand in front of her face. "Wow, those guys are moving fast."

"Go get a coffee," he said impulsively. "Meet me over there." He pointed to a park bench across the street.

"You want to have coffee with me?"

He nodded. "I want to know how things are going." He swallowed. "How the baby is." He met her gaze. "How you are."

"Okay." She gifted him with a smile he'd never seen before, not for him at any rate, not joyful or sexy. Just sweet.

When she went into the bakery, he crossed the street and sat on the bench, opened his coffee and took a sip. He studied the town.

Main Street used to be lined with old shops that had already been tired when Nick left for Seattle thirteen years ago.

A half dozen years ago, town council had put their heads together and had come up with this idea to bring in tourists—update and upgrade all of the shops. Bring in new business with the offer of cheap rent and low taxes.

Several trendy clothing shops had moved in. An upscale organic market had opened up. Tammy had transformed an old gift shop into a treasure palace that Nick had seen for himself was packed on Saturdays and Sundays.

The town had decided on a Victorian theme to match the Accord B and B. Imagine Nick's surprise to find, when he'd stayed there and had expected the worst, that it was an exceptionally fine and gracious hotel with an excellent menu.

The businesses had taken that Victorian theme and had made it fresh and new—a mix of old-world charm and new-world flash.

He'd noticed around town that homes were gussied up with gardens, some with plaques that announced wins in garden competitions. Verandas were bedecked with hanging baskets of ferns and trailing vines and riotous floods of flowers.

Strategically placed around town were murals painted by a local artist depicting scenes from the town's past.

An old train engine restored to perfection and parked at the far end of the street was a nod to the railway, the source of Ian Accord's wealth. Without the railroad baron's wealth and bringing a spur line to this part of Colorado more than a hundred years ago, the town wouldn't exist.

Apparently, town council had decided in the spring that park benches should be stationed along Main, beside huge stone planters filled with annuals to beautify the street. It worked.

Tourists flocked to town all summer.

Nick could almost swear the feeling clogging his chest was pride for his hometown.

His gaze swept the street and landed on Laura as she walked toward him. Her legs drew his eye because, really, they were the prettiest legs he'd ever seen. Bar none. He'd thought that as a teenager and he still thought it now.

"Like what you see?" she asked.

He grinned and openly stared at her legs. "Oh, yeah."

"I was talking about the town." She sat beside him and put a tall glass of lemonade on the bench between them.

She unwrapped a sandwich made on dense homemade bread that looked as if it was filled with seeds and nuts and healthy stuff.

The sandwich was sliced chicken covered with a lot of vegetables.

He glanced at her lemonade. "No coffee?"

"Nope. Until the baby is born, there'll be no caffeine." She sighed. "And no wine. I like a good glass of wine."

So did Nick. For the next twenty minutes, they discussed wines.

"Stop doing that," he said.

"Doing what?" she asked, her drink arrested halfway to her mouth.

"Being interesting. Having things in common with me. Making me like you."

She laughed. "Poor Nick. You don't want to like me, do you?"

He shook his head. "If you weren't pregnant, I'd be all over you, but I don't want another baby and I don't want another wife and, no, I don't want to like you."

"I know."

Her understanding embarrassed him. "The baby scares me."

"It scares me, too. I mean, I'll love the daylights out of her—"

"It's a girl?"

"I don't know. That's just what I call her. I don't want to know until he or she is born."

"I like things to be planned and organized ahead of time."

"Not me. I like surprise." She placed her hand on her belly. "Although this was a big one that really threw me for a loop."

She shifted on the bench until she was facing him more fully. "I've come to terms with how this happened. I've let go of regret. I'm putting my heart into having this baby alone and giving her a good life."

"Laura, what I said before, at Ty's, about contacting my lawyer. Don't do that. Talk to me. I'll give you child support. I'll be generous."

"You just can't escape your heritage, can you, Nick?"

"What are you talking about?"

"You tried to escape this town and your background, but you just can't. You turned yourself into a cold-blooded businessman, but when push comes to shove with me and this baby, your natural generous Jordan spirit comes out. You can't help being one of those Jordan boys."

"I used to hate being 'one of those Jordan boys.'"

"I always sensed that, but the longer you're staying here this summer, the more you're growing out of your discomfort. Being a Jordan boy is not a bad thing. It's special, Nick. Look at the good men that Gabe and Ty are. What's embarrassing about them? They're fine men. Don't be afraid to embrace who you really are."

She stood and took their garbage to a bin nearby, her flowered summer dress swirling around her thighs.

He was still uncomfortable with his past, but being involved with the town, coaching basketball and offering the youth an education if they wanted it, was changing him. Relaxing him. Or *forcing* him to relax, which was a good thing.

The headaches he'd been suffering all winter were nonexistent now. His shaky stomach was now rock solid.

Opening up to the town had done him good. Even more rewarding had been opening up to Emily—one of the best things he'd ever done in his life.

Helping Mort to overcome his dependence on alcohol had been fulfilling.

But laying himself bare to Laura that one night had upset and confounded and angered…and pleased him. It had given him a ridiculous amount of pleasure.

He was on a journey for which he had no road map, leaving him vulnerable but strangely unwilling to turn back and return to his starting point.

She sat back down on the bench.

"How much longer are you staying in town?"

"It's supposed to be another couple of days."

"Might as well stay until the end of the summer. It's only another couple of weeks. Or you could consider moving here since your daughter loves it so much."

After firing that salvo, she left.

He struggled to breathe steadily. Move here? *Live* here?

The woman was insane if she thought this was his destiny.

He might be on a journey, and he might be having fun here

this summer, but surely the end of it wasn't Accord, Colorado, the town he'd wanted to leave his entire childhood? The town he couldn't wait to kiss goodbye after high school?

Weren't journeys supposed to lead us forward, not backward?

The town had changed, yes, and so had he. It was pretty and popular with tourists, but, when it came down to it, Nick's favorite view of it was still in a rearview mirror.

AFTER THAT, NICK PUT everything he had into resisting everything the town had to offer. There would be no more extensions of the holiday. The second Davis returned to Accord, he and Emily were heading home.

Move here, my ass.

It's a nice place to visit, but I don't want to live here.

When he set his mind to something, it was hard to shake him.

He coached basketball and encouraged his boys to give their all. He pushed himself on the court with them in drills. He shouted and supported and cajoled at the next game until they won.

The townspeople came out and supported the team and him as coach. That was all he would take from them.

Where a week ago, he'd reveled in the feeling of belonging, now he drew away, set himself apart again. He appreciated their support, but that was all.

Laura sat in the front row, cheering on Salem.

He refused to look at her, or to acknowledge her. Look at what happened when he had sex with her. She got pregnant, dragging him into a drama that would last a lifetime.

Look what a simple conversation with her got him—an exhortation to move here. To live here. To make Accord his home.

No way.

Never.

Wasn't going to happen.

He was a man who looked forward, not backward.

His life was in Seattle, in the business he ran so well, and with the daughter he adored. He didn't need this town, the townspeople or another child.

His life was perfect the way it was.

At their next practice, Jamie Cosgrove came to tell him he wouldn't be able to finish basketball camp.

"Why the hell not?" Nick knew that Jamie loved it. The kid was damn good, too.

"I'm in summer school for math, but I'm not getting it. I failed during the school year, and I'm flunking out of summer classes, too."

The boy looked miserable.

"My mom and dad said I could take basketball only if I passed math and I'm not, so I have to quit."

"No way," Nick said. "I'll talk to your parents."

Nick was good at math. It was one of his skills as a problem-solver. He loved the challenge.

The next day, he sat down with Jamie and reviewed everything that Jamie needed to understand to pass the final exam, went over it and over it again, spent hours with the boy, until Jamie understood enough to pass.

The kid did. He brought in sixty percent on the test.

And he stayed in the basketball camp.

Nick had loved helping out the kid. He resisted yet another pull toward staying in town.

CHAPTER SIXTEEN

TAMMY STOPPED AT the fence to say hello to the bison. She'd missed them.

Hirsute ran over and shoved his head into her hands.

She scrubbed him and petted him and cooed, and he lapped it up like a big baby. "I missed you, too."

Over her shoulder, she stared at the house. *I missed* him.

She knew that Ty was working and wouldn't get home for at least another half hour. She had time to put her plan into action.

She'd heard through the grapevine that Ty had driven Ruby to the airport yesterday, sending her home for the coming school year. Nick, Mort and Emily had gone home last week. How was it almost the end of August already and there had been no further movement forward with Ty?

She knew the answer to that, though. He'd made the first steps toward reconciliation. It was now up to her to either reject or follow through.

Since the Fourth of July, she'd kept her distance so Ty could have a relationship with his daughter without Tammy getting in their way, but she'd thought long and hard about what he'd said about holding on to past resentment.

Her talk with Ruby had been illuminating. She knew that Winona hadn't returned to town since January. She knew there was no chance of reconciliation with Winona. She knew that Ty said he wanted her and their baby.

It was time to take him at his word. To trust him.

This evening, Tammy was putting a bold plan into action.

She wanted Ty and she wanted a family. She planned to get him back tonight for good, in the most daring way possible, to fix his attention firmly on *her*. She was going to make an impression, a lasting one, to leave him with a memory he wouldn't soon forget.

She planned to obliterate any trace of Winona from Ty's mind and claim him for herself.

If there was any way possible for a pregnant woman to be sexy, she was pulling out all the stops. Ty would love it, or he would find her pregnant body gross and she would have humiliated herself, and there would be no hope of a future between them.

But wasn't love worth taking a chance for?

Go bold or go home.

Using her own key, she entered and closed the door behind her, her hands shaky, but her jaw tight. She was nothing if not determined, committed.

She unbuttoned her light summer cardigan and dropped it from her shoulders onto the floor in the front hallway, where it landed…in a lump.

Bending gingerly because her eight-months-pregnant body had a mind of its own, had a different balance than her normal body, she rearranged her sweater so it looked more graceful lying on the floor in the foyer.

Next, she took off her skirt and dropped it a few steps away, close to the bottom of the stairs.

She took off one black stocking and draped it on the bottom step, then hung the garter on the newel post.

A third of the way upstairs, she draped the second stocking and garter. Putting on the stockings with her big pregnant belly in the way had been a real pain. Ty had better appreciate her efforts or she would never speak to him again. Ever.

At the top of the stairs, she dropped her black lace bra onto the carpet.

With difficulty—thank God Ty wasn't here to witness her

ungainly striptease—she stepped out of her black lace panties. This evening, she'd eschewed maternity panties for a tiny
pair that sat under her belly.

She hung the underwear on the doorknob of his bedroom
then closed the door. She pulled the bedsheet to the foot of
the bed then lay down.

At that moment, she heard Ty's truck come barreling up
his driveway.

She struggled to arrange herself into a sexy pose. How did
an extremely pregnant woman do that?

Her hands started to shake. What if she was wrong about
this? What if she turned Ty off? What if he ran for the hills
rather than love her elephant body?

Since last January, when she had learned of Winona's existence, and how eerily Tammy resembled the woman, she
had been living half a life. She'd adored Ty for too long to let
what they'd had slide off into oblivion.

Her baby needed a father, but Tammy needed Ty even
more for herself. In the past, she had pushed Ty about marriage and he had always balked. It sounded as if he'd changed.
She had to hope that was true. She wanted happiness. She
wanted a family.

They belonged together.

She ran her hand over her stomach.

Oh, Lord, what if she was making a fool of herself?

Ty ENTERED THE house and stopped, arrested by the sight of a
pale yellow sweater on the floor of his entryway.

He would think it was Ruby's, but she had left yesterday.
Besides, the sweater hadn't been there this morning when he
had left for work.

Farther along the hallway, a yellow skirt lay on the floor.
What the—?

He picked it up and recognized it. Tammy had worn it on

the Fourth of July, to his barbecue. He hadn't realized then that it had a big elastic insert for her expanding belly.

What was it doing in his house, on his floor? A black stocking lay on the stairs, and farther up, another one hung on the banister. He picked it up and rubbed it between his fingers. Soft, like silk. Maybe it was silk. He didn't know these things.

A garter circled the newel post. He picked it up and scrunched it in his fist. Tammy was in his house. His breath caught in his throat. Thank you, Jesus.

Tammy was here and, unless he missed his guess, was naked upstairs, or wearing pretty damn little.

He took the stairs two at a time.

A bra lay on the carpet and a pair of lacy black panties hung from his doorknob.

His hands shaking, he opened the door...and there she was, naked on his bed and blooming with pregnancy, and beautiful enough to break his heart. To rob him of breath. To send him to heaven.

He approached slowly, afraid that if he moved too quickly, she would disappear, that he would find she'd only been a mirage.

Her body fascinated him. Her breasts were bigger, the nipples swollen and ready to feed their babe after she gave birth, and her belly was large, round, hard.

"Take off your shirt," she whispered.

He did, unbuttoning slowly because his fingers were clumsy. He would do anything Tammy asked of him, if only she would stay. He shrugged out of his shirt and she smiled.

"Take off your pants."

He unbuckled his belt, unzipped his jeans then pulled them off, taking his boots and socks off at the same time. She watched his every move, the look in her eyes avid.

"Take off those." She pointed to his underwear.

He took them off, unhooking them from the erection that had already started to burgeon.

When he stepped toward the bed, she asked, "Who am I?"

He shook his head, trying to catch his breath, to regain his senses. "What?"

"Who am I?" she repeated.

A slow smile crept across his lips. "Tammy."

"Right answer." Tammy smiled and opened her arms.

He stepped into them, his weight dipping the mattress. She rolled against him.

"You're really here." His voice broke, backed up as it was with tenderness and gratitude and relief. And love.

They kissed and Ty had never tasted anything as beautiful as Tammy's lips. He drank in hints of her favorite black tea with orange zest. At some point this afternoon, she'd eaten something with cinnamon in it.

He ran his hands over her shoulders, her collarbone, her breasts and her stomach.

She touched every part of him she could reach. "Oh, Ty, it's been so long."

She turned her back to him and he positioned himself to enter her, taking it slow and easy. He'd never made love to a pregnant woman.

"I don't want to hurt you."

"You won't."

"I don't want to hurt the baby."

"Just take it slowly."

He did. Her body welcomed him by degrees, with warmth and moisture and womanly acceptance.

He cupped her breasts then reached a hand below her belly to arouse her. Her breathing hitched and she moaned.

Slowly, delicately, her scent tinted the air. Ty drank in the beauty of it.

For hours they loved each other with their bodies, with

hands and lips, with promises whispered in dirty words. In sweet phrases.

"Ty," Tammy whispered, "marry me."

Ty closed his eyes, wrapped her in a loving embrace and said, "Yes."

CHAPTER SEVENTEEN

"I'VE SPENT MORE TIME in Accord in the past six months than I have for my whole life." Nick pulled his stiff shirt collar away from his neck.

The tuxedo rental shop hadn't got the size right. He should have brought his own.

He stood at the altar beside Gabe, who stood beside Ty. Nick had expected Ty to be nervous on his wedding day, but no. The man was as cool as a cucumber.

Nick could never get married again, let alone look so confident doing it.

A few stragglers still entered the church.

Laura Cameron walked in just as a shaft of September sunlight flowed into the church, setting her chestnut hair on fire. She wore a purple dress that he suspected was a maternity dress because she looked wider than when he'd left.

The baby was growing.

His baby was growing.

Her skin shone. He didn't know what kind of vitamins she was taking, or whether hormones did that to a woman, but she glowed from within.

Five months later, he still didn't know what to do about the baby. For a man of decision, it rankled.

Laura slipped into a seat in the back row.

The church was full. Ty was respected not only in town, but also in the county, for his law-keeping skills, his cool head and his steady character.

The wedding march started and Ruby and Emily walked

down the aisle, pretty in pink ballet-length gowns with big white bows at their waists. At least, Emily had called them ballet-length. What did he know?

Pride constricted Nick's throat, made his vision mist.

His preteen daughter was already a striking beauty, not to mention a smart cookie, and growing up too quickly for comfort.

He winked at her and she grinned.

Tammy entered the aisle behind the girls, breathtakingly gorgeous in a one-shoulder white gown that started with a small bow on her shoulder and draped across the oversize beach ball she carried in her belly then ended at her knees.

Even at nine months, she looked elegant.

Apparently, she was due in two weeks. Nick thought they should have waited until after the baby was born, but neither Ty nor Tammy would agree.

Despite what a pretty bride Tammy made, Nick's eye was drawn to Laura. He hadn't seen her since that last game he'd coached before he and Emily returned home for the rest of the summer.

Funny that he'd been dying to get back home, but life in Seattle had felt flat.

He pushed himself at work, but hired a second assistant so he could continue in his promise to spend more time with Emily.

He took her out to shows and museums.

Seattle was his home, where he did business, so why did it feel so flat even while he spent more time with his daughter? Because they'd had more fun here in Accord.

Laura noticed him watching her and stared back, her eyes wide, as caught up in the moment as he. When he'd left Accord, they'd been friends, a concept foreign to Nick—to be friends with a woman to whom he felt so attracted. Shared interests and their few warm conversations added depth to that confounding crazy-hot attraction.

Time stretched on until Gabe nudged him with an elbow. Startled, he turned to his brother.

Oh. Tammy had already arrived at the front and they were all supposed to be facing the minister.

His face burned, which was strange. He never blushed.

The ceremony was beautiful and Nick felt for his brother. He and Tammy were making their own brand of happiness and Nick couldn't be more proud of Ty for taking that huge chance on the Fourth of July to bring his family together as best he could.

Good for him for marrying the woman he loved and for Gabe, too, for marrying Callie.

Later, after the ceremony and after the couple's first dance, people started coming up to him and asking questions like, "When are you going to make an honest woman out of Laura?"

It seemed that everyone in town knew his business, and what he should do about it.

He cornered Laura and asked, "What the hell is going on?"

Her eyes widened. The soft smile fell from her lips like water.

He went on, angry and heedless, "Did you tell everyone that I was the father and wouldn't marry you? They're all acting like you're the pretty little sheep and I'm the big bad wolf."

She stiffened. "I told no one anything. I don't know how they found out. If I'd told them I wouldn't have slanted the story that way. I've tried to be more than fair with you." She looked down at his fingers wrapped around her upper arm, wrinkling the fabric of her sleeve. "Let go of me."

He did and she walked away without another word, head high. She looked confident, strong, but he'd already figured out that he had the power to hurt her. He'd certainly shot down their fledgling friendship.

By the time Ty and Tammy were ready to cut the cake,

Nick was ready to plant a fist into the face of the next person who tried to meddle in his life.

While servers handed out cake, Tammy turned her back on the crowd to throw her bouquet. Single women lined up behind her. A bunch of women coaxed—and pushed—Laura into the line with the other women. The bouquet barreled toward her and she put her hand out to stop it from hitting her face.

Unfortunately, instinct kicked in and her fingers curled around it. She'd "caught" the flowers.

Nick smirked. Some lucky sod would marry Laura someday but it wouldn't be him.

An older man he couldn't remember—Nick must have known who he was at some point because the man had lived his entire life in Accord—said, "Laura deserves better than to be given the shaft. When are you going to marry her?"

"Never," he shouted, no longer worried about what people thought. He was sick to death of his life being everyone else's business. "I'm never going to marry Laura Cameron. Got it?"

"Yeah. I think the whole room got it."

Too late, Nick noticed his surroundings. The room was quiet. Laura stood a short distance away clutching the bouquet. A waiter shoved a small plate with cake on it into her other hand. She dropped the flowers, stepped close and said to Nick, "I haven't asked you to marry me. You would be the *last* man I'd choose."

She rammed the cake against his chest and walked away.

Damn it. She shouldn't have heard that. He picked up a napkin from a table and wiped the cake from the front of his shirt. Pink-and-blue icing stained the white cotton.

Later, he saw her dancing with a muscled handsome man.

"Gabe," he said, "who's the guy on steroids dancing with Laura?"

Gabe glanced down at Nick's shirt. "Battle scar?"

Nick shot him a repressive look. "Who's the guy?"

"Her former fiancé."

Vin. "He's got a lot of nerve showing his face."

Gabe shrugged. "He was part of the community for years. Things didn't work out between them. It happens."

Nick didn't care. "That man hurt Laura."

"And you didn't?" Gabe shook his head, his voice ripe with disgust. "Your hypocrisy is showing. The whole room heard what you said about her."

Gabe walked away and Nick stared after him. He'd only said he wouldn't marry her. That guy, Vin, had promised to and had then backed out. Vin had hurt her more. Nick honored any commitment he made in business. He might be ruthless, but at least he followed through on promises.

He stalked onto the dance floor.

"I'm cutting in."

Laura stared at him. Muscle boy asked, "Are you the guy who knocked up Laura?"

"Are *you* the guy who knocked her up and then ran out on her?" Nick countered.

"Hey, man, I would have stayed around and supported the baby."

"Lucky for you she lost it and you can't prove that."

"Who the hell are you? You aren't sticking around, either."

"I'll pay her child support. I won't leave her hanging in the breeze."

"I wouldn't have, either."

"And yet, you left her the second she lost the baby. Nice support."

"Listen, you—"

They realized at the same moment that Laura was no longer there. They muttered expletives at each other then walked away.

Nick needed to find her and apologize. He should have never shouted to the entire room, in effect, to the whole town, that he wouldn't marry her.

He found her outside sitting on a bench with her eyes closed and her face turned up. A cooling September breeze had kicked up and had sent the day's stifling humidity packing.

"Are you okay?" he asked.

She opened her eyes, but didn't look at him. "I'm too busy to talk to you."

"Doing what?"

"Digging more deeply than I've ever had to in my life for patience." Her index finger popped out of her fist to point at him. "I've just had one man yell to the whole world that he will never marry me. I don't want you to. I neither expected nor asked you to."

Her middle finger popped up to join the first. "I've had Cro-Magnon man, who ran out on me when I lost my baby, chastise me for getting pregnant with a man I didn't plan to marry and I, an intelligent woman, never once realized in five years what a chauvinist he is."

A third finger joined the first two. "And last, but not least, I've had the two of you fight over me on the dance floor in front of God and the whole town and who knows who else."

Her fingers curled back into her fist.

"I'm responsible for my life. I hold no one else accountable for my mistakes. I will take care of this baby and will never, ever make her feel like a mistake. I will take child support payments from you because it is the right thing to do, because this baby shouldn't have to pay for *our* mistake. But do I need either you or Vin? No. I'm blessedly, happily independent. Take your posturing and fighting elsewhere. From now on, I won't have anything to do with either of you. I'm stronger on my own."

She left the garden, alone and independent and strong and magnificent. She was right. She didn't need him or spineless Vin. He felt the loss of their fledgling friendship.

Warrior woman Laura would raise a strong, independent

child. Unlike him, she would parent her baby beautifully. The child would get the attention and the guidance she deserved.

Laura would do a hell of a lot better raising this baby than he had ever done with Emily.

He thanked the higher power, whoever or whatever it was, and Marsha for doing for Emily what he had failed to do.

Rushing through the wedding guests, he found Emily sitting in the side garden drinking punch with Ruby and giggling.

"Hey," he said.

She started, guiltily.

"Give me that." He took the punch from her and tasted it. "Someone spiked this. Give me." He flicked his fingers at Ruby and she handed over her glass. He poured both into the bushes. "Come on. Let's get you something nonalcoholic to drink."

He shook his head while they followed him. "God, girls, you're only twelve."

They giggled behind him. Lord save him from everything he knew he was about to go through in Emily's adolescence.

He handed them both cans of soda, unopened, so he knew they hadn't been tampered with.

On impulse, he took Emily's face between his hands and leaned his lips on her forehead. God, he loved her. Oh dear God, he loved the daylights out of her.

He thanked God that he hadn't screwed her up, that she had a father who had finally seen the light, and he prayed that he hadn't come to his senses too late for his daughter.

He let her go and the girls walked away. He caught a glimpse of Laura. A breeze through the open window pressed her dress against her expanding belly.

That baby would have no father.

But it would have the monetary support it would need to grow up healthy and safe.

But it would have no father.

Déjà vu.

Just like Emily in her younger years.

Maybe Laura would find a man who loved her, who was more developed than either he or Cro-Magnon Vin, who would take on the baby as his own and give it the fathering it would need.

Acid burned in his stomach. Acid? No. Anger. He didn't want another man raising his child. He didn't want another man touching Laura.

You don't want to raise the baby yourself, though, do you?

Nor do you want to commit to Laura in any way, so grow up and let her move on with her life. Let her find someone else.

He headed to the bar and ordered a Scotch. Neat.

OLIVIA STOOD AT the bar alone having a martini when she heard Nick Jordan yell that he would never marry Laura Cameron.

She watched Laura smash a slice of cake against his chest then walk away. A moment later, she managed to find her daughter in the washroom.

"What was that all about?" she asked. "Why would Nick Jordan be talking about marrying you?"

"You mean talking about *not* marrying me," Laura replied, her tone bitter.

"What's going on?"

"You haven't heard? I don't know how the word leaked out, but I guess it was only a matter of time. Nick is the baby's father."

Laura might as well have slapped Olivia. "What?" she said faintly. "Nick Jordan? But I thought you hated him."

"I did."

"Apparently, not anymore."

"Not for a while. I might start again, though. He's behaving like an ass tonight."

"What is he going to do about the baby?"

"He has offered child support and I have accepted it."

"How about paying medical bills?"

"I haven't asked him to."

"Ask him. Having a baby costs a small fortune."

"I'll see what I can do."

"Will he be around for the baby?"

"I don't want him here. This is my baby and no one else's."

"Are you sure that's wise?" Olivia touched Laura's shoulder. "You've always wanted a whole family."

Laura leaned her cheek against Olivia's hand. "I know, but I don't have a choice. This wasn't what I had planned at all."

"All of those things I said about not wanting to be a grandmother?"

Laura nodded.

"I take them back. I want this baby, too." Olivia had been doing some hard thinking. She was what she was. Her age couldn't be changed. It was what it was.

"Oh, Mom, thank you. I want this baby to know her grandmother."

Olivia held Laura until she said, "Mom, I need to be alone for a few minutes, okay?"

"Okay, sweetie. I love you." She kissed Laura's forehead and then left the washroom.

Aiden leaned against the wall, waiting for her. She'd known he was at the wedding, but she'd been avoiding him.

"I want to dance with you," he said.

"I'd like that." The band was playing a slow song. Why not? Why the hell not? Here, in public, she could hold him, she could be held by him, without worrying about Aiden wanting to take it further. Without fighting her own almost-overwhelming temptation to give in to the man.

She could be held by him here where it was safe.

He danced as well as he did everything, with a natural athletic grace.

She reveled in the warmth of his embrace, in the divine strength of his arms around her.

"You dance well," he said, his voice a rumble in his chest and an exhalation of breath near her ear.

"So do you," she murmured with her eyes closed, savoring the moment.

"Have you changed your mind? About us?"

"No."

His embrace tightened, briefly.

"I'm going to bring your metal piece over tomorrow."

"I'll have a check ready for you."

"No. I told you. It's a gift from me."

"But—"

"Be quiet." He softened the order with a "Please."

"Okay. Come over at two."

The following afternoon, Olivia opened her front door.

Aiden stood with the melting vaginal petal in his arms. Goodness, the man was strong.

"Where do you want it?"

"Upstairs."

He followed her up the stairs and she led him to her bedroom.

"In here. Over there."

He put it down where she directed then turned and studied her.

"Aiden, no," she whispered. *Don't tempt me.*

He left without another word.

Olivia stared at the petal and wanted to weep that fate would have them come onto this earth at the wrong time for each other.

CHAPTER EIGHTEEN

NICK SAT IN HIS HOME office going over documents that had been sent to him by a client. Since the contracts leaned far too far in the client's favor, Nick's pen hadn't stopped marking them up in the past ten minutes.

He didn't know where the autumn was going. It was already late November and he hadn't finished work on the Fellows contract let alone starting work on the new O'Connor deal.

His door slammed open, startling him.

"Dad! I know you told me not to bother you, but I have to." Emily ran into the room clutching the telephone.

"What's wrong, Emily?"

"It's Uncle Ty on the phone. He needs to talk to you. Right now. He sounds really tense."

Nick took the phone. To avoid interruptions, he purposely hadn't put one in the office. It allowed him to get through whatever work he had to bring home more efficiently so he could spend more time with Emily.

"Ty? What's up?"

"You might want to get down here. Laura's in the hospital."

Nick had been leaning back in his seat, but shot forward. "Why?"

"Something to do with the baby. I don't know if she's losing it or what, but an ambulance was called to the bakery. Apparently, there was blood on the floor in the kitchen."

"I'll be right there."

He handed the phone to Emily. "I have to go to Accord."

"I'll come, too."

"Not this time, Emily. You have school."

She followed him upstairs to his room. He took a carry-on out of the closet and tossed in jeans and a couple of sweaters and underwear.

"Why are you going?" Emily asked. "What's wrong?"

"Laura is in the hospital."

"So what?"

"I don't know. I think there's a problem with her baby."

"So why does she need you there?"

"She doesn't need me." She really didn't. She was strong. She would survive whatever happened, but he didn't want her in pain. She didn't need more sorrow and grief. She'd been through enough. He didn't want anything to happen to her. He didn't want her to lose her baby.

"So if she doesn't need you, why are you going?"

"She might lose the baby."

"So what? That would solve all of our problems."

His pulse lurched. He didn't want that kind of solution to this problem.

"It would devastate Laura." She would need a friend. Despite his asinine behavior at Ty's wedding, he didn't want Laura hurting. He did want to support her.

Besides, he'd slept with her that one night. He hadn't planned it and, with the different perspective that time and distance allowed, he knew she hadn't planned it, either.

He wasn't a man to sleep around easily. She wasn't a woman who slept around. They didn't do one-night stands. So, in effect, for that one night, they'd become involved with each other. They'd had a relationship.

He'd wanted her. Not just any woman. *Her.*

As far as he could tell, Laura had wanted *him.* Not just any man. Not a father for her baby. She'd wanted a deep, strong, emotional, insanely hot relationship with him. In the nature of their relationship with each other, it had lasted one night.

Because their night together had been more than a one-night stand, because they *knew* each other and cared in their screwed-up way, he had to go to her now.

"I have to go," he said.

Emily started to cry and left the room.

He couldn't go to her or he would miss the only flight going out to Denver today.

He phoned Mort to ask him to come stay with her. He said he would head right over.

The flight to Denver took too long, as did the drive to the hospital outside of Accord.

At Information, he asked to see Laura. She'd been admitted and he took the elevator to the second floor.

He rounded a corner and found the correct room.

Laura lay in a bed hooked up to an IV, looking pale and tired.

Her hands were swollen. He touched one. She woke up. When she saw him, her eyes widened.

"Sorry," he said. "I didn't mean to wake you."

"I was only dozing."

"What happened?"

"I started to go into labor."

Because Marsha had handled all of the details of her pregnancy while Nick established himself in her father's company, he knew little about pregnancy and complications.

"Isn't it too early?" he asked, figuring that much out at least.

She nodded. In her eyes lurked fear. She'd had a miscarriage before. She must be scared to death to lose this baby.

"What are you doing in Accord?" she asked.

Nick frowned. "I came to see you. Ty called. He thought you might be losing the baby."

"You came for this?"

"Of course."

Her fingers tightened perceptibly in his. "I thought you hated me."

He felt a lot of things for her, a weird amalgam of affection and resentment and who knew what else. He never did look at those kinds of things too closely.

"I don't hate you and I don't want you to lose the baby."

"I don't want to, either, Nick."

"I know. Tell me what's happening." Without letting go of her—he didn't think she would let him—he hooked a chair with his foot and dragged it over to the bed before sitting down.

"It's premature labor. Oh, Nick, if the baby were born now, it would be so tiny. It would have to fight for its life."

He tried to imagine being so small and helpless, hooked up to machines for survival. Right now, it was where it was supposed to be, inside the safety of Laura's warm and giving body.

"What can we do about it?" he asked. "How can we prevent it from coming so early?"

Her fingers tightened their grip on his. "Bed rest."

"What's wrong with that?" he asked, responding to the bitterness in her voice.

"I've got a grand opening scheduled for two weeks before Christmas. I'm closing for a week to take that dividing wall down and to finish the place and to bake like there's no tomorrow. I'm big and I'm slow and tired all of the time and now I've got to stay in bed."

He kissed her fingers. "It's for the baby's health."

"I know. I'll do anything for the baby, but I don't know what to do about my other obligations. I've hired all of these servers who think they have jobs starting on Opening Day."

She stared at the ceiling. "I was trying to get it all done before the baby arrived."

"Who is the doctor taking care of you?"

She gave him a name.

"I'm going to talk to her."

She nodded, her eyelids drooping. In a minute or two, she would be asleep.

While he watched, something…happened. Under the thin sheet, her belly moved, a bump rippled along under her skin.

He placed his palm on the huge mound that was her pregnant stomach, and a second later, a tiny elbow or knee brushed his hand.

He snatched it back, the wonder of it backing up in his throat. He put his hand on her again and the baby brushed against him, as though they were communicating, as though the baby were saying, "Daddy, play with me!"

All of those missed times with Emily came back to haunt him, all of those moments when he'd been too busy for her.

Another child would be born and would live through all of those missed moments, through opportunities squandered.

All hail the god of commerce and business.

It was his life, though. He didn't know how to leave it, didn't know who to be without it. In his office, in his world, he felt real, needed, useful.

This was real, too. This baby he'd thought of as a tiny amorphous thing was real, was "talking" to him from the uterus. He was overwhelmed by the responsibility.

He might not be able to help the unborn baby, knew he would spend the rest of his life missing her growing up, but he could help her mother. And he would.

He went in search of her doctor and finally found her.

"Can you tell me what's going on with Laura Cameron?"

"It depends. Who are you?"

"Nick Jordan. The baby's father."

The doctor nodded. She was only a few years older than him, trim and tall with short dark curls and eyes that had seen a lot.

"Laura is in preterm labor."

"What does that mean?" Nick asked.

"In layman's terms, premature labor."

"What will happen?"

"If she gives birth now, the baby will be very small and at risk."

"Meaning it could die?"

"Oh, yes."

"How can you change it? If her body wants to give birth now, how do you stop it?"

"I've put her on a tocolytic to suppress labor and inhibit contractions. In case she does deliver, she's also on a corticosteroid to help the baby's lungs mature. We want to give the baby a fighting chance."

"So, will she be hospitalized until she gives birth?"

"No. We'll keep her overnight for observation and then send her home. She will be bedridden, though. We don't want to take chances."

"But she's got a business to run."

The doctor stiffened so subtly, Nick almost missed the movement.

"She'll have to make a choice between the baby and the business."

"No contest," he said. "She'll choose the baby."

The doctor seemed to relax. "Good. She'll need support in the coming weeks. Despite our best efforts, anything could still happen."

"Okay. I'll stay to help her until the baby's born."

Once more, Accord beckoned, and once more, he answered the call.

He phoned Emily and explained what was happening.

"You're going to stay there?" Her nose sounded stuffy. Had she been crying all this time? "For how long?"

"I don't know. Until Laura seems stable, I guess."

"Come home soon."

"I will. Guess what. I felt the baby today. It moved against my hand."

Silence.

He cursed. He'd said the wrong thing. She didn't want to have anything to do with the baby. She especially didn't want to hear him express anything that remotely resembled happiness.

Nick was in a foul mood.

He phoned Ty. He needed to talk to him. "Do you mind if I stay at your place tonight? Or should I go to the B and B?"

"Go to my place. I'll pick up something for dinner."

By the time he got to Ty's, his mood wasn't any better and he guessed that the root of his mood was fear. He was smart enough to figure that much out. The doctor had scared the daylights out of him. The baby could die. They should have got rid of it right at the beginning.

Wasn't it funny that neither he nor Laura had ever thought of that? They had accepted that she was pregnant and that she would have the baby and that was that.

They would do what they had to do to keep the baby alive and inside of Laura for as long as possible. So why this foul mood?

Was it because Emily didn't want to accept the baby? So what? Neither did Nick, not really, despite those moments of magical touch with the baby still in Laura's womb.

The plan hadn't changed. He would give her child support and that was it. The purpose of this trip? He was here to help a friend.

He took a beer out of the fridge, but his hands shook when he tried to open it. He slammed it onto the counter.

What if the baby died? How on earth could Laura lose another baby? He'd seen her grief at the cemetery his first afternoon in Accord.

Ty walked in, his arms full of grocery bags with the organic market's logo on them.

"If you're going to buy organic," Nick said, his tone peevish, "you should use your own reusable bags."

He couldn't stand anything illogical in life.

Ty put the bags on the counter, crossed his arms and stared at Nick.

"What's wrong with Laura?"

Nick handed the can of beer to Ty. "Open this."

Ty did and gave it back to him.

Nick took a long draw on it and then said, "Preterm labor."

Tammy walked into the kitchen with her baby on her hip. She'd given birth a week after the wedding. That's what Nick called cutting it close.

The baby stared at Nick, wide-eyed. It wore a pink polka-dot sleeper.

"Laura? Oh, that's far too early," Tammy said. "Is she still in the hospital?"

"Yes."

"I'll go visit her tomorrow." She kissed Ty.

"You manage to get a nap while Rebecca napped?" he asked.

Tammy nodded. "That's what I was doing when I heard Nick come in."

"Sorry if I scared you when I barged in," he said.

"You didn't. Ty called to warn me you were coming to town and would probably stay with us."

She sat down at the kitchen table. The baby had been fussing. Tammy threw a small blanket over her shoulder then reached up under the top she wore and fooled around with something.

To Nick's horror, he realized she was getting ready to breast-feed the baby. Didn't women do things like that in private? He spun around and glared out the window at Ty's backyard.

"What's really wrong?" Ty asked. "You seem madder than you should be that there are complications in the pregnancy."

"Yes," Tammy said while tiny snuffling noises came from her chest area. Nick peeked over his shoulder. The baby, and Tammy's breast, were hidden under the blanket, thank God. "Preterm labor is bad, but you seem more angry than worried."

Nick felt bile rise into his throat just thinking about it. "What if the baby dies?"

"Nick, the baby won't die. Preterm labor doesn't have to be a death sentence," Tammy said, watching him carefully. "Wait a minute. You're worried about Laura, aren't you?"

"She's already lost one baby. It would kill her to lose another."

"It's more than that. You're afraid for Laura's health, too, aren't you?"

He nodded.

"The doctors will take care of her. She'll take care of herself. She'll do everything to keep her baby safe."

"Who will keep her safe?"

"You?" Tammy asked.

Him. What a responsibility.

Still she watched him steadily while the baby made snuffling noises under the blanket.

"What?" he asked. "Why are you staring at me?"

"You love her."

"No!" he shouted, rounding on her, breast-feeding be damned. "I don't. I really don't. I'm just worried. You don't know what the hell you're talking about."

"That's it," Ty said, grabbing his shirt and manhandling him into the living room. "I get that you're angry and worried about the situation with Laura, but you can't take it out on Tammy."

"I wasn't taking it out on her."

"You raised your voice to her."

"Sorry," Nick mumbled. He brought his temper under control. "This has got me tied up in knots. I don't know why."

He paced from one end of the room to the other. "I handle everything life throws at me. I have control of my business, and trust me, there's a lot of stress there. I mean, these are million- and billion-dollar deals. I handle it all. I can't take this, though. I don't know why."

"Were you this stressed when Emily was born?"

"No."

"Why not?"

"I wasn't around that much. Marsha handled the pregnancy and the birth on her own."

"Laura's handling the pregnancy on her own. She's willing to raise the baby on her own. She can, too. That woman can do anything she sets her mind to."

"I know, but I feel more responsible this time." He struggled to remember. "I don't think I ever saw Marsha breastfeed Emily."

"You don't plan to be around for this, other than sending a monthly check, so I still don't get what's so different this time."

Nick sat on the edge of an armchair and leaned his elbows on his knees. He dropped his face into his hands and rammed his fingers into his hair. "I guess I've come to care more for Laura than I did for Marsha, which is weird because I've spent a fraction of the time with her that I did with my wife."

"I always thought Marsha was a means to an end with you."

"Yeah, she was. I wanted to work for Mort."

"Poor Marsha."

"She knew what she was getting into. I never lied to her."

"How about Emily?"

"Marsha wanted a child. I never had time for Emily when she was young. I'm making amends for that now. She seems happy with me."

"Are you happy with her?"

"I couldn't care for her more. I treasure our time together. I love her."

"You could come to the same place with this baby."

"I had Emily without thought. I know better now how much children deserve. I can't give this new baby what it should have."

"Our parents really did a number on us."

Nick jumped up out of the chair. "What about our parents?"

"Look how much trouble Gabe and I had finally claiming some love for ourselves. Look how much trouble you're having with this."

This was what had been sending a chill down Nick's spine the entire drive from the hospital to the ranch. "Something about our parents wasn't right. I keep having these vague thoughts, memories. Darkness. What happened with them?"

He stared out the front window. "I mean, Dad wasn't there. He climbed a lot and then he died when I was only five. What did he have to do with my life?"

"You need to hear some things so you understand this family better."

Darkness rippled along Nick's nerve endings. "Something happened before Dad went away the last time, didn't it?"

"Do you remember what it was?" Ty asked.

"I remember yelling. I remember hiding in my room."

"Five-year-olds don't always understand what's going on around them. What do you remember about Dad?"

"He was big, gregarious, fun. Everybody loved him. Right?"

"Right. He was more than that, though. He was driven and ambitious and inclined toward getting his own way. Made him hard to live with."

"So what? Mom adored him."

"Yes and no."

"What the hell does that mean?" They'd had a good marriage. Nick knew it. Mom had idolized Dad. She'd told him so often enough.

"I mean exactly what I said. Dad could be incredibly hard for her to live with. I don't know all of it. Gabe would know more. He was older. You should ask him about it sometime."

Maybe he would talk to Gabe at some point, but Ty was here. Nick was here. He wanted answers now.

"Tell me what you know."

"Dad's climbing put a heavy load on our stretched resources. When he climbed Everest he paid $25,000 to the Nepalese government for a license. Do you know how much food that can buy a family of five? How many pairs of shoes that kids run through like they're made of paper? That's just the license. What about the cost of the gear? There was no point in going if he didn't have the right gear to make sure he would survive."

Good Lord, he'd never realized.

"While Dad was training and climbing, he wasn't bringing in income. They fought about money. A lot. Loudly."

Ty looked queasy, as though there were more to come that Nick wasn't going to want to hear, that made Ty uncomfortable, too.

"The night before he left for Everest, she actually said, 'If you leave tomorrow, don't come back.' He didn't."

A train might as well have flattened Nick. Oh, Mom. Oh, God. The guilt after Dad's death, after saying something like that to him in anger, would have devastated her. No wonder she hadn't coped well.

Ty had heard it all. No wonder he looked sick. Nick could imagine how loud the fight must have been in that small house. There would have been nowhere to hide from the angry voices, from the things Mom and Dad said, hurtful words hurled at each other like missiles. Nick suspected that part of the darkness inside of him was a room where those words still lived. After all, he had been only five. He would have been in the house. He would have heard that fight.

"Mom would have never meant it," Nick whispered.

"No, but she would have lived with terrible guilt after he died up there."

"She was scared about money."

"Probably feared for his life, too. Was afraid that he'd be injured or die. Unfortunately for all of us, he died."

"Knowing Mom, for the rest of her life, she would regret that instead of telling him she loved him, she told him to not come back."

"She did love him. She told me so. I once asked her about that fight. She couldn't talk about it much, but she did say that she'd loved Dad and regretted everything she'd said that night."

It explained so much. So, all of those things Nick had offered her over the years, including a new house? She hadn't been keeping the old one as a shrine to Dad. She hadn't taken the things he'd offered because of her guilt. She'd been paying a penance in keeping things as they were, in thinking that she deserved no more than what she lived with.

Oh, Mom, you deserved.

Nick wished he'd known this information years earlier. Then again, he might not have been ready for it. He felt as if he was only just growing up now. Finally.

"Gabe had to do everything, Nick."

"I know. He had to cook and clean and watch out for us."

"No," Ty said, his voice quiet. "I mean, immediately after we learned about Dad's death, Gabe had to take over. Mom fell apart."

"Can you blame her?" Nick asked sharply.

"No, but Gabe was only ten. He grew up overnight. He talked to a funeral director about organizing a service to celebrate Dad's life. We needed something to aid our grieving. To bring closure. There was no body to bury. It was too dangerous to bring the body down from Everest. Besides, how

could we have afforded to send an expedition up there to re-
trieve his body? Gabe arranged the service."

Nick had always known Dad's body was still up on top of
Everest but had never thought about what that would have
meant to the family immediately after his death.

"Gabe called neighbors, Mom's friends, church ladies,
anyone he thought might help, and asked if they would bring
food to the house after the service. He bought paper plates
and serviettes and plastic forks. Jesus, Nick, he was just a
kid."

Nick's vision misted, for the first time his grief directed
toward Gabe. Jesus, what a burden for a boy to bear.

Nick couldn't deny that what Gabe had done was pretty
miraculous for a boy his age. Saint Gabe, all right.

For the first time in his life, he regretted that he'd been
so young when his father died. He would have helped Gabe
with everything.

"What do you think that has to do with now?" Nick asked.
"With Laura and the baby?"

"You must have been in the house that last night. Their
fight was nuclear. You would have heard everything. My
guess is you blocked it out, but it would have gone underground, Nick. You would still be carrying scars from that
battle."

"Yeah, but *what* scars?"

Ty shrugged. "I don't know. I imagine they're the same for
all of us, but unique, too. Don't forget that our lives changed
in different ways after that. You became Mom's favorite. I
think that was good for you, but screwed you up, too. It kept
you apart from me and Gabe. It made you think you deserved
more in life than you had. It made you work pretty damn
hard to make a lot of money. What a great marriage you entered into with Marsha, one in which you really didn't have
to care, which engaged none of your emotions. You sure do
care about Laura, though, don't you?"

Nick could only nod. What a mess.

He rubbed his temple where one of his old headaches was forming—the first one in months.

He wasn't flying back to Seattle and leaving Laura in the lurch for the next month. Neither could he sit here for a month doing nothing.

He called Rachel. "Get down here to Accord."

"But Thursday is Thanksgiving. I'm visiting my family in Olympia."

Nick cursed. He'd forgotten about the holiday. "Go celebrate with your family, but send the most urgent work to me at the B and B. Go to my house and pack up the contracts on my desk and ship them to me."

After he hung up, he sought out Ty and Tammy in the kitchen.

"I'm going to stay in town. I can't leave Laura now, but I need to get a bunch of work done. Rachel's going to ship work to the B and B."

"You can have one of the bedrooms to use as an office."

"Thanks, Ty, but it's probably smart for me to be in town. Kristi has an office in the hotel that I can fax from. I can receive them there, too, in case there's something urgent to be taken care of."

Ty looked worried.

"Take it easy, Ty. I just don't want to leave Laura in the lurch."

"Tell her I can come right over if she needs me," Tammy said then ran off to change a diaper that reeked.

"God, breast milk makes baby's poop stink? It's all natural. Shouldn't that mean it's pure, or something? That the poop should be pure and natural."

Ty laughed at Nick's expression. "It's still shit, Nick."

"Babies are messy."

"Life is messy."

After settling in at the B and B and spending a restless night, Nick drove to the hospital to pick up Laura.

CHAPTER NINETEEN

NICK FOUND LAURA sitting on the bed trying to put her socks on.

"If you dare laugh," she said, the strain in her voice so dark it swallowed sunlight, "I will personally eviscerate you, slowly and painfully."

Nick hid a smile and got down on his knees to put her shoes on for her. His humor disappeared when he saw how swollen her ankles were. He rubbed her instep gently with his thumb.

"On the other hand," she said, sounding infinitely better because of that simple touch, "if you keep that up, I'll bake a cake for you, a chocolate layer cake with the best chocolate icing on earth. Not too sweet. Light as a feather. The whole thing just for you."

Her eyes were closed and her head was hanging back. Lord, she was a sensual creature.

He smiled and put her shoes on. He would give her a massage when they got home. To her apartment, that was.

He helped her up her back stairs. She'd put on a lot of weight, the baby weight spreading across her hips more than it had on Tammy.

"No comments about how big my behind is, no *thoughts* about how big it is, or that chocolate cake never gets made."

Upstairs, she went straight to an armchair and sat down. She looked tired. They'd stopped at the pharmacy to fill her two prescriptions.

"Here," he said, handing her a glass of water and today's pills.

Under her sink in the kitchen, he found a bucket with two compartments, obviously for washing the floor, with one side for soapy water and the other clear for rinsing. It would be perfect for soaking Laura's feet.

He filled it with cool water and found bath oil in the washroom that smelled like incense. No wonder Laura always smelled so sexy.

In the living room, he set it down in front of her feet.

He searched through her CDs and put on Joni Mitchell's *Mingus*.

"Close your eyes," he said.

He took her shoes and socks off then lifted her poor swollen feet into the cool water.

She sighed.

"I'm going out for food. Stay put, okay?"

She nodded.

"I mean it. Don't get up for anything. I won't be gone long."

"Oh, don't worry. This feels heavenly. I'm not moving." A smile hovered on her lips.

He shopped at the organic market down the street, returned and loaded everything into the fridge.

Then he ran downstairs and looked in on the shop. It was busy. He went around behind the counter.

Two of the farm women Laura had hired in the summer were cleaning up the kitchen.

They looked up when he entered.

"Hello, Nick," they both said, and Nick was embarrassed that he didn't remember their names. Man, he had to get his head out of his rear end and start paying attention to those around him.

"Is there any chance I could hire you two to come up to Laura's apartment after you finish here today to cook her some meals and freeze them."

"Of course. How is she doing?" Wanda—or was it Norma?—asked.

"It was premature labor. The doctors have stabilized her and she's on bed rest."

"Poor thing."

"I picked up groceries."

He named everything he'd picked up. "Should I have got anything else?"

"It sounds like you bought out the store. We should be able to manage."

"I'll leave Laura's back door unlocked and tell her to expect you. Thank you, ladies." He pulled a couple of hundreds out of his wallet and handed them to the women. "Will that cover your labor?"

"It will do." They both grinned.

Okay, that was taken care of.

He slipped across the street to the B and B. He found Kristi in her office.

"Kristi, I'm going to be eating with Laura for the next few days." He'd already explained the situation to her when he'd checked in. "You have this pudding, though, that's really good. Some kind of custard with rice in it."

"It's rice pudding, Nick. Simple rice pudding."

There was nothing simple about it. It had wild rice and golden raisins in thick creamy custard.

"Do you have any?"

"How much do you want?"

"Four servings?"

"You got it. Want it packaged up now or do you want me to deliver it to Laura later?"

"Can you bring it over when you have a minute?"

"That would be after tea and before I start on dinner service."

"You're busy. I'll come back over and get it from you if you can have it boxed up by then."

He had this weird nurturing thing going on all of a sudden. He wanted Laura happy and taken care of.

Next, he went into the second storefront Laura had bought to see what needed to be done before the opening.

The interior took his breath away, just as the bakery had on his first day in town with Emily in the spring.

Except for that one brick wall on the far side, the colors Laura had chosen for the walls were deep and rich and stunning.

Paintings lined the wall, resting on the floor and still wrapped in brown paper to protect them.

He introduced himself to the contractor, who showed him around the kitchen. Once that dividing wall came down, it would be a baker's dream kitchen.

In a little more than a dozen years or so, Laura had taken a small normal bakery and had baked her way to success, living with odd, long hours and hard work, and this was what it had all led to. The woman was brilliant. He didn't know of many small businesses that were such a success.

"When is the wall coming down?"

"Laura's giving us three days in December—Sunday through Tuesday—to bring it down and then scour the place. She's hiring someone else to come in with the tables and chairs."

"Why do you need three days to knock out one wall?"

"It's a supporting wall, so we'll need to use supporting beams and then camouflage them so they go with the rest of the decor."

He brought the man up-to-date on Laura's medical issues. "If you need any questions answered, bring them to me. I'll either be upstairs at Laura's or across the street at the B and B."

"You got it. I won't bother Laura."

Nick returned upstairs to see how Laura was doing. Her feet must be prunes by now.

She was asleep, her feet still in the bucket.

He got a towel from the bathroom, knelt in front of her, lifted her feet out of the water and dried them.

She roused. "Oh, that was amazing."

"You need to get into bed."

"I can't. I have so much to do."

"Doctor's orders. Remember?"

She nodded. "This is going to be hard, Nick. I'm used to giving orders, not taking them. Doing, not sitting back and watching others work."

"I saw the renovations on the extension."

She perked up. "What do you think?"

"They're brilliant. It's warm and inviting. It's going to be the busiest place in town." A thought struck him. "Who did last night's baking?"

"Norma and Gayle came in early and followed some of my recipes."

Nick whistled. "Wow, two women doing what you usually do on your own."

"If they're any good, I'll keep them on as bakers. I've been working too hard for too many years. Maybe that's why I'm so tired with this pregnancy. I don't know."

Another thought struck. "They're going to be tired. I asked them to come up here and cook a bunch of meals for you when they finish downstairs. I didn't know they'd been up since the middle of the night."

He took her hand, helping her out of the armchair and leading her to the bedroom.

"You don't have to do so much, you know. I'm not an invalid."

"Change into something comfortable to sleep in while I rinse out the bucket."

He washed the bath oil out with soapy water then returned to the bedroom. Laura was already in bed.

Nick glanced up. He missed the colorful, beautiful, inspired gauze. "Why did you take it all down?"

"I was angry with my impulsive nature."

"With your passion?"

She nodded.

"That represented your passion?"

"Yes."

"Might as well try to deny that you need to breathe to live. You're a passionate woman, Laura."

"I know and look at the trouble it got me into." She raised her head to look at him at the end of the bed. "What are you doing?"

"Massaging your feet."

She moaned.

He moved up to her calves and then the backs of her knees. She yelped.

"Sensitive spot?" He grinned.

"Yes. That felt good on my calves. They ache sometimes with the extra weight I'm carrying."

He skimmed his hands back down and massaged them some more.

"I have to get back to the B and B. I have work to do. If you don't mind, I'll join you for dinner. The ladies will come in at some point to cook, but they won't disturb you."

Her eyes drifted shut.

The baby took a lot out of her, or was it the medication she was on that made her so sleepy? He didn't have a clue, but it looked as though sleep was exactly what she needed.

His fingers grew itchy and he couldn't help himself. He touched her belly. A tiny appendage grazed his palm.

Daddy, play!

Dear Lord, what a miracle. He left before he started to blubber all over Laura like a great big baby.

HE CAME BACK at five with rice pudding and a briefcase full of work in case Laura was still asleep.

As he walked down the hall to the living room, he noticed what he hadn't before. Laura had turned a small bedroom into a baby's room, with a crib and pale yellow walls and ducks that waddled along a white border. A white rocking chair sat in the corner, presumably for breast-feeding, Nick thought, but what did he know?

She was up and sitting in the armchair reading a book.

"Did you get enough sleep?" If his tone sounded censorious, too bad. She needed to take care of herself and the baby.

"If I nap any more, I won't be able to sleep tonight."

"What did the ladies cook for you?"

"I don't know. I was still in bed. The place smelled amazing, though."

He checked out the casserole dishes in the freezer. They were all clearly labeled. They'd made and individually portioned lasagna. There were also containers of macaroni and cheese.

"I take it pasta is good for babies?"

"The calcium in the cheese is."

He checked out the fridge.

"We have fried chicken and potato salad for dinner."

"Sounds great. Can we eat now? I could eat a horse."

Nick laughed. "Sure."

He laid out dinner on the small dining table and set out glasses of decaf iced tea.

"I brought over dessert from Kristi."

Laura stilled. "What?"

"Rice pudding."

"Oh my God, I love you. I'm making you two chocolate cakes after I deliver the baby." She sobered. "How am I going to spend the next month in bed? I'll go stir-crazy."

After they ate, Nick washed the dishes and worked on contracts while Laura read, then went home to his own bed in the B and B.

He called Emily to tell her good-night, but she was blue, grumpy.

"Honey, don't waste this time we have together now. Let's talk. Tell me about your day."

She mumbled a bit about classes then perked up when she shared the latest tidbits of school gossip. "I talked with Ruby today on Skype. She's going to see her dad in Accord for Christmas."

"Sounds great."

"Can we have Christmas there, too?"

"I'll see whether Ty is okay with that. Tammy lives in the house now with the baby so I don't know whether he has room. I'll find out."

"How is the baby?"

"She moved against my hand again today." He didn't bother to hold back his excitement since she'd asked about the baby.

She was quiet for so long he knew he'd said something wrong.

"What?" he asked.

"I meant Tammy's baby, Rebecca."

"Oh." He'd screwed up. "She's great. Pretty. You know, for a baby."

The call ended awkwardly. He'd spent so much time spring and summer and thus far into the fall building a relationship with his daughter, but tonight, it felt as though he was back to square one.

THE NEXT COUPLE of days settled quickly into a routine.

Early mornings, he worked on contracts then had breakfast downstairs.

Then he visited Laura and cooked her breakfast, made sure she had everything she needed then stopped in at the bakery to get the latest updates from Tilly and the Gems. He dropped in to the adjacent storefront to check on renovations then brought all of the news up to Laura.

He picked up lunch for her from one of the local restaurants, went back to the B and B while she napped and got as much work done as he could. He made necessary phone calls. He conferred with Mort. He had Rachel send more work.

Late afternoon, he returned to Laura's to warm dinner for both of them. He spent a couple of hours with her because he knew she was going stir-crazy. At about nine, he went back to his hotel room and called Emily.

Tonight he had good news for her. "Grandpa Mort's flying here with you tomorrow morning. I'll pick you up at the airport in Denver. We're having Thanksgiving at Ty's."

Emily squealed. "Thanks, Dad."

"Go pack. Grandpa's driving the two of you to the airport at noon. Don't keep him waiting. Okay?"

The call ended on a happy note and some of Nick's tension eased.

He worked until well after midnight then fell into bed.

The following afternoon, he left Laura sleeping soundly and drove to Denver to pick up his daughter and Mort.

When she saw him waiting at the gate, she flew into his arms. "Daddy!"

So now he was Daddy again. He twirled her around. "I missed you so much."

"I missed you, too."

Nick shook Mort's hand. "Let's go."

They drove to Ty's house because Emily wanted to see Rebecca.

Tammy greeted them and Emily was all over the baby. "Can I hold her? Show me how."

Tammy had her sit on the sofa and then settled the baby onto Emily's lap, showing her how to support Rebecca's neck and head.

She looked so happy that he asked Tammy, "Is it okay if I leave Emily here for a couple of hours?"

Emily's gaze shot to his. "Why, Dad?"

Dad again.

"I need to check up on Laura and warm some dinner for her, then I'll come back."

"No! I don't want you to go."

"Come with me, then."

"I don't want to see that woman. She tricked you into having a baby."

"Actually, Emily, she didn't. To be honest, we both screwed up."

Sensing how deep the tension was between them, Tammy said, "I know Laura well. She isn't devious. Why don't you go with your dad and get to know her a little better."

Emily looked panicked. "I don't want to get to know her better. I don't want my dad to, either."

"Then just go so you can spend more time with him. He's made this commitment to help a friend. Keep him company while he runs this errand and then both of you come back here for supper."

"Okay." Tammy took the baby back from Emily.

Over his daughter's head, just before he stepped out of the house, Nick mouthed, "Thank you."

Tammy nodded and closed the door behind them.

In Accord, they dropped Emily's bag at the B and B and then Nick ordered three portions of the rice pudding.

He led Emily up the back stairs to Laura's apartment and entered without knocking.

Laura was reading by the window.

"Hey," she said, smiling. Then she saw Emily. Her "hi" sounded less certain.

Emily stared at her without speaking.

"How's your back?" Nick asked Laura.

"Good."

"Your feet?"

"A bit swollen. My calves are aching."

"I'll heat supper for you. Emily and I are eating at Ty's."

"How's Rebecca?"

Nick shrugged. "A baby. They don't do much at that stage."

"She's beautiful," Emily said, her tone strident. "The most

beautiful baby ever." She stared at Laura. "Tammy didn't get fat when she was pregnant."

"Cool it," Nick snapped.

"It's true."

"If you can't behave then wait outside."

Emily flounced to the door and slammed it behind her.

When Nick finished preparing Laura's dinner he left to find Emily sitting on the top step waiting for him.

"Why can't you be polite? Laura is Tammy's friend. She told you Laura didn't get pregnant on purpose."

"I don't care. I hate her."

Nick's patience was strained. He was tired and overworked and trying his best to juggle too many balls. He scooted past her and rushed down the stairs.

"Grow up, Emily."

He waited for her in the car. She got in quietly and remained that way throughout dinner, with him at any rate. She loved her uncle Ty, she loved Tammy and she loved Rebecca, and she loved her grandpa Mort, but she was angry with her father and Nick didn't have a clue how to change that.

CHAPTER TWENTY

TY HAD INVITED Laura for Thanksgiving dinner so Nick drove her out with Mort and Emily.

She insisted on sitting in the backseat so Emily could sit up front with him.

At the ranch, Tammy and Callie embraced her into their fold so Nick didn't have to worry about her.

He kept Emily close with his arm around her shoulders, trying to make up for being so harsh with her the day before. She kibitzed with his brothers and seemed to be in a good mood as long as she didn't have to spend time with Laura.

Dinner went well until dessert was served when Laura jumped up and ran to the bathroom. She returned moments later, wide-eyed and nervous.

"Callie," she said, "may I borrow Gabe for a few minutes?"

"What's happening, Laura?"

The tension among the women had Nick jumping out of his seat. "What's going on?"

Laura picked up the purse she'd left in the living room. "Gabe, would you drive me to the hospital, please?"

"What is it?" Nick stepped in front of Laura. "I'll drive you."

"I'm spotting. Stay here with your daughter." She walked to the front door, her back ramrod-straight, her neck stiff, trying to shrug into her jacket. "Gabe, can we go? Now, please."

"You don't have to bother Gabe. I'll take you."

"No, Nick."

"I'm the baby's father," he shouted.

"Nick, calm down." Ty took his arm, but Nick shrugged him off.

"Why is Gabe taking her? If anything goes wrong, I should be there."

Ty leaned close and whispered, "She's right. Emily is here right now. Stay with her."

Nick turned to find Emily staring at him, her eyes huge saucers in her pale face.

He walked to her, pulled her out of the chair and held her while Laura left the house with his brother.

"What's happening, Dad? What's spotting?"

"It means the baby might be coming. Laura's going to the hospital to make sure that isn't what's happening."

"So what if the baby came?"

"It would be so small, it might not live. Or it could have medical complications."

Emily shook in his arms.

"Emily," Tammy said. "Do you want me to make some hot chocolate? You look cold."

"Yes, Auntie Tammy."

Ten minutes later, Tammy returned with a steaming mug. Everyone sat down again to dessert, but the mood had shifted, worry evident on everyone's faces.

Callie began to talk about Gabe's preparations for the dog-sledding season and Nick sat with his arm across the back of Emily's chair, his fingers resting on her shoulder, and everyone knew it was all for Emily's benefit.

She sipped her cocoa, but then said, "I don't like this, Dad. I don't like that she's having a baby and now might lose it. She's making everyone feel sorry for her."

Nick straightened away from her. "This isn't something Laura's manufactured to make us feel sorry for her. This is real life. It's a real life-and-death situation. I don't want this baby, but I don't want Laura to lose it, either. She's in love with it already. She'll make a great mother and deserves to have a shot at having a healthy child. Understand?"

Emily nodded. Why was adolescence so hard? Had Nick screwed up Emily so badly that she would never accept another child into her father's life? He was only thirty-two. He had no plans to marry and no plans for more family. But what if he *did?* Would Emily never be okay with that? Was the problem immaturity or had she been screwed up by him beyond the point of repair?

By the following morning, when he left Emily asleep at the B and B to pick up Laura from the hospital, he still didn't have an answer.

Gabe had returned to Ty's late last evening to tell them that Laura and the baby were fine, but that they were keeping her overnight for observation.

When Nick said he would pick her up in the morning, Emily had started to object, but he'd stopped her with one look.

He knew enough about this fatherhood business, even if he was coming to it late in Emily's life, that sometimes you just had to be tough.

At the hospital, Laura was sitting up in bed waiting, dressed and with her socks and shoes in her hands.

"I thought Gabe was coming to get me."

"You're stuck with me instead," he said, not too happy about the game of war he felt part of between Laura and Emily.

Without a word, he put on her socks and shoes and took her home.

"Don't come over today, Nick. Stay with Emily."

"I'll come later, the same as I did earlier in the week."

"That wouldn't be wise. Stay with Emily."

Despite what Laura said, he came over later, but the back door was locked and he didn't have a key.

He knocked, and knocked, and then knocked some more, but Laura didn't answer.

He went downstairs and took a look at the renovations. Everything was running smoothly, so he picked up Emily and Mort and drove out to Ty's, where they helped him do chores with the bison.

The following day, he dropped Mort off at the home and took Emily out to Gabe's, where they admired Gabe's progress on the house and where Emily could talk and laugh with the dogs to her heart's content.

On Sunday, he put them both on the plane for home.

He hugged Emily hard. "I love you. I wish you would believe me."

"I do."

"Then stop worrying that Laura's baby will come between us."

"I'll try, but she is already coming between us. I'm going home and you're staying here."

"I don't feel comfortable leaving her. She needs a friend right now. Someone who can run errands for her because the doctors won't let her do anything. How's she supposed to eat if she can't shop for groceries or cook?" He tucked a strand of hair behind Emily's ear. "Tammy has her baby to take care of. Callie is a bit more pregnant than Laura is and she's got her hands full with her job and with getting ready for the baby. Laura needs a friend and that seems to be me."

Emily stared behind his left shoulder, no longer mulish or sulky, but thoughtful.

"Call me?"

Nick hugged her again. "You're my shining star. I need to talk to my star every night."

He watched while she boarded the plane and, despite the tension of the past few days and despite his using his brothers and their wives as a buffer between him and Emily, he didn't want her to go. He missed her already.

On Monday morning, Nick drove to Callie's long-term-care facility.

She smiled when she saw him.

"Nick! What are you doing here?"

He'd come on an errand, but now that he was here, he found himself curious about Callie's adventure and how she was doing.

Funny, in the past few months, he'd come to terms with her having "defected" to his brother. He wasn't so blind that he couldn't see that what they had between them was a powerful love. He wasn't so petty that he couldn't be happy for them.

He asked Callie for a tour of the home and got it. He was impressed.

"You're doing a great job, Callie. This place is warm and homey rather than institutional."

"Thank you, Nick. Your opinion matters to me."

The quiet honesty of the statement touched him.

"Do you want to see Johanna while you're here?"

"I'd love to see her."

"She won't recognize you."

"That's fine."

He visited briefly and Callie was right. Johanna didn't recognize him, but then, she didn't realize Callie was her own daughter.

After they left her room, Nick said, "She doesn't know us, but honestly, she's doing well here. She seems calmer. Happier."

"She is." Callie gave a brief instruction to a passing nurse then turned back to Nick. "Why are you here? I know it wasn't for a tour."

"I want to borrow or rent a wheelchair from you."

"A wheelchair?" Her eyes widened. "Oh, Nick, not for Laura. She would hate to be wheeled around."

"I know, but she's stir-crazy. I want to get her downstairs and into the wheelchair so she can visit her café and see her

renovations and maybe even take a ride down Main Street
without exerting herself."

"That's so thoughtful. You're good for her, Nick."

He shrugged. "I'm helping a friend."

"You've come all the way from Seattle to do it. You're staying in a hotel at your own expense. From what I heard, before
Emily came for Thanksgiving, you spent every day with her."

"There's no better communication than the small-town
grapevine."

Callie laughed, a musical sound that Nick had forgotten.
Then again, she laughed a lot more now than she had when
she'd worked for him, so he hadn't heard it often.

"Someday soon it wouldn't hurt," Callie said, walking with
him to the front door, "for you to admit that you love her."

"I don't."

"Here's your wheelchair." She picked up a folded chair
from a rack by the entrance. "Keep it until Laura gives birth."

Nick hugged her. "I still like you, Callie. I won't hold that
'you love her' remark against you."

Her laugh rang again, following him through the open
door to his car.

He'd joked with her, but God, when were people going to
stop shoving Laura down his throat?

HE HELPED HER down the stairs. She took them carefully,
scared to death of falling and making her baby come early.

When she saw the wheelchair she frowned. "I'm not an
invalid."

"No, you aren't. You're going nuts inside your apartment,
but you have to take it easy for the baby. Sit."

She did and then he wheeled her down the narrow alley-
way onto Main. "This is embarrassing."

"What do you think of the weather? Nice, isn't it?"

"People are staring at me."

"The breeze keeps the sun from getting too hot."

"Would you quit with the weather already?"

"Just trying to get you to stop complaining."

She huffed out a laugh. "I am complaining, aren't I? The sun is nice." She closed her eyes and raised her face toward the sun's rays.

He wheeled her into the café and everyone turned.

"Bringing your own chair with you?" someone who Nick didn't know called out. "Good for you, Laura."

Nick bought himself a coffee and Laura an herbal tea and got her to carry both of them while he wheeled her next door.

When he pushed her into the shop, he heard her breath catch.

"Looks good, doesn't it?" he asked.

"It's gorgeous."

"Happy with the colors you chose?"

"I love them. Geordie," she called.

The contractor stepped out from the kitchen, his coveralls stained with plenty of white and beige paint, but also plum and orange and red. Laura's colors.

"What do you think?" Geordie approached, leaned forward and bussed her on the cheek.

"You've done a fabulous job."

"You chose the colors. All I did was apply them to the walls."

Nick sat on the floor and Laura in her chair and they talked about her plans for the place and the Opening Day party.

Later, he took her back upstairs, put her to bed and started to head to the B and B to concentrate on his own business.

On impulse, he stopped in to see the Gems, stepping around the counter because they worked exclusively in the back now, baking.

"Do either of you women know where I can find more of you?"

"What do you mean?" Norma asked. Or maybe it was Gayle.

"I want to hire more women for the Opening Day party that Laura's planning after she opens up the wall."

"We've already got our sisters on the front counter to replace ourselves."

"Do they bake as well as you do?"

"Yep. Our mothers taught us."

"Okay, all of you are hired to work overtime. How does time and a half sound?"

"Sounds good. I've already been to Denver twice since I started work here. I'm collecting a whole new wardrobe."

"Okay, I'll get Laura to write up a menu for you."

He worked all afternoon, but got little done because much of the time was devoted to calls he needed to make. He was late getting to Laura's and therefore late calling Emily. By the time he'd finished putting dinner together and eating it and cleaning up and then making sure that Laura was in bed, it was past nine-thirty.

"Dad, I thought you weren't going to call." He could hear her uncertainty and disappointment in her voice.

"Sorry, honey. Tell me about your day."

By the time he hung up, he was yawning, but still had hours of work to do.

He thought it might have been sometime after three when he fell into bed.

His days fell into a routine in earnest after that.

As hard as he worked, he seemed to slip further and further behind at work. Mort called and chastised him for missing client phone calls and for not getting contracts returned on time.

If he could just get through the Opening Day at Sweet Temptations, things would slow down.

The day arrived with great fanfare. Nick had handbills printed up and delivered to every citizen in town and for miles around.

When he wheeled Laura around to the front of the building, there was a lineup down Main. They stepped aside so she could enter, then followed her in.

Tilly and the Gems and their sisters and the extra staff Laura had hired for the day all waited at the new counter to serve everyone.

Geordie had outdone himself. The place shone. The missing wall opened the room into a huge airy space full of tables and chairs covered in cloths to match the colors of the walls.

There was a coffee and a cinnamon bun free for everyone, along with trays of sweets that the ladies handed around. The children got either cold drinks or hot chocolate.

Even with the larger space, there weren't enough chairs for everyone. The café would never house this many people on a normal day, though.

Laura glowed. The townspeople loved her.

Nick talked to everyone, helped the Gems clear tables, handed around sweets, but never lost track of where Laura was in the room, watching her for signs of fatigue or stress.

The music for the day had been chosen by both of them. They'd spent a pair of evenings burning CDs with Laura's favorite artists. The music added to the ambience of the space.

At noon, he approached Laura. "Time to go upstairs."

"Already?"

He nodded and smiled. "It's a smashing success."

She sighed. "It is, isn't it?"

He made them a light lunch.

"I'm going home tomorrow, Laura."

She shot him a startled gaze. "Really?"

"You won't need me now. The shop is open and up and running and I've got bucket loads of work to catch up on."

She fingered the crackers he'd served with the soup. "I don't know how to thank you for what you've done for me."

He stood to leave. She stood, too.

He leaned forward. Their lips touched. They stared. This close her eyes were golden, the hazel overtaking the brown.

"It was my pleasure," he said and, to his surprise, meant it.

She walked him to the door, well, waddled really, but even this ripe with pregnancy, she was still beautiful. Radiant. Aglow.

He left with mixed feelings, sort of lost and lonely.

In Seattle, his daughter welcomed him home with squeals and opened arms.

They spent as much time as he could carve out of his evenings with her, then worked long into the night.

Two days before Christmas, they flew to Accord, he and Emily and Mort, to spend Christmas with the Jordan family. On the 28th, Nick put Emily on a plane bound for France and he and Mort headed back to Seattle.

Nick worked through New Year's Eve and then fell into bed alone, the house hollow and still.

He had an early dinner on New Year's Day with Mort and then went home and caught up on more work.

He wondered what his brothers were doing.

CHAPTER TWENTY-ONE

OLIVIA CAMERON STEPPED out onto Main Street in the driving snow, leaning into the wind. She needed to get across the street to pick up some lunch. She hadn't brought anything to work today, it was after two and she was starving.

A gust blew snow against her. Every January, she swore she was going to sell the house and the gallery and move to Florida. Year after year, she stayed put. She turned her face away from the stinging cold, trying to keep her makeup dry, and hopped over a small bank of snow onto the road.

She landed wrong and lost her footing.

Tires screeched and a bumper hit her hip. She screamed and fell, landing on her other hip.

"Olivia, what the hell were you thinking?" Lester Hughes ran from his car to her where she lay on the wet pavement in dirty snow. "You don't step into the road without looking both ways."

Olivia tried to breathe, but the fall had knocked the wind out of her.

Lester crouched beside her. "How bad are you hurt?"

She finally caught her breath. "My hip…hurts."

"Which one?"

"Both." One from the bumper and the other from hitting the road.

"Are they broken? Can you stand?"

They weren't broken. Standing was painful. She was stiff. She managed, though.

"I'm okay," she said.

"I'm taking you to the hospital."

"No." She took a few steps. "I'm fine. I'll be bruised tomorrow, though."

Tyler Jordan appeared beside them. "I heard the squealing tires. What happened?"

Lester explained and Olivia agreed, "It was all my fault, Sheriff. I didn't watch for cars when I stepped out."

"Tell her she's gotta come to the hospital with me," Lester said. "I want her x-rayed for internal injuries."

"He's right," Ty said. "You need to get checked out."

"Okay." Olivia sighed. She'd have to call Monica Accord in on her day off. "You go on about your business, Lester. I'll drive to the hospital myself."

"That ain't right, Olivia. What if you conk out on the drive?"

"I didn't hit my head when I fell. I'm fine to drive."

"But—"

"I insist."

"In that case," Ty said, "I'll follow you to make sure you arrive safely."

"Give me a few minutes. I have to call Monica in from her day off to cover at the gallery."

"I'll wait for you out front."

Back in her office, Olivia sat down and put her head between her legs. She hadn't hit it, didn't have a concussion, but the incident had scared the daylights out of her and had left her dizzy and shaken.

She raised one hand. It shook so badly she couldn't use her phone. What if Lester hadn't been able to stop? What if he hadn't had the presence of mind to jerk the steering wheel so she got only a glancing blow rather than being hit head-on?

If she'd been hit squarely by his car, would she be dead now instead of able to drive herself to the hospital?

Or worse, would she be crippled or unable to lead a normal life, the life she took for granted?

In those few precious moments suspended between life and possible death, she'd seen a lot. It had happened so quickly, but not so fast that she hadn't had immediate disgust for herself.

How much time had she wasted in her life? How much had she let fear rule her?

Tyler entered her gallery and called her name.

She left her office and handed him her phone. "Please," she said. "Call Monica."

Five minutes later, she was on the road and Tyler was following her.

X-rays showed neither internal nor permanent damage.

She sent Tyler home. She had a stop to make before returning to downtown Accord.

She was fifty-eight years old and deathly afraid of aging. She was a coward. A man loved her, had told her he wanted her exactly the way she was, flaws and all, and she'd thrown it back in his face.

All it took was one brush with her own mortality to set her head on straight. She wanted Aiden, her age be damned.

She turned down the road to his home. Her cell phone rang, but she ignored it, her mind on one purpose, one goal, and nothing else.

She dashed through the snow to his door and rapped on it hard with her knuckles. *Please be home. I need you, Aiden McQuorrie.*

He opened the door, opened his mouth to set her down with something scathing, something she probably deserved, but then saw her face and stopped.

"What happened, love?"

Love. Was there a more perfect word in the English language or a more perfect man for her on the face of the planet? Without another word, he took her into his arms. She wrapped hers across his back to hold him tightly, to savor every muscle and sinew of his vibrant body.

"Make love to me," she whispered and he slammed the door and pulled her down the hallway.

God, it had been so long. Her body throbbed with un-relieved sexual tension. She hadn't been with a man in ten years and, during the years after her husband's affair, their lovemaking had been spotty, impeded by grief, resentment and distrust. She was growing older by the minute, and dry-ing up by the second.

She wanted to know love again.

Her body ached.

There'd been a time when she'd been crazy about sex, she and John active as young lovers well into their marriage, even after their three children had been born.

Since then? Next to nothing. Her body cried out for release. She wanted vitality flooding her veins.

They entered a bedroom and she barely had time to regis-ter an enormous king-size bed before Aiden pulled his T-shirt over his head then closed the blinds.

What she'd seen before the room went dark dried her mouth. He was beautiful. Hard. Lean. Sculpted. Muscular.

And she was soft and wanting to accept, to take.

He found her in the darkness as though she were phos-phorescent. His fingers worked quick magic, divesting her of her clothes.

Then they were on that massive bed and he was on top of her, his big body pressing hers into the mattress, and kissing her and licking her neck and breasts and running his hands in places only she had touched for years, and he smelled, touched, felt like quintessential Man. Then he was inside of her and she was climbing a golden mountain.

He filled her, stretched her, and quickened her blood. She spread her legs wide and put her hands on his behind to hold his body hard against hers, to savor him inside of her, to cher-ish the filling of a space empty for far too long. He moved and she wanted more. Her hands urged him deeper, harder, faster.

More.

More.

He touched her between her legs and she sang. Flew. Shattered.

Still, he moved inside of her and their bodies ran with sweat and her spirit rose again, to fly, weightless, timeless, without context.

This.

Only this.

Aiden roared then collapsed onto her, his weight crushing, heavenly. Essential.

Rolling to his side, he took her with him, threw one heavy leg across hers and wrapped his arms around her, as though he would take her into his core.

Her heart pounded. Eased. Drifted back to earth.

In this divine darkness, she was only a woman. She was not age, or society, or business. She was only a sensual, tactile creature.

Aiden's lovemaking was a revelation, a balm to a body in need and to a soul aging too quickly.

Finally, he pulled away from her and left the bed. He returned with towels. They cleaned themselves, then he tossed them into the corner.

He did something at his dresser and music filled the room, classical and moody.

When he returned to the bed, he pulled her back against him, spooning with her, kissing her neck, nibbling her earlobe. His arms came around her and he took her breasts into his hands, calluses abrading her nipples and threatening to make her orgasm again.

"No condom," she whispered. How utterly freeing to be a woman her age and no longer have to worry about birth control.

"I haven't been with a woman in a long time. I'm clean."

"I only ever knew one man and it's been years."

She felt him smile against her neck. "It's only us in this darkness. Man. Woman. Flesh and bones."

Aiden's lips trailed down her spine, kissing each and every bone, all the way to her ankles and back up, spending time on the backs of her knees, nearly sending her through the ceiling.

"So soft. Every part of you is silk."

But she wanted more than his homage. She wanted to explore. John had been strong, but slim. There was so much more of Aiden. She ran her hands and lips over all of him, loving the feel of him, the contrasts between his body and hers.

When he could wait no longer, he turned her to spoon again and entered her, with his hand to her belly to arch her back so he could go deeply.

Her body opened to him, spread wet warm petals to enfold his bulk.

Olivia murmured, hummed, whispered then cursed when she nearly came but he drew back.

"We have all day." His voice, lazy and deep, laughed at her. She smiled. She had ideas of her own and set about torturing Aiden the way he was torturing her.

He hissed and lifted her to her hands and knees and continued to rock inside of her with his hands holding her breasts.

Sated quickly the first time around, they went slowly now, loving thoroughly. Completely.

Time's relentless march halted and stood still, preciously, blissfully still.

NICK STOOD AT the window on the third floor of the B and B.

Two days ago, Gabe had called. Callie had given birth to a baby boy. Caleb. Nick had flown down and had seen them all at the hospital.

Caleb looked like a newborn. What else was there to say? Babies looked like babies.

He received a call in the middle of the afternoon.

"You screwed up, Jordan." Mort's words were slurred. Had he started drinking again? Why?

"What are you talking about?" Nick gripped the windowsill.

"She's gone."

Nick stilled, afraid that he knew what Mort meant, but hoping that he was getting it wrong.

"Emily's moved to France to live with her mother."

Nick's blood turned to ice. Was there a better word for how his body felt? Gelid, maybe. Glacial, even better.

Emily, he thought, misery painting her name dark. He'd been so afraid of this. He felt the edges of his world turn black. What would he do without Emily?

She'd come home after Christmas and things had been fine, but as January progressed and he'd worried more about Laura, the more sullen Emily had become.

Nick needed to be in Accord when Laura gave birth. He had felt compelled to be here, ironic given that he didn't want another baby. Laura's baby was costing Nick his daughter.

Before he had left for Accord, Emily had cried. "Dad, don't go. She doesn't need you."

"She might. Honey, I don't know what else I can say or do to convince you that I love you."

He'd left two days ago. Neither last night nor the night before would Emily take his phone calls.

"I tried to stop her," Mort continued, bringing Nick back to the present, his words uneven but every one driving a nail into Nick's heart. "Nothing I said made a difference."

"She's a minor. You could have prevented her from getting a plane ticket."

"Not when she had her mother's permission."

Nick swore.

"You really hurt her this time. She doesn't believe your promises anymore."

"I can't leave here. Laura could have the baby at any moment. Yesterday was her due date."

"I know. Emily thinks that baby is more important to you than she is."

"That's absurd. I couldn't love Emily more."

"Your history led her to believe otherwise."

Nick cursed all of those times he had said he would be there for her, but hadn't been. He cursed his needs and his drive. So what if he'd made less money? So what if they'd lived in a smaller house? So what if the world hadn't seen Nick as a huge success?

None of that mattered now. When he went home, Emily wouldn't be there. It hurt too much to think about.

He stared blindly through the window of the B and B. He hadn't wanted to stay out in the country at Ty's, had needed to be close to Laura.

While he stood there, she emerged from the alley beside her bakery. In one hand, she carried an overnight bag, moving carefully in the snow.

While he watched she stopped beside Lester's cab and handed him her bag then grasped her belly. Her face scrunched up in pain.

Jesus. She was in labor.

Jesus.

For one terrified moment, Nick was frozen, his feet nailed to the floor. Then he grabbed his car keys and flew from the room. When he got outside, the cab was already gone and there was nothing for Nick to do but drive to the hospital.

When the nurses would have stopped him from following Laura in a wheelchair at the far end of the hallway, he called her name.

She turned, surprised to see him.

"I told you I'd be here. Let me come with you."

She looked calm, composed, but a trace of wistfulness

peeked through her confident exterior. She didn't want to be alone.

She wasn't.

He approached.

"I called my mom," she said, "but she isn't picking up."

Nick had a few thoughts about Olivia Cameron and her self-centeredness, but then, who was he to judge?

"I'm here," he said, defiant in the face of her composure, but buoyed by that trace of need he'd seen in Laura. "I'm not leaving, so you might as well let me into the delivery room."

She stared at him for long moments that left him unsure. He couldn't force his way in. He wanted to be there, though. Needed to be there for her.

She saw something she must have liked because she smiled with the serenity of a Madonna and nodded.

LAURA SCREAMED AND YELLED and cursed the day Nick was born. Never mind that there had been two of them making love that night, and that she'd been a more than willing participant.

The pain looked horrendous. Nick didn't care that it was natural, that millions of women had done this down through the ages. He didn't want Laura hurting so much.

"Give her something," he snapped at the doctor.

"She told me *not* to give her anything."

"She changed her mind."

"Laura." The doctor took her hand. "Have you changed your mind about having an epidural?"

"No!" she shouted.

"Laura," Nick said, "be reasonable."

The doctor shook her head as if to say, *You poor sod, you don't tell a woman in labor to be reasonable.*

The string of invectives Laura let loose was so inventive, Nick was impressed. Still, there was so much pain.

He opened his mouth, but both Laura and the doctor gave him warning glares. Right. Mother knows best.

Pearl Cameron Jordan was born an hour later at four in the morning.

After the nurses checked her thoroughly then gave her to Laura for a while, they swaddled the baby and handed her to Nick.

He balked. What the hell did he know about holding babies?

The baby was in his arms before he could mount a coherent protest.

He stared at the tiny fingers with perfectly shaped nails, at her tiny face and unfocused gray eyes…and fell in love. Head over heels stupid in love. Drunk in love.

He sighed, long and contentedly. He'd never felt so good in his life.

He heard Laura sigh and said, "You must be exhausted."

"I'm tired but happy. Isn't she lovely?"

He studied the exquisite creature in his arms. "She's beautiful." He took Laura's hand, overwhelmed by love, by rightness. "You did it. You kept her safe inside your body and carried her to full term."

He kissed her forehead and, in that moment, realized how much he truly loved her, how much he'd loved her since his fifteenth birthday when he'd first realized he wanted his brother's girlfriend, and how much he admired her strength and commitment.

She'd wanted a café and had built up a dated little bakery into the most successful business on Main Street, Accord, Colorado.

She'd wanted a baby and, under less than ideal circumstances, including the baby's hostile father, had carried her to term, to a healthy, successful birth.

Wasn't sleeping with a woman without protection a commitment, unspoken, but binding nonetheless? Didn't a man's obligation extend to more than just the financial? Didn't it extend to a lifetime of caring?

He watched Laura smile.

A lifetime of caring.

He realized he was talking about more than just a commitment to Pearl. He was also thinking about Laura—and not in terms of passion or sex or companionship, or easing his loneliness.

He was talking about love.

He was thinking about love even when it wasn't easy, about giving *because* it wasn't easy. Because it was the right thing to do. Because it was the *only* thing to do.

He stepped closer to the bed. Laura glanced up and her hazel eyes widened when she saw his expression. Everything he felt, the love he hadn't known had existed for years for this woman, most likely since the first moment he'd seen her in town, when they'd been nothing more than children, poured from him.

Allowing her no time to protest, he leaned forward and set his mouth on her beautiful full lips...and kissed her as though he'd rather do nothing else on earth than honor and worship her.

He pulled back only far enough to look into her eyes. When he whispered, "I love you," his breath feathered stray chestnut hairs around her cheeks.

"Marry me," he said.

Laura smiled, sadly, and touched his face. "It's the baby," she said. "The birth. This is an emotional time. Ask me again when Pearl has been up all night teething and crying. Today, here in the birthing room, this isn't real life, Nick."

"I know. I want it all, Laura. The good *and* the bad."

"You're feeling the euphoria of bringing a life into the world. It doesn't last. Real life will set in."

"Laura, I know what I'm talking about."

"Come back to me in a few months. I need to get my baby home and take over my business again."

My baby. Not *ours*.

From the best high he'd ever experienced in his life, Nick came crashing to earth.

He'd never before told a woman that he loved her.

Laura had turned it back on him, didn't believe he was telling the truth, or that he knew his own mind.

The two women he'd loved most in the world had rejected him. How could this be both the best time in his life and the worst? How could he be so close to heaven, but so far from the women he loved?

Anger flooded him along with determination.

For the first time in his life, he was surer than he'd ever been of what he wanted. When he'd kissed the dust of Accord goodbye after high school graduation, he'd thought he'd known how his whole life would go. He'd thought he'd mapped it out so cleverly.

He'd make his first million by the time he reached thirty. To his credit, he'd succeeded beyond his wildest dreams. True, he'd used Marsha, but she had gone into their marriage with her eyes wide open. He'd never deceived her.

Everything had come crashing down around his ears. Money was fine and dandy, was great to have, was security in a wild and crazy world, but it wasn't all it was cracked up to be.

Like the old cliché went, it didn't keep you warm at night.

Laura would. She would keep a man warm every night, would meet and exceed his wildest dreams.

He had to convince her that he loved her and truly wanted to marry her.

This time around, he was marrying for love.

Except that the woman he loved wouldn't accept it.

He left the hospital without a game plan, the great and

successful Nick Jordan knowing only that he would grovel if he had to.

He returned to the B and B, brushed his teeth and showered. Papers littered every horizontal surface in the room. He used to be neat. He used to need everything in its place. Lately, his world had fallen apart and he didn't care. He didn't know where one contract ended and the other started.

He was making a mess of his business and he just didn't care.

His parents' marriage, and its disastrous consequences for their sons, had finally loosed its hold on Nick. He was making decisions with a clear head, with full awareness of the consequences to him and those around him, and was willing to take on the responsibility.

Laura had turned his world upside down, had shaken his carefully planned and ordered life to the core, had taught him about what really mattered in life, had given him passion and pleasure.

Considering that they'd only ever slept together twice, wasn't that extraordinary? With the force of her character, she'd brought color into his life. She'd brought *life* into his life. She'd shown him what commitment to a better cause looked like, what love looked like, and how much one had to give up for it.

For a woman who thrived on doing, a physical, passionate woman who craved experience and people and life, she'd willingly locked herself away for a month to keep her baby safe.

Yet here, today, the reward was exponentially huge, thrilling, real.

A child existed and would thrive because of the level of Laura's love and commitment. She would carry that commitment through every day of her child's life, without fear, knowing that she was doing the right thing.

He knew her well. He loved her.

She'd taught him so much, how to strive for something

more elemental and powerful and important than the almighty buck. Had he learned too late?

There was only one way to find out. He packed his carry-on and drove to Denver.

Back in Seattle, he entered Mort's office.

"Mort, I'm moving to Accord."

Mort glared at him. "And do what?"

"I'll run the business from there, long-distance. I've been doing it off and on from Accord for the past seven or eight months anyway."

"And Emily?"

"I'm flying out tonight to bring her home."

"Home meaning Accord?"

"Yes. I'll sell the house here and either buy or build in Accord, depending on what Emily wants."

Mort looked lost.

"You could come, too," Nick said softly. "You could live in Accord. You like it there."

Mort stared out of his window to Seattle below. Slowly, he nodded. "Yes, I could."

"I'll call you the second I get Emily back."

He reached for the doorknob to leave, but turned back. "Mort?"

"Yeah?"

"Kick the bottle."

Mort nodded and smiled. "I can do that."

"Yes." Nick grinned. "You can."

For the next twenty-four hours, he took every last-minute flight he could snag, flying to France by way of Chicago and New York and London and finally Paris.

He needed Emily.

Marry me.

Laura couldn't believe Nick had said those words, had offered her those beautiful strings that she craved so badly, had dangled in front of her the culmination of her dream.

A family.

So close and yet so far away.

She'd been right, though. Men said things in the heat of passion, in the midst of emotions they didn't understand and that overwhelmed them, and then took them back later in the calm light of day.

She wanted her dream, but only if it was real. True.

She'd sent him home to get some sleep.

Tomorrow morning, he would see things differently.

She stared down at her precious baby. Her Pearl.

"You're my miracle."

Pearl slept peacefully, as though she hadn't spent hours banging against her mommy's pelvis to make her grand entrance.

It had all been worth it.

The chance she'd committed to, that she was taking, in vowing to raise this baby alone would be worth it, worth every second of time and energy and passion that she would devote to it.

She kissed her baby's soft forehead.

A rustle at the door had her glancing up.

"Mom! You heard. Sorry I didn't call after she was born. I'm kind of tired and dazed."

"I got your message."

It must have taken her a while to check them. Laura had left it hours ago. Mom checked her messages regularly, all day long.

Someone else entered the room behind her mother. Aiden McQuorrie. One of her mother's artists. What was he doing here?

Laura noticed what she hadn't earlier. Mom was a mess. Her hair was askew and smudges of mascara colored her lids.

Her yellow coat had dirt stains on it, as though she'd been rolling on the ground.

She limped a little.

Under Laura's perusal, her cheeks turned pink.

Aiden, wild too-long hair unkempt, stepped behind Olivia and placed his palms on her hips, watching Laura steadily, sending her an unmistakable message.

He and her mother were involved. By the looks of the two of them, they'd driven straight over from being *involved*.

Oh, myyyy. She thought hard, but couldn't remember a time when she'd ever suspected her mother of being with a man.

The pair looked defiant, maybe with good reason. Laura didn't know what the age difference was, but knew it was broad and it astounded her.

She grinned.

"Good for you, Mom."

Olivia let out a breath she'd been holding and rushed to her daughter, wrapping her in a hug.

"Is this what's been bothering you for the past months?" Laura asked.

"The stubborn woman wouldn't give in." Aiden's dormant Scottish accent took center stage, a testament to his emotional involvement with Mom? Laura hoped so. She wanted more for Mom than just sexual love. "She's obsessed with age and with what people will think."

"And you aren't?" Laura asked.

"Not in the least." He kissed the back of Olivia's neck.

Mom looked as though she'd died and gone to heaven. "Let me see my grandchild," she demanded and Laura became weepy. Oh. Mom was going to be involved after all. She'd been telling the truth at Ty and Tammy's wedding. Laura had been afraid to believe, but here Mom was making it true.

Pearl might not have much of an extended family, but she would know her only living grandmother.

Aiden was obviously helping Mom come to terms with her age. Thank God.

Olivia's eyes misted when she held Pearl and Laura knew there would be a loving relationship between the two.

She mouthed "thank you" to Aiden. His grin took her breath away.

Dear Lord, her mother had chosen an inordinately handsome lover.

NICK DIDN'T RETURN that day or the next.

It wasn't until she brought Pearl home that she found out he'd left town.

She wasn't surprised, but oh, she was hurt.

He'd gotten a good night's sleep, as she'd directed, and had seen that he didn't care enough, that he wasn't committed enough, that he didn't love enough to stay with her and with his baby.

It shouldn't hurt as much as it did. She'd seen it coming, but she was only human and her heart more susceptible to hope than she'd thought.

She'd figured out that men couldn't be trusted to keep a commitment or to stick around when the going got tough. She'd betrayed the only man she'd known who could be trusted. Gabe.

She'd made her bed and now she would have to sleep in it.

She laid Pearl gently into her crib and touched her tiny perfect cheek. She had no regrets where her baby was concerned.

"It's you and me against the world, sweetheart, exactly as I'd thought."

She lay down on her own bed and turned on the baby monitor on the bedside table, determined to sleep while Pearl slept.

The next phase of her life would test her strength and endurance.

She refused, absolutely refused, to think about Nick.

When sleep overtook her, it came swiftly and deeply, without dreams.

CHAPTER TWENTY-TWO

NICK'S PLANE LANDED in Paris after midnight, but he didn't know which day it was. He'd lost track of time.

He should have taken a hotel room for the night, but instead, rented a car and drove to the villa Harry Fuller owned outside of Alençon, arriving in the middle of the night.

He pounded on the door.

Harry answered, disheveled, pulling the belt of his robe tight.

"Qu'est-ce que c'est?" he asked before realizing it was Nick. "Oh, it's you. What do you want?"

"Emily."

"Not sure she'll see you. You couldn't have come in the morning?"

"I want to see her now."

"You might as well come in. I'll go wake her."

Nick waited in an expansive, beautifully appointed sunken living room.

It wasn't his daughter who finally entered, but Marsha.

"Nick? What are you doing here?" She looked at a tiny gold watch on her left wrist. "At 2:30 in the morning?"

"I want to see Emily. I want her back."

She nodded, but made no move to fetch his daughter. "Sit down."

Gracefully, she sat across from him on a settee that had probably been made two hundred years ago. What did he know? Marsha had furnished their home.

"Did you know," she said, "that she used to idolize you?

From the moment she first started to notice the world around her, she honed in on you and couldn't get enough of you. Unfortunately, you were never around."

"I know, Marsha. You have no idea how much I regret that now."

"When I married Harry, I left Emily with you because that's where she wanted to be." She leaned back in her chair. "Mort said you were trying to make time for her."

"Yes, and it was working, but then…life got complicated."

"You got some woman pregnant."

"Not just some woman. The one I betrayed my brother with. I love her. It's taken me this long to figure it out."

"I'm happy for you." She looked reserved.

"You can go ahead and gloat. She turned me down when I asked her to marry me."

She smiled. "These days, things don't seem to be coming to you as easily as they used to."

"Marsha, you have no idea." He cracked his knuckles. "I have another daughter. Pearl. Do you know what I realized when I held her for the first time?"

"What?"

"How much I love Emily. How much love there is in my heart. How much I have to give to this new baby, but even more so to Emily."

"Dad?"

He turned at his daughter's voice.

"Emily?" Before he barely registered how sleepy and grumpy she looked, he strode across the room and hauled her into his arms. "I missed you," he breathed. "I missed you so goddamn much."

"Nick, language. Please," Marsha admonished.

"I can't help myself, Marsha. I missed my baby."

"Dad, I can't breathe."

He eased his grip. "I don't want to let you go. Come home with me. I never want to be apart from you again. Never."

"Really?" She sounded so hopeful, but her hope had been dashed so many times by him in the past. She became suspicious.

"Did Laura have her baby?"

"Yes. A little girl. Her first name is Pearl and her last is Jordan. She's your baby sister."

"Are you sure you still want me?"

"I want you more than ever. Do you know what I've learned?"

She shook her head.

"How much love I have inside of me. How much I love *you* and want *you* in my life. I want to share everything with you, including your baby sister."

When she would have objected, he said, "I have boundless, infinite love to give. The more I love the more I want to love. I'm learning so much, Emily, and so much of it is from you. *You* started me on this journey way back in the spring. If not for you, I would still be sitting behind my desk doing nothing but earning more and more money, and letting you slip through my fingers."

He rested his forehead on hers. "You saved my life. I want you back in it. I'm going to quit my job."

He heard Marsha gasp behind him. He'd had a lot of time to think on his flights and the thought that popped into his head over and over was *It's time.*

Instead of the panic, the hollowness leaving his job in Seattle should have brought on, he felt only peace and rightness. What would he replace it with? He didn't know, nor did he care at this moment.

"I want you to come home with me," he told his daughter. "I want us to buy a house in Accord and live there. Or we can build one that you like. We can design one together."

His happiness, his optimism, knew no bounds. "I want you to meet Pearl, because she has shown me that I love you to pieces."

"Daddy?"

"Yes?"

"I love you so much. I want to go home with you."

He'd never been so happy. Or so tired.

"Do you want home to be in Accord?"

"Oh, yeah! It's awesome."

"Marsha?" he asked, still holding on to his daughter with every ounce of his strength.

"Yes?" He heard a smile in her voice.

"Do you have an extra bed? I haven't slept in two days. Or it might be three."

Nick slept for ten hours. He and Emily left the following day.

Two days after he returned to Seattle, after he'd slept twelve hours straight, he walked into his office. His heart rate tripped along too fast.

He knew he was doing the right thing, had achieved an epiphany on the flight over the Atlantic with Emily asleep in his arms.

It had taken losing his daughter for him to finally get his head screwed on right.

The room was neat, tidy, nothing out of place, the way he liked to work. He had no idea what had happened to the work he'd left on the top floor of the B and B in Accord.

He studied the sterile symbols of the success he'd once thought vital to his life, his soul.

He stepped to the window with the stunning view and touched his hand to the glass, just as he'd done that day last spring when Mort had told him that he was losing his daughter.

He remembered thinking that this life was real, that he existed here while he knew no Nick Jordan other than the businessman.

Convinced that he was making the right choice, he walked to Mort's office. He nodded to Mort's secretary and said,

"Good morning, Sarah," surprised that he remembered the woman's name.

"He's expecting you." Sarah smiled the vapid, generic smile of the professional. No laughing here. No husky voices. No real caring.

Mort appeared to be sober. He leaned back in his desk chair and studied Nick.

"You got her back."

"Yes. Emily's home again."

"Good."

Nick had thought of no way to soften the blow. "I'm here to tender my resignation."

He knew Mort's explosive temper, understood that Mort had put time and effort and years into grooming Nick to be his successor. Nick was throwing it all back in his face.

Mort didn't look surprised and that shocked Nick. The decision had been a tough one, but something had to give in his life.

"Why?" Mort asked.

"I've taken stock. The area of my life in which I'm least happy is work."

Mort continued to watch him but said nothing.

"I'm most happy with Emily and Laura and Pearl. I'm most happy in Accord."

"We can't have everything we want in life. What makes you think you can?"

Nick shrugged. "I can only give it my best shot. I became a success here in this world through grit and determination. If I apply that to my private life, just think how far I could go with a family. I could make Emily happy. I could make Laura and my newborn infant happy. *I* could be happy."

Mort nodded and stood. He held out his hand to Nick to shake.

Nick stared, too shocked to take it at first. "You're not angry?"

"You've come to your senses. I've made a hash out of my life, but you're young enough to save yours."

Nick took Mort's hand and shook it, hard. He had a lot of respect for the man. What impressed him even more was the affection. The love. Mort had been a mentor, but he'd also been the father Nick had lost at too early an age.

"I've decided to run the Accord Resort," he said quietly. "It makes perfect sense. I'm not sure why it took me so long to see it."

Mort smiled. "I figured that might be the direction your life was taking. You've come to terms with your past. You do what you have to do. Expect company, though. I'm coming to live there, too."

Before he left, Nick looked back at Mort over his shoulder. "Accord would be a great place to retire."

"Yep. It's time to sell the company."

With that he was gone, leaving the building empty-handed. There wasn't a thing he wanted or needed from here.

HE FLEW WITH Emily to Accord, not at all sure how things would go, but determined.

Her relationship with Laura had been combative.

He called the hospital. Laura was already at home with Pearl.

Before trying to work out some kind of reconciliation between his daughter and the woman he loved, he thought he should see Laura alone.

After settling himself and Emily in the B and B, he drove her to Gabe's for a day of dogsledding. She'd wanted to try it ever since coming to town last spring and meeting the dogs for the first time.

Then Nick headed back into Accord, to Laura's.

He pressed his face to the glass of the bakery. The place was busy. To his surprise, he spotted Laura behind the counter. Working already?

He stepped inside.

The café was full, almost every table taken, but the lineup was short. Tilly, another woman, a young man and Laura worked behind the counter.

Laura laughed at something someone said and the huskiness, the earthiness of it, thrilled his nerve endings.

She looked tired but happy. She glowed every bit as much now as she had during pregnancy. Her breasts were heavier, full of milk. She looked womanly and wonderful.

Then she saw him.

After the initial unguarded look of shock, her expression closed.

He stepped up to the counter.

"We need to talk."

She nodded, stepped into the back and then returned with Pearl on her shoulder.

He followed her out of the shop and upstairs and into her apartment. She put Pearl down in her crib then walked to the living room and turned and watched him quietly.

"I meant what I said in the hospital." He stepped closer to her. "I love you and want to marry you."

"You have an odd way of showing it. Where did you go?"

"I flew to France. I picked up Emily and brought her home. I quit my job. I put my house up for sale."

By the time he'd finished with his list, her eyebrows had shot up.

"I'm committed. Emily and I are moving to Accord. I don't know where we'll live. With you, if you'll have me. If not, somewhere else, but close enough that I will be involved in Pearl's life. Daily."

He stepped even closer. "I'm never leaving again. I'm here for the duration. I love you, Laura, with all of my heart."

She grasped the back of his head and pulled him to her for a searing kiss. When she finally released him, they were breathing hard.

"Don't change your mind on me, Jordan," she said. "I'll hold you to every single word. To every commitment. I love for life, Nick. I don't do divorce."

"I'm here for good, love."

They sat on the sofa, together, and talked and touched and murmured words of love until Pearl woke up.

Laura brought her to the living room and sat beside Nick. "Can I hold her?"

"After I feed her." Laura unbuttoned her blouse and unhooked her maternity bra then lifted out one breast, unashamed. Pearl latched on and started suckling and Nick didn't think he'd ever seen anything more beautiful in his life.

Laura's breast was large, full with the life-giving force that would help Pearl grow and become strong.

Why had Nick never seen it as the beautiful miracle that it was? Why had it always made him squeamish?

Laura let him hold Pearl and taught him how to burp her. Then she put the baby to her other breast.

Nick watched, couldn't get enough of it. He touched one finger reverently to the velvet skin above where his baby nursed.

He ran his fingers through Laura's hair, pushed it back away from her face and kissed her.

When he thought he couldn't leave Emily with Gabe any longer, when he was bursting with so much excitement he couldn't wait another second, he left to get her.

Gabe's house was coming along. Work was stalled for the winter, but he'd managed to complete enough of the rooms for them to live indoors with the baby instead of in the prospector's tent.

Nick walked around the house and back to the clearing where the dogs lived.

Emily was helping Gabe to feed the dogs. When she saw him, her face lit up, as though the sun had come out on this dreary day.

She flew into his arms.

"How was the dogsledding?" he asked.

"Awesome. Amazing. The most incredible thing ever. Dad, you have to try it."

Gabe approached. "Anytime, Nick. Come out and I'll show you how it's done."

"I will, Gabe." Something fundamental had changed between them. With Nick's happiness had come peace. He'd let go of childish resentments. These days, he had room only for the good in life.

"Heard Laura had her baby."

Nick nodded. "Pearl. She's beautiful."

While Caleb, and even Rebecca the last time he'd seen her, looked like average babies, Pearl was stunningly beautiful.

Gabe laughed and Nick stared at him. "What?"

"You're in love with her already, aren't you?"

"Madly."

Emily stiffened at his side. He looked down at her. "You will be, too. Come on. Let's get you over there to meet her."

When he returned to Accord, she walked into Laura's apartment beside him, her face flushed from her dogsled ride in the winter wind.

"Laura?"

"In here."

She was just putting Pearl into her crib.

"She's asleep." Nick's disappointment must have shown on his face, because she laughed. "Don't worry. She'll be awake again soon. Trust me."

"You look tired," he said. "Do you need to sleep?"

"I could use some, but I'd rather get to know Emily better." He understood the reservation in her voice.

They followed her to the living room. She poured three iced teas and handed them around. Then they all sat down.

"How do you feel about the baby, Emily?"

No beating around the bush for Laura.

Emily shrugged. "I don't know."

"It's a big change for you."

Emily nodded.

"So is moving to Accord. How does that feel?"

Emily launched into a description of her morning with Gabe and the dogs.

"I'm so envious. I've never been dogsledding." Laura might have been trying to put Emily at her ease, but her enthusiasm sounded real.

Emily had also met Caleb and gushed about him.

She stopped abruptly. "Dad, I just realized. I'm starving."

"Will you two be okay if I run down for sandwiches?"

"Sure."

"Emily, you want our regular?"

She nodded.

"What's your regular?" Laura asked.

"Turkey on rye with avocado."

"Sounds good. Can I have the same?"

Nick flew down the stairs and out onto Main on weightless feet. This might work. It just might work. Emily and Laura were talking!

Emily hadn't met the baby yet, though. That would be the real test. She had to decide whether her dad was telling the truth, that he had endless, boundless amounts of love inside of him for all of the women in his life.

When he returned, they were still talking.

Laura seemed to be filling Emily in on the schools in the area.

They ate their sandwiches in harmony, but Nick knew that was relative. They weren't fighting, were having a decent conversation, but relationships took time to grow.

A tiny wail sounded from the baby's room and Laura left to get her.

Back in the living room, she prepared to feed the baby, but had brought a small blanket with her and draped it over her shoulder, as he'd seen Tammy do. She was being modest for Emily's sake. Nick's heart warmed. She was trying so hard.

When the baby finished at the first breast, Laura rubbed her back to burp her then said to Emily, "Do you want to hold her?"

"I'll try."

Laura put her into Emily's arms.

"She's so tiny," Emily whispered. "When I saw Rebecca she was a lot bigger. Caleb is bigger, too. I've never held such a small baby. What if I hurt her?"

"You won't. You're holding her properly. You're supporting her head well."

"Tammy taught me how to hold a baby the right way."

"You're doing a good job."

Pearl stared at Emily.

"She's watching me."

"She's listening to you, too. Learning what her sister's voice sounds like."

"She looks like you." Nick touched Pearl's cheek with his forefinger. It looked ridiculously large against her tiny pink face. "Do you remember that picture of you as a newborn that your mom kept on top of the piano?"

They'd had delusions that their daughter would someday be a world-class pianist. Trouble was, she'd shown no aptitude for or interest in it. She'd loved the violin, though. She'd brought it here with her.

"I remember that picture. Mom took it with her to France."

"Pearl looks so much like you in that photograph."

"She really is my sister, isn't she?"

"Yes. You have a sister."

"Awesome," she whispered and Nick caught Laura's eye above her head. They smiled, because life just might be working out for them.

IN THE FOLLOWING DAYS, Nick was careful to give Emily as much attention as he gave to Pearl.

Without the burden of the work he'd always carried with him wherever he went, it was easier to juggle the time spent with his two daughters.

Nick enrolled Emily in school, then he and Laura set a wedding date, for May.

"May?" Nick yelled. "Why the hell do I want to wait so long? I want to get married now."

"Do you have any idea how long it takes to organize a wedding?"

"It didn't take Ty and Tammy very long."

"Nick, I'm only getting married once. I want everything to be perfect."

They decided that Nick and Emily should stay at the B and B until then, for propriety's sake. As well, Emily would need her sleep to stay alert for school, so her grades wouldn't drop. Pearl was feeding every four hours—she would wake Emily up during the night.

Emily spent a fair amount of time after school every day with Laura and the baby. In fact, she went straight there instead of coming to the B and B.

Laura made sure that the Gems set one cinnamon bun aside for Emily every day. She picked it up on her way upstairs to see Pearl.

Nick would join them and Laura taught him how to cook. Soon, while Laura took care of Pearl and Emily did homework at the dining room table, Nick cooked their dinners.

Feelings of harmony flooded him in those times.

His favorite times were when it stormed outside. They lost their power once and had to do everything with emergency candles, bundling up in heavy sweaters. Emily loved the adventure.

Rather than fight the storm to cross the street, they slept over that night.

Laura piled heavy quilts onto her bed and put Pearl in the middle between her and Emily.

Nick slept on the sofa.

In the evenings, he and Emily designed the house they would all live in. Nick bought a piece of land adjacent to the resort.

When Mike Canning came to town to oversee parts of construction, to make sure that all was being built according to plan, he would review the work that Emily and Nick had done on the design of their house.

Nick built in an extra room. He wanted another baby with his wife.

Mort lived at the B and B while he scouted out a place to live. He had dinner with them often.

One night, he showed up with an expensive bottle of wine that Laura swooned over. Then she grimaced. "I can't drink it because I'm still breast-feeding."

"I'll buy you a whole case of it when you finish breast-feeding."

Emily and Laura drank milk while Mort drank iced tea.

"What the hell," Nick said and left the wine unopened. "I can't drink alone." He joined Mort in a glass of iced tea.

"We're celebrating tonight," Mort said.

"Celebrating what?"

"I found a small house a five-minute walk from the home. I bought it today."

"Squeeee!" Emily hugged her grandfather. "I'm so happy, Gramps. You love the home."

"When I'm too old and decrepit to live alone, it will be a short walk to move into the place."

The relationship that had developed between Mort and Johanna was heartwarming. Every day, Mort started their relationship anew, because Johanna would have forgotten who he was from the day before.

"I've given the home a donation to help Callie get it running to full potential." He blushed. "What do I need all my money for? Especially here in Accord."

Unless Nick missed his guess, his ex-father-in-law had fallen in love with Johanna.

Throughout those perfect months, only one thing marred the perfection of Nick's life. He wanted to sleep with his wife. Laura became more desirable by the day. Her joy in motherhood and life were an aphrodisiac stronger than anything Nick had known.

He wanted her.

BEFORE THEY MARRIED, there was one other problem Nick had to take care of. Laura's brother.

Noah had hated Nick from the moment he'd slept with her all of those years ago for petty revenge. A changed man, he wanted no disharmony in his life. He needed to build a bridge with Noah.

He found him in his Army Surplus shop.

Nick could give Noah tips on how to run a business a hell of a lot better than Noah was doing, but he doubted Noah would be open to listening, suspecting instead that the man didn't mind living on less. Probably took pride in it.

When he saw Nick, Noah scowled. "You'd better take care of my sister. If you hurt her, I'll rip your throat out."

"I thought you were a pacifist."

"Not where Laura is concerned. You screwed her up so badly the first time around. I don't want to see you do it again."

"I won't. You have my word on it."

"How do I know you're telling the truth?"

"You don't. You'll just have to trust me like your sister is doing. Think about this, though. I've quit my job in Seattle and brought my daughter here with me. Would I do that if I planned to turn around and abandon Laura later?"

"I guess not."

"Laura says you don't plan to attend the wedding."

"Nope. I'd rather see her marry a snake."

"Be there. Trust that Laura is smart enough to make her own decisions. She's a grown woman. She doesn't need your support, but she could use your acceptance."

Noah studied the counter in front of him and came to a decision.

"Okay. I'll be there."

"Be there and be happy for her."

"Don't push it, Jordan."

Nick turned to leave, but Noah called out before he got to the door. "I'll be watching you."

"I would expect no less."

Nick had done as much as he could with Noah.

CHAPTER TWENTY-THREE

ON THE INTERNET, Nick ordered lush, colorful silks and put them away for later, to use as a surprise for Laura. He ordered a beautiful pale yellow sari. Laura would look amazing in it.

When Pearl was old enough to be left with her grandmother, and when he and Laura could finally have sex, he wanted an orgy of the senses with the woman he planned to make his wife as soon as possible.

The wedding took place when Pearl was four months old.

The night before, he shooed Laura out of her apartment for the entire night and made her take Pearl to stay with her mother.

Nick worked into the wee hours draping the silks he'd ordered around Laura's ceiling. He still hadn't finished building the house where they would all live permanently, but that seemed a small problem. They would be together—he, Laura, Emily and Pearl—and that was all that mattered, whether in Laura's apartment or in a larger home.

He left the pale yellow sari on the bed for Laura to wear later.

The following morning, Nick walked down the aisle with his daughter. She stood beside him at the altar with Gabe and Ty on her far side.

Callie and Tammy were matrons of honor on his other side.

Laura made a beautiful bride.

Nick watched her walk toward him up the aisle and held his breath, clutching to himself all of the deep-seated emotions—joy, love, wonder—that threatened to explode out of him.

She walked with her mother on one side and her brother on the other, in a white dress that showed off every one of her glorious curves. They'd filled out more with Pearl's birth. Laura complained about the extra fifteen pounds she still carried.

He planned to love the daylights out of every one of those extra pounds tonight.

When the minister asked, "Who gives this woman away?" Noah and Olivia answered, "We do."

When he asked, "Who gives this man away?" Emily said, "I do," then beamed up at him. He leaned down and kissed her nose.

After a beautiful ceremony, they held a celebration in the community hall.

Later that night, Nick and Laura returned to the apartment alone. Pearl was staying with Grandma and Emily with Ty and Tammy and Rebecca and Ruby. Ty had shared the good news that Ruby was moving to Accord to live with him permanently.

Nick turned to Laura. "I left something on the bed for you to change into."

Laura raised a brow. "You did?"

Nick's kiss lingered on her lips. When he pulled away, he said, "You use the washroom first."

"Nick?"

"Yes?"

"No condoms, okay?"

"You want to get pregnant again?"

"Yes. Okay?"

"Yes. A thousand times yes."

While Laura washed up for the night, he lit candles and incense in the bedroom and turned on a CD he'd made for tonight, music for them and them alone. It featured masters of the sarod and sitar and tabla, East Indian pieces he'd found that were sensuous and uplifting.

Laura finished in the washroom, then he cleaned up and returned to the bedroom.

She lay across the bed wrapped in the nearly sheer yellow sari, her hair luxuriant on her shoulders, her body's curves abundant, everything hinted at with contours and shadows.

She'd foregone the skirt and short top that belonged underneath the sari. Thank God.

She'd found the bracelets and anklets and necklaces of tiny golden bells that he'd left for her and had adorned herself.

While he undressed, she stretched sinuously to the exotic music then rested on her elbows and arched her back. Her breasts rose and fell with her breathing. Her nipples peaked against the delicate fabric, all of her hidden or exposed at the whim of flickering candle flames.

Nick leaned one knee on the edge of the bed and hovered over her, running his hands along her body. Laura sighed and purred.

"You're a happy cat," he whispered, smiling, his voice deep with desire.

"Mmmmm," she murmured low in her throat. He'd never met a more sensual woman.

He ran his hands under the sari, watched as they traveled her body beneath the pale fabric. Her nipples hardened against his palms while the silk caressed the backs of his hands, the contrast sexy and startling.

Taking the gold chains between his fingers, he played them over her nipples.

He loosened the garment and touched her belly. She gasped. He smoothed his fingers lower and touched her wet core. She arched again, gracefully, like a panther, her heels digging into the mattress and her knees falling open to give him access, the music of the bells at her ankles ringing with the sitar floating through the room.

She eased the sari open and held it out, inviting him in. He lay with her and she closed the fabric across his back, the silk soft on his spine and her skin silky against the hard planes of his body.

His fingers inflamed her, wrought gasps from her. She writhed against him, her thigh brushing against him, hardening his flesh.

The bells on her wrists and ankles tinkled, a musical counterpart to her earthy moans.

He kissed her and she sucked on his tongue. She lifted her ankle to his waist, opening herself to him, and the bells tinkled. His fingers went deeper.

He knelt between her legs and spread them wide, bringing his mouth to her moist flesh while his fingers filled all of her, every bit of her, and she shuddered. He kissed and licked her until she writhed, until the edge of her control.

He sucked hard and she came. He would never desire another woman as he did this one. Laura was every woman to him, every desire and need fulfilled. He held her while she shivered then quieted.

Her husky laugh filled the room.

"I love you, Nick Jordan," she said. "I always have and always will."

"I love you, Laura Cameron, and will until the end of my days."

How right to discover that love was an aphrodisiac. He'd never known.

She took him in hand and used skillful fingers to harden and lengthen him, to please him and to prepare him for her.

Finally, he entered her, flesh against flesh. She took him in as though molded, sculpted for his body.

The music changed tempo, became smoky, and someone's husky voice sang of love while he performed love, while Laura took from him and gave to him all of her self, of her being, of her bold and generous spirit.

Her perfume floated around him, mingled with her sex,

with her essence, fomenting his passion, fanning flames higher.

Silk floated across his back.

"Look," he whispered and she followed his gaze.

She hadn't noticed. He'd put up a mirror on the wall on the far side of the bed.

"You're so beautiful."

She watched them move together, in harmony, in lust, in rut. He screwed her until they nearly turned inside out, transforming the most basic animal needs into transcendent beauty.

He touched every part of her and she him. They left nothing to the imagination, nothing unloved.

The tempo of the music picked up again and so did Nick. Laura drove him higher with her vocal demands and with her body's strength, with her body's ability to keep up and to want more, more, more.

He drove her higher. She keened long and loud, the most beautiful music he'd ever heard.

He followed her into oblivion.

Minutes later, he rocked her in his arms, whispered inanities, feathered love nips along her neck.

Her heavy breathing slowly calmed until they lay still in each other's arms.

Unwrapping the sari from around them and getting out of bed, she walked to the bathroom, returning with two warm wet towels.

They cleaned each other, because it was more fun than cleaning themselves.

She walked to the mirror and ran her fingers over the reflection of her body.

Glancing over her shoulder with her hair running down her glorious back, she said softly, "This is brilliant, Nick."

She looked up at the swooping falls of color across her ceiling. "Thank you."

She lay beside him and he enfolded her in his arms. He

draped the sheer sari across her body. She arched when the silk whispered across her skin. He played with the fabric, with her. She turned over and he ran it across her back, along the chasm of her full behind.

She took the fabric from him and played it over his body like a maestro. When he began to harden, she took the silk and bound his wrists to her bedposts.

Moving slowly, she straddled him, settled onto him, her moist and ready flesh embracing his. When he responded and hardened enough, she took him into her body.

She sat up straight and proud on him and he glanced at the mirror. In the smoky candlelight, her breasts, her hips, her bounteous body glowed. Then she moved and his breath caught.

She rode him hard while the bells of her jewelry played a delightful symphony.

They bathed by candlelight then gathered apple and pear slices and a warm triple cream Brie and carried them to bed. They sliced off the top of the cheese and dipped the fruit into it and fed each other.

Later, Nick used the yards of silk to bind both Laura's hands and her feet. He drove her to a frenzy and brought them both to a resounding release.

In Laura's sexy grotto, in her love palace, they played long into the night.

CHAPTER TWENTY-FOUR

THE GRAND OPENING of the Accord Golf and Cross-country Ski Resort was held on a sunny, perfect day in September.

Nick held baby Pearl in his arms. Laura tried to take her, but he shooed her away.

There was a bond between Nick and his baby daughter that he had missed the first time around. He planned to miss nothing this time. He would be there for every first—her first word (he was angling for *Daddy* and repeated it umpteen times a day), first solid food, first step.

The new clubhouse sparkled like a diamond in a setting of emerald trees. The air swam with the scent of meat on the grill.

All of Accord had come out. Mort showed the investors around, with pride in his every step.

Nick's brothers and their wives were here.

Gabe and Tyler stood beside him admiring the resort, both with growing babies in their arms.

"You did a good job, bro." Ty nodded his approval.

"Thanks for not carving up my mountain," Gabe said.

In the end, Nick had respected Gabe's wishes and hadn't carved ski runs out of the mountain.

Visitors could hike or climb it, but it wouldn't be desecrated.

They could cross-country ski in the winter and golf in the summer. Shuttle buses would take them to Gabe's dogsledding in the winter. In the summer, visitors could watch archaeology students as they conducted ongoing digs. If they were very careful, after copious instruction, they could even participate in a dig.

Nick was going to run the resort. He'd have his wife and children to fill his nonworking hours, including entertaining his wife in the new bedroom they'd designed for the new house they were having built.

He wandered to the clearing, where Salem's Cathedral (his and Emily's nickname for the Native American Heritage Center) showcased every artifact found on the land. There was so much more digging to do, but they were taking it slowly so they wouldn't destroy anything.

One resurrected skeleton, a young female, had been lovingly carried to a small cemetery created on a portion of Ron Porter's land that Nick had bought. She had been buried with a moving ancient ceremony. Nick had attended, loving the reverence and the sense of peace that settled over him. A simple message, *Peace,* written in Salem's native Ute, had been carved into a small headstone that Nick had paid for. Before burial, DNA samples had been taken, in case local Utes wanted to determine whether this might have been an ancestor of theirs.

"Dad." Nick turned and grinned. Emily flew toward him on legs getting longer by the second. She was growing into them. One day soon she would be a woman and gone. She was thirteen now. These days, he treasured every second of their time together.

"Em," Pearl squealed and Emily grinned from ear to ear. She nuzzled Pearl's neck and got a big smile for her efforts.

"Hey," Nick said, "she hasn't smiled at me yet today. Besides, her first word was supposed to be *Daddy,* not *Em.*" He frowned in mock disapproval.

"That's because you're not her favorite sister."

"So? I'm her favorite dad."

"You're *my* favorite dad." Emily kissed his cheek. "The best."

Before he teared up and disgraced himself by crying, he said, "What do you think of the cathedral?"

"I *love* it!" She ran ahead of him. "Salem's going to give me a tour. I have to go. See you later!" Emily seemed to be running everywhere these days—to school, to violin lessons, to gymnastics—but that was okay. She always had a smile on her face and it warmed Nick's heart to see her so happy.

Salem and Nick's architect had fashioned a three-story glass house with minimal brushed steel for support.

Once inside, Nick felt like a part of nature while embraced by the modern architecture of wood, glass and muted steel.

Every wall was glass, including the display cases and Salem's office.

Artifacts were lovingly tucked into corners with rounded edges that cradled them. As it turned out, Salem had an artist's eye and ability and all signs were painted by his hand in English and in his native Ute.

The gentle flow of paths and stairways was a testament to his old soul. Nick didn't know what had happened in the boy's life, but it had shaped him into a wise, but sad youth. Nick had no idea what more he could do for Salem. He'd given him a career, a beautiful home for his treasured history and a free hand in running the museum.

The only one who consistently brought a smile to Salem's face was Emily. Good. The kid needed it.

Laura stood beside him. "It's breathtaking."

"Yes. Mike and Salem did a good job."

"More than good. Stunning."

Nick stared down at his wife. She was pregnant again, just barely. They weren't wasting any time.

He remembered when he'd stood in his office that day that Mort had stormed in. He'd thought his work was the only real thing in his life. He'd been so wrong.

He'd learned about depth of love from Emily.

His love for Laura and Pearl was real and deep and everlasting. His life in Accord was more real than ever before.

He was no longer that invisible poor Jordan boy. Nor was he the arrogant businessman who had to flaunt his worth.

His wife looked up at him, her smile sexy and promising, and he wished they were alone.

"Stop doing that," Nick said.

"What?"

"Making me love you."

Laura grinned as she moved close for his kiss. "Not a chance."

* * * * *

If you were to visit Laura's bakery in fictional Accord, Colorado, you would be able to sample her tasty adult version of chocolate chip cookies. To bake them at home, try her recipe.

LAURA'S CHOCOLATE CHUNK COOKIES

¾ cup butter
¾ cup white sugar
¾ cup brown sugar
1 egg, beaten
2 tbs Frangelico
1 tsp vanilla extract
1 ⅔ cups all-purpose flour
½ tsp baking soda
¼ tsp salt
1 Lindt Excellence 70% chocolate bar (100 g or 3.5 oz),
chopped into chunks
¾ cup whole hazelnuts

Preheat oven to 375 degrees F.

Toast hazelnuts in oven for 7 or 8 minutes. Be careful they don't burn. Put them on one half of a kitchen towel, fold over the other half and rub them to get most of the papery dark skins off. Set hazelnuts aside.

Cream butter until soft then add both sugars. Cream until smooth. Add egg, Frangelico and vanilla extract and mix well.

Mix together flour, baking soda and salt. Add to the butter/sugar mixture and mix well.

Add the chocolate chunks and the whole hazelnuts. If desired, chop hazelnuts before adding.

Drop by tablespoonsful onto greased or parchment paper–lined baking sheets.

Bake for 11–12 minutes.

Caution: whole nuts could pose a choking hazard for children. Save these cookies for adults, or chop the nuts.

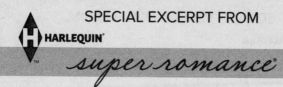
Talk of the Town
By Beth Andrews

Maddie Montesano shares a history with
Neil Pettit...and a daughter. Their relationship
has been rocky and it could get worse with
Neil back in Shady Grove...
Read on for an exciting excerpt!

Maddie Montesano swung her crowbar at the wall, focused on finishing this demolition. The back of her neck prickled with a warning of being watched...and let her know who stood there.

When it came to Neil Pettit, it was like some sort of homing device was imbedded inside of her. *There he is! The man of your adolescent dreams!*

It was annoying and as powerful as it had been when she'd been young and stupid with love for him.

Well, she'd gotten over Neil a long time ago.

Neil leaned against the doorjamb, his broad shoulders filling the space as he lazily slid his gaze from her head to the toes of her work boots.

There should be a law that when a woman saw her ex, she looked hot. Sexy hot…not sweaty, I've-been-working-and-am-a-total-mess hot.

"Hey, babe. Looking good." His greeting was the same as in high school when he'd wait by her locker. Oh, how her heart had raced with so many wonderful, conflicting emotions.

"It's the tool belt," she said, not bothering to keep the flatness from her voice.

He grinned at her tone, one of his slow, panty-melting smiles. It was more potent now than it'd been twelve years ago. "It's not the tool belt." He came closer until the toes of his sneakers bumped against her boots. "It's the whole package."

She rolled her eyes. "Please."

Golden stubble covered his cheeks and she noticed the dark circles under his eyes. He looked tired and that hint of vulnerability had her weakening. Not allowed.

"Something I can do for you, Neil?"

His expression changed. "Is Bree here? I'd like to see my daughter."

What are Neil's intentions?
Find out in TALK OF THE TOWN
by Beth Andrews, available April 2013
from Harlequin® Superromance®.
And be sure to look for the other
three books about the Montesano siblings
in Beth's IN SHADY GROVE series
available later in 2013.

REQUEST YOUR FREE BOOKS!
2 FREE NOVELS PLUS 2 FREE GIFTS!

H HARLEQUIN®

super romance®

Exciting, emotional, unexpected!